THE Misadventures OF Lady Ophelia

THE UNDAUNTED DEBUTANTES
Book 3

CHRISTINA McKNIGHT

DEDICATION

For my readers~

The Undaunted Debutantes heroines are very near and dear to my heart. I do so hope you have loved them as much as I have. They are strong, confident, and deserving of love and happiness…just as every woman is!

ACKNOWLEDGMENTS

To Marc, my amazing boyfriend, partner, and soul mate—thank you for always encouraging me to push myself!

To Lauren Stewart, my critique partner and best friend, you pushed me to explore new avenues of thought that I never dreamed possible. If we were in a true relationship, it would be one based on co-dependency, but in a good way. My writing would not be what it is without your comments, criticism, suggestions, and guidance.

I'd also like to thank the wonderful women who've supported me in both my writing career and life, including (but not limited to): Erica Monroe, Amanda Mariel, Debbie Haston, Angie Stanton, Theresa Baer, Ava Stone, Roxanne Stellmacher, Laura Cummings, Dawn Borbon, Suzi Parker, Jennifer Vella, Brandi Johnson, and Latisha Kahn. I know I'm forgetting people…Thank you all for accepting me for, well, me.

A very special thank you to my editor, Chelle Olson with Literally Addicted to Detail, your skill and professionalism surpass all that I expected. Chelle Olson can be contracted by email at literallyaddictedtodetail@yahoo.com.

Also, a special thank you to historical and developmental editor, Scott Moreland.

And to my proofreader, Anja, thank you for embarking on yet another journey with me.

Cover design by The Midnight Muse.

Wraparound cover design credit to Sweet 'N Spicy Designs.

Finally, thank you for supporting indie authors.

.

PROLOGUE

Devonshire, England
December 1813

AS THE RESOUNDING gong subsided, Lady Ophelia
Fletcher glanced up from her book to note the fire in
the hearth had died to mere glowing embers and a cold
draft blew through the room, raising the hairs on her
arms.

The other women in the salon, her dearest friends,
all laughed, and Ophelia joined in, having lost the train
of conversation long ago.

"…you will tell us everything on the morrow? At
breakfast, and not a moment later. I truly must know if
everything is as I've been told." Lady Lucianna
Constantine raised one brow with a wicked grin. Her
green eyes sparkled with mischief as she wrapped Lady
Abercorn, formally Miss Tilda Guthton in a tight
embrace. "You look breathtakingly innocent."

Ophelia glanced at Tilda, their newly married
friend, and was surprised to notice that the young
woman did, in fact, look far too innocent for her new
status as a duchess. Her mousey brown hair was tied
back with a simple white ribbon, the pure shade
matching Tilda's nightshift perfectly, making it all the

more clear that at age seventeen, barely introduced to society, their friend was far too young to wed a man over twice her age.

Again, it was none of Ophelia's business—the heart loved who the heart loved.

She only found it peculiar that Tilda, the daughter of a mere baronet, had been the one to capture a duke's notice. She was lovely enough—adequate at household matters, graceful as expected, and cultured in her speech—however, Abercorn was a worldly, wealthy, and influential lord.

The duke had seemingly plucked Tilda from obscurity, their courtship developing far quicker than normal.

But, that was none of Ophelia's business either.

She was happy for her dear friend, even if her love match did not resemble that of the star-crossed lovers in her current novel.

Ophelia stood, along with Lady Edith, Lady Lucianna, and Tilda, preparing to leave the room—at least, that was what Ophelia assumed they were doing at such a late hour. Tilda's bridegroom would certainly start to wonder where his young duchess had disappeared to if he approached their marriage bed only to find it empty.

Edith stepped forward and wrapped her arms around Tilda and whispered something in the new bride's ear. Ophelia wasn't privy to the private exchange, but an easy smile lit Tilda's face, removing any trace of unease that may have been there, however subtle.

"Thank you, Edith. You have always been a great friend." Tilda hugged Edith a bit tighter before pulling back. "I must hurry. It will not do for my *husband* to arrive and find that I have fled. He said he would arrive by half past midnight, after attending to a few business matters."

Luci slipped her arm through Tilda's, while Ophelia

grabbed her book from the settee and held it to her chest as she followed her friends toward the door, suppressing the tingle of envy that began to blossom at Luci and Tilda's close relationship.

Now was not the time to allow the hurt of being left out to surface and thus drag her into despair.

"Now remember that thing we spoke about, with your ton…" Luci's whispers trailed off as the women departed the room, their heads leaned together much like conspirators, as if Ophelia could not possibly understand the things they tittered about. The pair had likely never even opened a book and lost themselves to an adventure, or a sensual tale of exploration and discovery.

Such a pity, but Ophelia would not be the one to share her private collection of leather-bound tales of love, lust, and escapades.

"I will extinguish the candles," Edith called as Ophelia reached the threshold.

She paused, turning to the petite blonde who'd long been the only one in the group to understand Ophelia's thirst for knowledge and her reserved tendencies. "I will help you."

"No, hurry along," Edith said, waving her off. "I know you are eager to return to your book. It will take but a few moments. I will meet you in our room as soon as I am done."

"If you insist." Ophelia smiled before glancing over her shoulder to see Luci and Tilda had reached the stairs. "I am eager to see how the fair Lady Daniella escapes the rogue pirate, Xavier."

Edith laughed softly. "Well, do get back to their story."

She needed no further encouragement as Ophelia stepped from the room and opened the blue, leather-bound volume to the place she'd marked with a slip of stationery, always hesitant to mar the pressed pages of her books.

Oh, how Lady Daniella flipped her long tresses over her shoulder before giving Xavier a narrowed look and demanding he listen to her, heed her words well, or the pirate would never again taste Daniella's womanly charms.

Ophelia longed to be so bold, commanding, and beautiful as to gain the notice of…well, anyone.

Instead, Ophelia's hair was an ungodly shade of bright red, her nose sprinkled with freckles, and her hips far too curvy to fit with popular fashion. Never could her wild tresses be tamed, unlikely was her complexion ever to be clear and pale, and it was doubtful she would ever embrace London elite's current affection for bold fabric choices.

She sighed, focusing on her place on the page.

A scream pulled her eyes from the author's description of Xavier's bare, hair-covered chest.

Thump, thump, thump.

"Edith!" Luci's blood-curdling scream stopped her in her tracks. "Ophelia!"

A sob escaped her as her book slipped from her grasp, hitting the polished floor with a resounding thud, unlike the hollow noise from a moment before. Her slip of personalized stationery drifted across the floor, coming to rest only when it partially slid under a closed door.

Tilda lay sprawled at the bottom of the staircase, her head turned at an odd angle, her eyes open wide.

Ophelia blinked several times.

She waited for Tilda to move. Or Luci to help her up. Or the floor to open and swallow them whole.

But nothing happened.

She blinked again when her sight blurred with tears.

Suddenly, time started again. The distant *tick-tock* of the mahogany clock in the room they'd just departed could be heard. Edith appeared at her side, and Luci crouched over Tilda, her black hair cascading over her shoulder to—mercifully—block the sight of their friend.

"Luci." Edith stepped around her toward Lucianna. "What is it—"

Edith's words cut off.

"No, no, no," Edith sobbed as she hurried forward. "This cannot be—"

"He did this." Desperation laced Luci's tone when she pointed toward the top of the stairs.

Ophelia looked to the darkened landing above them but saw nothing of consequence.

"Who?" Ophelia asked, swallowing the sob that threatened to escape if she opened her mouth again.

"That is not important at this moment," Edith scolded her, hurrying to Tilda's side. "We must wake her up, make sure she is all right and call for the duke—and a physician."

How is it not important, Ophelia longed to ask. However, she pressed her lips together and remained silent—as was expected of her.

If she were Lady Daniella, Ophelia would lift her chin until she stared down her slightly crooked nose at her friends and demand to be heard and answered. However, she was not Lady Daniella, a woman abducted from her village on the Scottish coast by a pirate most fierce. She was merely Lady Ophelia, a passably comely, reticent, self-professed bookworm. The women before her were beautiful, clever, and captivating. Everything the heroines in her novels were. Not red-haired, freckle-faced, and rounded.

"…he pushed her. I swear it."

Ophelia shook her head, feeling guilty at the continued wandering of her thoughts when she should be listening to Luci and attempting to make sense of the scene before her. She'd studied many novels where the hero, a shipwrecked man, had been forced to do battle. She'd read of blood-thirsty Amazon natives and murderous clansmen laying claim to neighboring villages, but witnessing the prone body of a friend was much different.

Actually, it was in no way the same.

Never could any tales have prepared her for the sight before her.

The way Tilda's eyes stood open but lacked any life. The angle at which her arm was bent. The thin trail of dark red blood leaving the corner of her slack mouth.

Uncertainty, confusion, and denial all waged war within Ophelia as her stomach tensed and her breath caught in her chest, locking her lungs and preventing the air from escaping. Perspiration broke out across her forehead and her neck heated at her collar.

Ophelia swallowed past the lump in her throat. "Wha-wha-what should we do?" She hated hearing the weakness in her voice, confirming what her friends already proclaimed about her. She was scared of her own shadow. Likely to faint at the slightest shock.

"We will rouse the house and tell them all what the duke has done!" Lucianna quickly stood, drawing Ophelia's eyes from Tilda. "Someone must have heard the commotion."

Edith glanced around the foyer. "You are correct. I heard her scream, and then the thump as she fell."

"She did *not* fall." Lucianna's tone reached hysterics, sounding much like Ophelia felt on the inside—panicked and terrified. "She was *pushed*, by Abercorn!"

They stared at one another. Hot tears began to stream down Ophelia's heated face, while Luci appeared to regain her composure. Her widened green eyes held no hint of the waterworks Ophelia had been reduced to. Edith reached out toward Luci, but the woman ignored her hand.

"How could this happen?" Ophelia asked, stooping to collect her book as she dashed the unbidden tears away.

"That is a question for him. You saw him, right, Ophelia?" Luci turned imploring eyes on her.

The heat drained from Ophelia as cold overtook

her, and her stomach roiled with unease.

"Tell her what you saw." Luci took an intimidating step toward Ophelia. "You were standing right here."

"I—I—I was reading." Ophelia turned to Edith, her book held tightly against her bosom as if she loosened her hold, Luci would snatch the volume from her. "I swear it, Edith, I did not see anything. I was reading about Xavier and—"

"What is going on here?" Townsend, the Abercorn butler, hurried into the foyer, his hair flopping from side to side like the caricatures depicted in the comical pages of *The Post*. He'd certainly been pulled from slumber. "Your Grace!" His eyes widened at the sight of Tilda as he rushed across the room to where she lay. His hand moved to her wrist and settled. "No pulse. She has no pulse!"

The servant shuffled to his feet, glancing around the room as if expecting someone to step forward and solve this major dilemma—his new mistress, lying dead at the bottom of the stairs on her wedding night.

"Petunia, Petunia!" Townsend shouted as he flapped his arms to and fro, rushing deeper into the Abercorn house. "Petunia! We must summon His Grace. Petunia, where in all that is holy are you, woman?"

Doors opened, and voices called from above as guests exited their rooms, hearing the commotion as Townsend continued calling for Petunia.

"Oh, Your Grace!" Townsend said, staring toward the top of the stairs. "Please, do not look. This is not for your eyes."

Ophelia pressed herself to the wall, praying she could escape notice for a few minutes.

As she took a deep breath, Ophelia watched Luci's hands ball into fists at her sides, and her face redden. Ophelia cringed. An angry Lady Lucianna could raise Satan from the depths of Hell with her fury.

Leaning away from the wall, the duke could be seen

making slow progress down the stairs.

The man seemed oddly unaffected by the sight of his dead wife only five steps below him. Truthfully, his gaze barely took notice of her before he stepped clear of the blood beginning to pool under Tilda's head.

Ophelia spun away from the foyer and hurried toward the sitting room they'd departed a few moments before.

Could it have been only precious minutes ago that they'd all sat close, gossiping about the night to come?

She'd been so distracted by her book she hadn't embraced Tilda one last time. She hadn't whispered good tidings before the new bride had left the room on Luci's arm.

Shame caused Ophelia's face to flush once more as she entered the darkened room and rushed to the windows overlooking the garden. She threw the windowpane open and allowed the cold night air in. Ophelia should return to the foyer, be there for her friends. Did they even notice she'd fled? She'd failed Luci and Edith, and especially Tilda.

If she hadn't been preoccupied with her reading, would she have seen Lord Abercorn atop the grand staircase? Surely, Luci was not mistaken, but Ophelia had been unable to voice her support of her friend's accusations.

Ophelia had frozen, her mind tangled and confused.

CHAPTER 1

It is with great pleasure that this writer speaks for the young women of the ton. Ladies who will not be taken for granted nor misguided by men of unsavory character. And with this article, this writer will no longer glorify the misdeeds of men, but celebrate the accomplishments of young, bright, charming females.

It is this author's opinion that lords far and wide heed th knowledge imbued by this column, as there is little doubt there will be postings regarding.

-The Mayfair Confidential

London
April 1815

LADY OPHELIA FLETCHER sat primly in a chair set against the wall, her ankles crossed and tucked under her with her hands folded lightly in her lap. She was the epitome of the proper miss as she watched Lady Lucianna discard yet another stationery sample. This time it was the color, the last was not an acceptable texture, and the one before that smudged when her friend placed quill to paper.

To all who viewed Ophelia, she most certainly looked at ease with a confident, serene smile.

Inside, she wanted to scream. She breathed deeply and released the air slowly to remain calm and in control. Her smile didn't falter, and her hands didn't so much as twitch, though she longed to clench something, even the delicate muslin of her morning gown.

If she'd brought her reticle, she would have thrown it against the wall.

Luci held up a thick, cream-colored stationery with gold leafing to elicit Ophelia's opinion, silent raising one brow.

"It is lov—"

"No, it is far too *cream* and not thick enough." Luci sighed, turning back to the proprietor and cutting Ophelia off. "Do you have anything with ebony trim?"

"Lovely," Ophelia finished in a whisper. The paper *was* lovely, as were the five other options presented during their hour in the stationery shop.

Her knees ached from sitting for far too long, so Ophelia stood and turned toward the storefront windows. The sun was nearly directly overhead, and Bond Street was now busy with the *beau monde* hurrying in and out of shops, their servants trailing behind, their arms heavy with purchases. It was the way of London. The only thing the *ton* enjoyed more than being seen was spending money on purchases one did not necessarily need and being observed doing it.

Certainly, stationery and calling cards were important, and since Luci was to wed the Duke of Montrose in under two weeks, it was imperative she select something with all due haste before she, Montrose, Lady Edith, and Lord Torrington left for Gretna Green.

Lady Lucianna's father, the Marquis of Camden, had refused to allow a proper betrothal between Montrose and Luci. The man had gone so far as to throw Luci from her home and ban her from seeing her mother and siblings.

And so, instead of waiting until her father agreed

and consented to the marriage, thus having the wedding blessed by her family, Luci had chosen to travel to Scotland to see the appropriate ceremony done. Odd for a woman who, only a few short weeks prior, was determined never to wed, let alone trust a man with her future.

Ophelia shook her head and focused on the passersby.

She breathed in and out. Deep inhale, slow exhale.

It would not do to allow unease to overtake her in such a public place—her cheeks flushing, her eyes widening, and her pulse racing to match the pace of a galloping thoroughbred. It would inevitably end with her vigorously fanning herself, or worse yet, falling into a dead faint. And would only serve to impress upon Luci—and Edith, once she heard of the incident—that Ophelia was less than capable of, well…anything.

Glaring out the window, she noticed an urchin slip past a finely dressed man, the boy's grimy hand snaking into the gent's pocket and back out again before the imp veered away and turned sharply, entering a shop across the street. By the time Ophelia tried to spot the thief's mark, the gentleman had disappeared, as well.

"…what about another choice with gold leaf on the edges?" Luci asked the proprietor.

Ophelia had been mistaken when she believed inviting Luci to live with her until the wedding was a grand idea.

If anything, it was tedious.

She sighed, meaning to turn and regain her seat, but a familiar gentleman strolled past the stationery shop with an elegantly garbed woman on his arm, causing Ophelia to press her face against the glass to watch the man as they moved farther down the street with their heads tilted together in a conspiratorial manner.

Glancing over her shoulder, Luci was busily flipping through another stack of samples on her quest to select the perfect paper product to announce her coming status as the Duchess of Montrose. There was little doubt she'd remain occupied for at least another hour.

Ophelia slipped out the open shop door just in time to see Lord Abercorn, the man responsible for their dear friend's death the Season before—and the man Luci's father had demanded she wed—step into Oliver's Book Shoppe with the spinster, Lady Sissy Cassel, at his side. It was not hard to peg Lady Sissy as Abercorn sister, although her greying hair and stooped shoulders made her appear more the age of the duke's mother. Ophelia had met the older woman only once, the previous month at the Abercorn townhouse, and Sissy had left little lasting impression on Ophelia.

The walk to the shop three buildings down took only a moment, but Ophelia didn't risk entering the business. She pressed herself to the wall bordering the shop and leaned around to peek through the windowpane, freshly cleaned to a shine. She pulled back when she noticed Abercorn turn down an aisle. Her nose left a print on the clean window, but Ophelia stilled herself from rubbing it off with her sleeve.

It would be possible, if she hurried, to slip into the shop and down another aisle without Abercorn noticing her. She needed to see what the man was up to.

As far as Ophelia and her friends were concerned, Abercorn should not be allowed out in polite society. She didn't trust him.

A bell sounded overhead as she entered the shop, and the owner, Oliver, issued a greeting from somewhere deeper inside.

The smell of old leather and candle wax assaulted her. She always enjoyed the mixture of scents, the comfort row after row of books provided, and, most of all, the silence of the bookstore; however, Abercorn's mere presence did away with any security and serenity she gained from being surrounded by her most favorite thing: books. This shop was not her safe haven or her sanctuary when Abercorn was near.

Safely in the aisle, she paused before hurrying toward the back of the shop. She'd been to Oliver's more times than she could count and knew the place well. Abercorn and Lady Sissy were three rows down in the History of the English Coast section. She'd scoured the section many times but found the books mainly about their country's many sea ports, including import and export routes favored over the last three hundred years. In short, the titles nestled on the shelves in that row lacked adventure beyond the mundane. No tales of swashbuckling pirates sailing across the seven seas in search of hidden treasure and their ladyloves. No tales of Arabian nights with hooded thieves and enchanting maidens. Not so much as a tale of a long-ago Robin Hood, stealing from the wealthy upper class and giving to the downtrodden paupers of Nottingham.

Abercorn was a shrewd businessman and tales of fancy were certainly not to his liking, but why would he be interested in trade in and out of England?

If she were utterly honest, Ophelia had little knowledge what men of vast wealth and power busied themselves with all day in their offices. Even her father, a duke much like Abercorn, did not concern himself with family matters, nor did he share news of his business ventures with his children.

"Can I help you with something, miss?"

Ophelia yelped with fright as she swung around to see the shopkeeper only a few feet away from her at the end of the aisle.

"No, sir, thank you," she hissed, putting her hand to her chest as her bosom heaved. "I am merely having a look around."

"If you need anything, I will be behind the counter." The shopkeeper nodded in the direction of the tall desk along the far wall toward the front of the shop before returning to his post.

Ophelia sighed in relief.

Taking in the shop—or the areas she could see through the opening in the shelf before her—it was only Ophelia, the shopkeeper, and Abercorn and his sister in the shop. She watched the duke closely as he moved down the row, scanning the shelves, his back to her. When he reached the end, he turned and started down the next aisle. Another row on England, these mostly featuring large, handwritten volumes depicting various countryside landscapes and their native plants and animals. The duke pulled a book from its place, and Ophelia shifted to see the cover; however, Abercorn moved down the aisle toward Oliver's desk before she could make it out.

"Good day, my lord," the shopkeeper greeted Abercorn. "And my lady. Will this be all?"

Abercorn responded, but his voice was too low for Ophelia to hear.

Oh, bother.

"Ask him, Franny," Lady Sissy whined, but again, Abercorn spoke too softly for Ophelia to hear what was said.

The shopkeeper and Lord Abercorn spoke for several minutes before Abercorn handed over his coin for the book he purchased.

Perhaps Edith and Luci were correct, and Ophelia was unequipped to undertake anything more than writing the articles for the *Mayfair Confidential* column in the *London Daily Gazette*.

The front bell chimed as Abercorn and Lady Sissy exited. Ophelia watched as they promptly entered his parked carriage. There would be little hope of keeping further watch on the man today.

Ophelia allowed her fingers to caress the spine of a book as she stepped around the tall shelf and into Oliver's line of sight. His eyes bulged, and his breath hitched. She'd startled him—and that might be enough to throw the proprietor off and allow her to ask the information she sought. She was here for a reason, after all. It was not enough to simply *follow* Abercorn. They were in dire need of information. Anything that could lead to the apprehension of the man for Tilda's death.

"Good day, Lady Ophelia. I did not know you were still here." Oliver busied himself with a stack of papers on his desk, giving her the privacy she normally needed, but she would not be turned away so easily. When she continued to stare at him, he set the papers aside and faced her from behind his desk. "Can I assist you with locating something?"

"I think you can." She smiled at the man.

"Anything, my lady."

Anything? She supposed she'd put his words to the test. "What was that man"—Ophelia glanced over her shoulder and pointed toward the door Abercorn and his sister had left through—"asking about? And what book did he purchase?"

The duke's trip to Oliver's Book Shoppe may very well have naught to do with Ophelia, her friends, or Tilda's death, but she needed to know. At least, for her own sake.

A measure of confidence infused and emboldened Ophelia. "It would be very helpful to know what Lord Abercorn was doing in your shop, Mr. Oliver."

The man's eyes narrowed on her, and Ophelia suspected she'd gone too far. But hadn't Edith risked it all when she'd climbed into Lord Torrington's father's tree? And hadn't Luci endangered her reputation by kissing Lord Montrose in that well-lit garden? It was Ophelia's turn to chance her name.

She could do this.

She had to do this.

She not only owed it to Tilda's memory but also to Edith and Lucianna.

"Come now, Mr. Oliver," Ophelia coaxed as she took a step toward the proprietor in the dim shop. "We have known one another for many, many years. My father used to bring me here when I was still in short dresses and childish frocks. I dare say, my hair mayhap still plaited. Please, I just want to know the reason for Lord Abercorn's visit to your shop."

His lips pressed into a fine line, and he tapped one finger on the desk. "I pride myself on keeping my clients' acquisitions private, my lady. I am certain you can understand that."

"I can; however, I am more than a client, am I not?" Ophelia's brow rose, and she stepped closer to Mr. Oliver. "It is a simple, unimportant, morsel of information I seek. Nothing more."

His eyes followed her as she advanced on him.

"My lady, you must—"

"My father will be greatly angered if I return to him without what he seeks." Ophelia detested bringing her father, the Duke of Atholl, into the matter, but she was running out of options, and Oliver seemed no closer to speaking. "He is a valued patron of your bookshop, is he not?" There was little need to wait for a reply, but Oliver nodded all the same. "What can it hurt to tell me what Abercorn was here in search of…that is, unless it has to do with my father's collection?"

Oliver's brow shot high, and Ophelia had the sense that she'd stumbled upon something completely unintended, but she pushed the notion from her mind. Her father had nothing to do with Abercorn.

The shopkeeper rubbed the back of his neck and sighed, pondering the limited options she'd given him. Certainly, the man would speak, and Ophelia would have the information she needed, as useless as it might be.

"Lady Ophelia, while your father is a valued client, he will understand I am unable to give you the information you seek." He glanced over Ophelia's shoulder toward the door. "Besides, would you want me sharing news of your purchases with anyone?"

Bloody bollocks. Ophelia certainly would not want

Oliver sharing with all and sundry her adoration for adventure tales or her love for romantic stories. She would not want her recent purchase of Coleridge's *The Rime of the Ancyent Marinere* to be known by anyone in polite society. She was not embarrassed by her reading pleasures, but she did enjoy anonymity regarding her purchases.

Glancing back toward the door, she noted that Lord Abercorn's carriage remained at the curb outside the shop. Lucianna would be completing her transactions very soon, no doubt. Ophelia headed toward the back door of the bookstore, knowing she could depart and re-enter the stationery shop where she'd left Luci without being seen by the passing carriages. She was nearly there when the front door sounded yet again.

Ophelia ducked into a small reading alcove she'd never noticed before at the back of the store and hastily pulled the drape closed to block her from view.

Heavy footfalls sounded across the wood plank floor and echoed through the empty shop.

Peculiar, Abercorn had made no sound as he traversed the rows in search of his book. Nor had his boots made any noise as he'd departed Oliver's. And Lady Sissy's slippers only shuffled along the floor.

A measure of relief flooded Ophelia, allowing her to take a deep breath before grasping the curtain. Her hand stalled when a deep, raspy voice sounded after Oliver's customary greeting.

She peeked through the slit in the hanging drape.

A man stood before Oliver, his hands hanging stiffly at his sides. His side profile showed a strong jaw, tanned skin, and fair hair that hung a bit too long over his collar. While Edith's hair was the color of pure spun gold or morning rays of sunshine, this man had hair so fair it was nearly white, though it could be the deep tan of his complexion that cast the illusion. His stance was wide, and he moved his hands to his hips as his voice rose.

"I would appreciate if you could check your records, sir," the man huffed, running his hand through his hair to return it to its place. "I have, on good authority, word you were at one time in possession of the book I seek."

Oliver's eyes narrowed, and he retrieved a ledger from the shelf next to his desk. "When did you say I might have had the book?"

"Ten years ago, perhaps longer," the man replied, his cultured tone and finely tailored jacket spoke of wealth. "It is called *Smuggling: A Journey from Kent to Denmark*, by Fair Wind Parnell."

"Ten years, you say?"

"There about, yes."

Ophelia dared pull the curtain open a bit further to hear Oliver's quiet reply.

"My apologies, but my ledger does not span more than five years of acquisitions, my lord."

The man rubbed his jaw and turned toward Ophelia's hiding spot, causing her to shrink back to avoid being seen eavesdropping.

"But you have other ledgers?" he asked. "This is of the utmost importance, and time is of the essence."

The man was clearly agitated, but why would a book, especially one over ten years old, be of any import?

Ophelia nearly giggled at the thought. Most of her collection was made up of books twice her age, and all were still relevant and captivating. She scooted closer to the curtain again as the man stared at something to the left of the alcove she hid in.

His eyes.

They were the most entrancing hue of green. They fairly glowed in the dimly lit shop and were only accentuated by his dark complexion—and the irritation rolling off him.

She envisioned that he must be the spitting image

of every pirate ever written.

It did not take much imagination to picture the man bare-chested, the salty sea breeze blowing his hair back as the noonday sun heated his skin. His grip on the helm of his impressively large vessel firm as he barked orders to his crew who worked frantically about the deck. His men would fear him, yet respect his leadership. He would be valiant, courageous, and chivalrous.

Was not every riveting man written of in books—tales of love and adventure—marked by those three traits?

He would be a captain in command of his men and his ship—or at least that would be how the tale went. But would he be a pirate? A naval captain? Or a mere merchant?

Certainly not a smuggler as intimated by his inquiry to the shopkeeper.

No, a smuggler would not sail into battle to win the heart of a woman.

Oliver offered the man a slip of paper and a quill, which the man gladly accepted before scribbling something.

Ophelia exhaled her pent-up breath as Oliver promised to inspect the ledgers kept at his home for the sought book and assured the customer he would send word to the address provided.

With a curt nod of thanks, the man returned the quill and paper to Oliver and strode from the store, the chime signaling his departure.

She exited her hiding spot and hurried to the middle row and a clear view of the front of the shop and the happenings outside the window.

The man, whoever he was, waited as his footman opened his carriage door and then entered the conveyance. Barely enough time had passed for the servant to leap back onto the perch before the carriage pulled onto Bond Street and out of sight.

Leaving Ophelia staring after him, puzzled and highly interested in his plight to secure a book.

CHAPTER 2

COLIN PARNELL, LORD Hawke, departed Oliver's Book Shoppe in no better mood than he'd arrived. He jammed his fingers through his hair, reminding himself for the tenth time he was in serious need of a trim as he threw himself against the velvety soft cushion of his father's town coach.

Blast it all, but the situation irritated him to no end.

"Well?" a raspy voice asked from across the enclosed carriage as it jerked into motion. "Did that fool Oliver have me book?"

"*Our* book," Colin corrected, bringing his glare to the woman. His tone and narrowed stare softened immediately when he took in his grandmama's hopeful look. "My apologies, Molly, it is only I am frustrated and tired of hitting dead ends with our search."

The old woman smiled, her teeth perfectly straight but stained by her love of Turkish coffee.

"Bollocks, but I detest disappointing you," Colin huffed. "Pardon my speech, Molly."

"Do not ye be worry'n 'bout disappoint'n me, lad," Molly chastised, crossing her thin arms over her nearly flat chest. Since the sickness had taken hold, she'd slowly diminished in size, though her demeanor was in no way less frightening, especially when she turned her anger on a subject. "None of this would be necessary if'n your scoundrel of a father was not so determined to prove your grandpapa, me dear Fair Wind, a debauched smuggler."

Colin massaged his temples, praying his headache did not return. Molly had arrived in London only a week prior from his family's country estate in Tintinhull, Somerset, under the guise of requiring a physician, but it hadn't taken long for her true purpose to present itself.

"You know how it angers Father when you call Grandpapa 'Fair Wind'."

"What do ye expect me ta call him, child? Porter? Lord Coventry? M'lord?" The woman huffed as her knuckles whitened on the head of her walking cane. "He be Fair Wind ta me, always has been, and always will be since the moment he entered that tavern in Sheerness. He was no gent then, nor when he went ta the good Lord."

The woman tapped her chest and left shoulder before winking twice and nodding her chin.

It had been the same superstitious ritual she'd performed Colin's entire life. As a child, he'd thought it peculiar and laugh-worthy, but as a grown man with twenty-three summers come and gone, he cringed each time Molly executed the foolish deed when his grandpapa, Porter Parnell, the first Earl of Coventry was mentioned aloud.

Colin desperately longed to make Molly happy. She'd been like a mother to him since his birth as his own parents had been far more interested in partaking of London Seasons and holidays in Bath than rearing their only child.

"I just cannot believe Oliver would sell the book," Molly sighed, shaking her head. "He and me Fair Wind were dear friends."

"If it is any consolation, he promised to review his old ledgers and determine who purchased the tome." It was the best Colin had been able to accomplish—and far more information than he'd expected to obtain. Who would have thought the old bookshop would still be operating after all these years, or that the proprietor would remember the book in question. "He has assured me he will send word, regardless of what he finds in his records."

"He best, or next time, I be forced ta speak with him," Molly threatened.

Yes, the woman was a force of nature, even at her advanced age, but her health was indeed failing.

She thumped her cane against the carriage floor, and her hat fell forward over one eye. She reached up, her fingers shaking slightly, and pushed the cap back. "I will bash him in the knees until he be remember'n exactly what he did with our book."

"You cannot go about hitting people, Molly." It had been a point of contention between Molly and Colin's parents for years. She lived by the old rules, the governances followed by the hardworking Englishmen and women of Kent during a time when she and Colin's grandpapa did all they could to survive. "And, I beg of you, do not cause another scene, or Father has made it clear you will be returned to Somerset where an adequate physician will be retained for you."

She snorted, a decidedly unladylike sound for a dowager countess. "Ramsey, my wayward son, would enjoy noth'n more than leave'n me ta rot in the wilds of Somerset while he lives like the grand nob he is."

The carriage hit a particularly large pothole, and Molly bounced from her seat, landing askew.

Colin immediately moved across the carriage to assist her back to a seated position, but she swatted his hand away.

"I'm not at death's door yet, lad," she scolded. "The carrion hunter won't be summoned for me today. I have important business ta attend before that day comes, and your rascal of a father won't be stop'n me."

And around and around it went.

"Of course, you are not in jeopardy of going to the hereafter as yet."

"And I won't be meet'n my love only ta tell him his son still thinks him a no-good smuggler." Molly turned sharply, likely to hide her teary eyes from her only grandson. "I won't be allow'n that ta happen, Colin."

"Neither will I," he said in agreement.

Colin allowed the silence to cloak him, to settle around him like a well-worn garment as he watched Molly, her head leaning back against the cushion as she continued to stare out the window.

Sometimes, he found himself beginning to believe his father's rantings surrounding Molly's mental state. The Earl of Coventry used words such as demented, addlebrained, and senseless when he spoke of his mother, Molly Parnell. However, Colin only saw a woman who'd cared for him during his infancy and childhood and who continued to dote on him even after his time at University. No one who came into contact with Molly could deny the old woman was set in her ways, or that she had a mouth worse than most seamen, the demeanor of a shrewd merchant, and the crass nature of a bar wench. And she'd been exactly that when she met and fell in love with Porter Parnell all those years ago.

Though before giving birth to her only son, Ramsey, Molly—and Porter—had been bestowed an Earldom by King George II with lands and a fortune to match, she'd never forgotten her humble beginnings in the coast town of Sheerness, Kent.

"Molly." He had the urge to say something, to reassure her that he was doing all in his power to find his grandpapa's book—the volume Molly was certain would prove that Fair Wind was not just a mere smuggler, but an honorable, king-fearing man who served his country well during the Seven Years' War. When his grandmama turned to him, Colin noted how much she'd aged since he last visited her. Her eyes were…tired. It was the only way to explain her heavily sagging lids. Her hair was now solid gray, though she'd always prided herself on her silky brown tresses. And her fingers firmly grasping her cane were gnarled. "I have not given up hope. Never will I give up hope."

"So much like me Fair Wind, ye are, lad." Her smile returned, but it was not meant for Colin. No, she was thinking of Porter "Fair Wind" Parnell, her lost love.

Colin was almost hesitant to call her mind back to the present, but they were nearly to Knightsbridge Townhouse—the Coventry home while in London— and he needed to remind her of the sensitive nature of their search. "You will keep this between us, correct? Father will return you to Somerset without a second thought if he learns we are trying to locate that bloody book again."

"Discretion is me middle name, boy," Molly replied with a grin.

"I thought you said it was Arabella-Louise," Colin teased.

"And ye are a far better listener than your father." She glanced out the window once more, and Colin was filled with a sense of pride—of accomplishment. His grandmama Molly was a determined woman, and with his help they would set history straight and prove that Fair Wind Parnell, later the first Earl of Coventry, was much more than a no-good, scallywag of a smuggler. They would establish that he was, in fact, the trusted friend of one of the greatest monarch's England has ever seen.

…if only they could hide their activities from his father for a while longer.

CHAPTER 3

OPHELIA SLIPPED INTO her room and leaned against the door, her eyes closed. She was beyond ready for a couple of quiet moments alone—and a few scarce minutes to lose herself in her current book, *The Buccaneer's Bounty*, without Luci droning on and on about the silly nature of adventure novels or, worse yet, her upcoming nuptials to the Duke of Montrose. Ophelia in no way felt ill will for the new pair, but she was rather jealous she'd been forbidden to accompany the couple on their trip to Scotland.

Another escapade she'd be left out of.

Oh, she'd known brief moments of adventure— their spying on Abercorn, their hand in the *Mayfair Confidential* column, and their trip to rescue Edith after she'd been kidnapped a few months prior—but none of those had been *hers*. Ophelia had had no control over any of those events, and a sense of helplessness came with that thought.

She sighed and pushed away from the door as she opened her eyes.

Only to recoil in horror.

The small bookshelf near her bed had been emptied of Ophelia's most treasured volumes.

She rushed around the mattress as dread heated her

skin.

Her books…they were haphazardly strewn on the floor with no regard for their value.

Glancing at her shelf once more, Ophelia was stunned to see several lengths of ribbon and a pearl-handled comb and brush set nestled where Ophelia had lovingly placed her collection of poetry.

The door opened and closed behind her with a resounding thud.

"Ah, there you are!" Luci's voiced rose the hairs on the back of Ophelia's neck. "I left the receiving room to call for tea, and when I returned, you had vanished."

Ophelia took a deep breath and exhaled slowly, reciting to herself that she only need share her private chambers for a few more days before Luci would be off to Scotland with Montrose, Edith, and Lord Torrington. Her bedchambers would once again be hers, and her friendship with Luci would return to normal.

"Oh, you are admiring my latest gifts from Roderick." Luci knelt before the shelf and caressed the handle of the delicate brush. "He is such a generous man, and he truly loves me," Luci sighed.

Yes, and before long *he'd* be giving up his personal space to accommodate Lucianna.

Ophelia *was* overjoyed that both of her dearest friends were betrothed to such fine, noble lords.

"Did you hear the brilliant news?" Luci moved to the wardrobe and collected a pressed set of cream gloves to match her sage-green gown—*Ophelia's* walking dress, the hem let out several inches to accommodate Luci's tall stature. "My stationery arrived this morning," she continued without waiting for Ophelia to answer.

"Splendid," Ophelia mumbled.

"When I return from Scotland, I am taking you to Mademoiselle Katerina for an entirely new wardrobe." Luci dragged her fingertips across the neatly hung gowns in Ophelia's dressing closet. "These colors…they are atrocious and in no way complement your complexion."

"But they are the same gowns I've been wearing all Season," Ophelia retorted, but even to her ears, the words held no bite.

"Yes, but now you are the bosom friend of a duchess and a soon-to-be marchioness." Luci pulled a muddy-brown riding habit out of the wardrobe and held it out for Ophelia to see. "You cannot possibly believe this dreadful excuse for a proper fabric is acceptable, O."

"I, well…"

"Do not fret." Luci rehung the habit and turned back to Ophelia with a reassuring smile. "I will outfit you properly."

A peculiar promise from a woman who was in all regards without a home at present.

Ophelia glanced at her still open closet behind Luci and then noted the pair of blue satin slippers protruding from beneath her dressing table, the pile of books continuing to collect dust on her floor, and the stack of shawls strewn across her normally neatly made bed. Luci moved through every room much like a windstorm, wreaking havoc as she did, and leaving destruction in her wake. Ophelia needs must remember to give her maid extra thanks for tidying up after her friend.

"Are you ready?" Luci took in Ophelia from head to toe.

For a brief moment, she had the urge to take in her appearance, as well; however, Ophelia had been dressed since shortly after dawn. She'd broken her fast with her siblings and mother. She'd written another article for the *Mayfair Confidential,* and she'd selected her next book to read—all before Luci had seen fit to crawl from her bed.

"Roderick will be here shortly to collect us for our outing."

"And we certainly don't wish to keep him waiting." Ophelia slipped her coin purse into the pocket of her cloak. "I am ready."

The way Luci's eyes lingered on her, told Ophelia her friend thought her anything but ready.

But, with no other protest, Luci slipped her arm through Ophelia's and pulled her toward the door as if Ophelia were a puppy to be manhandled and led about on a leash.

Not that Ophelia had anyone to blame but herself for the way Luci and Edith treated her—she'd always been happy to follow their lead, listen to their instructions, and do exactly as she was told. It was the same with her family. Ophelia's mother bid her keep watch on her younger siblings, and she readily agreed. Her father demanded she remain in London and not accompany her friends to Scotland, and Ophelia had not issued so much as an argument in favor of what she longed to do. When Luci had quickly taken over her chambers, making them her own, Ophelia hadn't objected.

They departed their shared chambers arm-in-arm and made their way to the main staircase. When an envelope had arrived containing a healthy amount of pounds, both Luci and Ophelia had gasped in surprise. The gift was from Lucianna's mother and was to be spent on proper clothing until such time that Lady Camden could convince her stubborn husband to hand over the rest of Luci's dowry after she wed Montrose.

Another day of shopping did not sound nearly as appealing as an afternoon spent reading. However, with Montrose, Edith, and Lord Torrington in tow, at least Ophelia wouldn't be alone in her plight.

AN EXASPERATED SIGH escaped as Colin pondered for the thousandth time why he'd agreed to allow Molly to accompany him to Atholl's townhouse. He leaned back against the velvet squabs of his father's finely adorned landau and gave his grandmama his most charming smile. Allowing the woman to know he was irritated would be unwise.

"You cannot accompany me into Lord Atholl's home," he repeated for the third time since they'd pulled into the drive. His footman waited outside the carriage to open the door, but Colin refused to depart the conveyance until Molly had agreed to remain inside and unseen.

"Why can I not go in?" Molly huffed, pounding the end of her cane against the floor to punctuate each word. "It is me book the man stole, and I will have it back."

"Atholl stole nothing," Colin said slowly, his imploring stare begging Molly to understand. "He purchased the book at Oliver's, bought and paid for."

"He is a bloody pisser, and ye won't be convince'n me no different."

"Molly." Colin pinched the bridge of his nose. Growing up on the docks of Sheerness, his grandmama's less than proper upbringing presented itself with increased intensity when she was angry or met by opposition. "This is exactly why I cannot allow you to accompany me. If you start in on one of your tirades, Lord Atholl will have no reason to give us any information about the book—that is if he even so much as remembers purchasing the blasted thing."

With a *humph*, Molly trained her eyes on the head of her cane. "We are too bloody close, Colin, me lad."

"I understand your impatience, I do. However, barging into Lord Atholl's home and demanding the book will not gain us what we seek." He was helpless to remain irked by her demeanor. "Besides, Oliver gave me the information in the strictest of confidence. It would harm his business if any hint of gossip escaped, concerning him giving out the personal information of his clients. Tell me you understand and will remain in the carriage until I return."

She took her narrowed stare from her cane and met

his eyes, her countenance immediately softening as she eased into her seat. "Ye are your grandpapa's offspring, that be for certain."

Colin smiled, knowing Molly could never refuse him anything when he presented her with his toothy grin—the mirror image of Fair Wind's smile, the mischievous smirk she'd fallen in love with all those years ago in a tavern taproom full of unsavory seamen.

At that moment, Colin did not feel a single ounce of guilt using the tactic against her to gain her cooperation.

"I know, Molly, and just as you did with Grandpapa, trust me to take care of you. Believe I will find Fair Wind's book and return it to you," he said on a rushed exhale. "Can you do that for me?"

She turned her head sharply to stare at the curtain-covered window.

"I will have your word, or we will leave now and I will return you home." He shrugged, content with either option depending on the choice she made. If she insisted on accompanying him inside, they would return home, and Colin would journey back to Mayfair without her in tow.

"I will wait here," she sighed.

"Thank you, Molly. That is a wise decision."

She snorted, refusing to look at him. However, she'd given him her word, and there was little his grandmama valued more than a promise.

He rapped on the side of the carriage, and his footmen opened the door and placed the step for him to depart.

"I love you, and I will return quickly with any information I discover." He leaned forward and pressed a quick kiss to the cheek she offered.

Colin leapt from the carriage, pausing to have a word with his footman and driver.

"Keep a watch on her. Whatever you do, do not allow her inside Lord Atholl's townhouse."

Both servants nodded in understanding and resumed their posts by the waiting carriage.

His clenched fist pounded on the door, quickly bringing a butler to greet him.

"Lord Hawke to see Lord Atholl," Colin announced, reaching into his jacket pocket for his calling card.

The servant accepted the offering but didn't take his eyes off Colin. "Is His Grace expecting you, my lord?"

"No. However, you can inform him that I've come in regards to information about Sheerness." The butler's brow rose, certainly familiar with the town on the Kent coast, known for its long history of smugglers. "It is a business matter."

"Of course, my lord, this way please."

Colin expected to be shown into the foyer or an empty receiving room, but the servant led him through the entrance, past two salons, and down a wide hall farther into the house.

"His Grace is in his study, sir." The butler stopped and opened a door to Colin's left before stepping into the room, leaving Colin in the dim corridor. "Your Grace, a Lord Hawke"—he glanced down at the card for the first time—"Baron Hawke, is here to speak with you in regards to Sheerness."

Bloody hell. He'd used the information as a ploy to gain entrance. Colin hadn't imagined the butler would announce his interests so boldly. When he'd gotten word from Oliver with regards to who had last owned the book, Colin had had his man of business look into the lord.

"Sheerness, you say?" The voice did not boom and echo down the hall, nor sound forceful in any manner—the robust volume Colin thought a duke would possess. "Do show him in."

"He is right here, Your Grace." The servant glanced over his shoulder to where Colin awaited. "His

Grace, the Duke of Atholl, will see you, my lord."

The comical nature of the exchange was not lost on Colin as he stepped into the room. The door shut behind him with a quietness not found in many homes—the hinges did not protest, nor did the latch clink.

"Your Grace." Colin bowed abruptly as the duke stood, his rounded spectacles and soft brown hair framing his heart-shaped face. "It is a pleasure to make your acquaintance. I apologize for not sending word before calling on you."

The man waved his hand toward the chair before him. "Do sit. I always relish the opportunity to meet and discuss locales of great British import. What do you know of Sheerness?"

Colin took a moment to take in the room around him, the walls were covered in maps spanning from England to Denmark and even Sweden and Russia. A wall lined with tomes of all sizes held titles of world travel and history. On any other day, he'd ask to walk the room and explore Atholl's fine collection.

But not this day. He was here on important business, though whether he should clue the duke in on that fact had still not been decided.

Sitting, Colin noted Atholl scrutinizing him from behind the large desk, its impressive size making the duke appear no larger than a child in comparison.

"My family is from Sheerness, or at least my grandpapa and grandmama on my father's side hailed from the area." Colin was satisfied when the man nodded at the information, making it unnecessary to share any further details surrounding his family's past in Kent. "I have heard you are purchasing property there."

A simple, innocent enough inquiry, but the duke's eyes narrowed sharply.

"Yes, well, the area is a prime locale for the import and export of goods." Atholl made a show of fussing with a stack of papers on his desk. "I have purchased several properties which I plan to utilize in the future."

"Have you been to Sheerness?" Colin spied the portrait hanging behind the duke's chair: five young children—a boy and four girls—all with red hair of various shades, cuddled around a mop-haired hound. "My grandmama speaks of the vast coastline and scenic walks. Mayhap you've taken your children there?"

Colin was baiting the man. He, himself, had never ventured to Sheerness. His father, the Earl of Coventry, was determined to erase their family's past, and doing that meant expunging everything his grandmama held dear, everything the woman had taught him growing up, including the connection to Porter "Fair Wind" Parnell, a known smuggler.

The duke chuckled at Colin's mention of family travels to the far reaches of Kent.

Atholl shook his head. "No, no, the children are too old to enjoy time away from London. Heavens, where would my son continue his fencing lessons or my daughters secure an adequate musical instructor, let alone a dressmaker in Kent?"

In the portrait hung behind Atholl, the children appeared to vary from ages seven to possibly twelve summers. Still rather young, as families went, though at the duke's age—certainly as old as Colin's father—toting around a brimming family of seven would be a task only a brave man would undertake.

Colin did his best to smile and laugh along with the man. If he hoped to bring any useful information back to Molly, he needs must be at ease in Atholl's presence—playact he was only here due to their mutual interest in Sheerness, not because his family's most treasured—and hotly debated—item was likely in this very room.

CHAPTER 4

OPHELIA COULD NOT remove her narrowed gaze from the closed door of the study the stranger had been escorted into by the Atholl butler. Here to meet with her father—but for what purpose? The man's appearance in *her* home, of all places, was highly suspect. Especially after Mr. Oliver had been nonresponsive to Ophelia's questions upon first seeing him at the bookseller's.

And for a second time, he hadn't noticed Ophelia's presence where she and Lucianna had pressed themselves against the stairwell wall to remain unseen.

Ophelia waved over her shoulder to her friend. "I think I will remain home," she said. "Edith and Lord Torrington will be meeting you, correct?"

"Yes, but—"

"No one likes a fifth wheel, as they say." Especially Ophelia. After Tilda's death, she was always the third of their small group—and since Montrose and Torrington had joined and made them five, she was the unneeded extra wheel of their carriage. There if needed, but forgotten more often than not.

"Shall we be off?" Roderick asked. "I believe she is duly occupied, and we have a bridal trousseau to gather before we depart for Scotland."

Their chatter faded as Ophelia approached her father's study, quickly pulling a book from the small shelf outside the closed door before she leaned against the wall. No servant would question if Ophelia were seen standing in the corridor with her nose in a book.

Flipping open the cover, she settled on a page about halfway through the book...a title on...oh, bother, the history of English imports from the Turkish Isles. While her presence with a book would not be viewed as peculiar, seeing her enthusiastically reading a volume on commerce and trade certainly would.

Ah, well, she was committed.

Besides, it was not necessary for her to actually read anything in the tome, only use it as a ruse to keep her true intent a secret.

She side-stepped several inches until her shoulder rested against the doorframe of the study and then crossed her ankles as if she were merely enjoying a few moments of silence for reading. However, her head was tilted ever so slightly toward the closed door, and her breath was held as she attempted to catch any stray words that might make their way through the closed portal.

Blast it all, but her father had always been a quiet man, never raising his voice in anger nor in exuberant joy. Level-headed, calm, and cool—all the things Ophelia strived to be but never fully achieved.

Her father's light chuckle sounded, accompanied by that of the stranger.

Rarely did her father allow himself the luxury of a moment of fancy—he worked hard every day to make certain the Dukedom was enough, would always be enough, for the care of the many Fletcher children. With four siblings—Jacob, Sarah, Elizabeth, and Jennifer—Ophelia could only imagine the pressure upon her father to see them all wed with proper families of their own, all while keeping Jacob in line to continue running the Dukedom after Atholl no longer could.

The laughter died quickly, and with it the sounds from within. If Ophelia moved any closer, she'd be perched in the doorway of the study, and eavesdropping was certainly not a proper activity for a young woman of quality. Ophelia bit her lip, keeping her eyes trained on her open book as she pondered her next move.

The man she was now convinced was a lord, had appeared rather tense and irritated at Oliver's a fortnight ago; however, she heard no shouting or anger from the study at present.

Was it possible that her father knew the man?

The words blurred together on the page before her, though she did not focus enough to sort them out.

"My lady?"

Ophelia yelped and nearly dropped the book when the Atholl butler cleared his throat to gain her attention.

"May I help you with something?"

She glanced around the deserted hallway in search of any excuse to send the servant on his way. "I—well—I was—" Ophelia closed the book and held it up for the butler to see, as if that should answer his question, but the man only continued to stare at her expectantly. "I was reading this book…and awaiting an audience with Father. Do you know how long he will be?"

"I do not, my lady." The servant appeared vexed at his inability to give her the information she sought. "His Grace is meeting with Lord Hawke, and I am uncertain how long they will be."

"I see." Ophelia did her best to appear perplexed by the situation. "I was under the impression my father had requested my presence while Mother and the girls were otherwise occupied."

"I will inform His Grace as soon as his guest departs, my lady."

"Wonderful."

The pair stood, staring at one another, clearly waiting for the other to depart.

Blessedly, a commotion in the foyer had the servant hurrying back to his post. It was likely only Montrose or Luci, returned to collect something they'd forgotten.

Alone once more, Ophelia glanced about quickly before boldly pressing her ear to the door. Her pulse increased at her daring act—something her father would punish her severely for if she were discovered.

And her cunning paid off in spades as bits of the conversation floated through the door, though many words were muffled.

Sheerness…a coveted book…smuggling…

The stranger's words were cut short by her father. "No, no, exports and shipping via the area's dock are all that hold my interest, though I can tell you that talk of age-old smugglers and pirates from the area has always piqued my curiosity."

Her father had an interest in anything other than matters of legitimate business?

She was uncertain which surprised her more; her father's bout of laughter a few moments before, or his admittance of curiosity regarding anything historical and, dare she say, adventurous.

The butler's raised voice sounded from down the hall in the foyer.

Ophelia drew away from the study door in case her father came out to investigate the commotion. It was advantageous Luci would be departing soon for Scotland, for if she continued making a ruckus in the duke's home, he may very well bid her find accommodations elsewhere.

Ophelia's slippered feet made no sound as she strode down the hall and around the corner into the foyer, a sharp rebuff on the tip of her tongue for Luci. Not only because of her disruptive nature, but also because Ophelia had, for once, been on the cusp of something—a bit of mystery surrounding the strange lord—and now she'd learn nothing more.

Maybe she did not rightfully possess Edith's inquisitive nature or Luci's cunning and daring demeanor.

She skidded to a halt the moment she rounded the corner and the foyer came into view.

"...I am a bloody fancy lady, ye yellow-feathered buffoon!"

"Madam, please!" The butler ducked as he tried to push the front door closed.

The pointy end of a stick shot through the opening and whacked the servant soundly on the shoulder, causing his hold to falter and the door to inch open as a footman rushed to assist.

"My heavens," Ophelia huffed. "Step back and allow the woman entrance."

The Atholl butler and footman leapt to attention, their movements allowing the front door to swing open—and crash into the wall.

In the doorway stood a tiny, silver-haired woman...swinging not a stick but a cane, her eyes wide with fury as they darted around the foyer in search of heavens knew what.

Ophelia took a hesitant step forward, and the two men retreated, keeping a watchful eye on the situation.

"Madam, may I be of service?" The woman was clearly confused, her cane coming to rest where it should as she stepped back from the open door. "Are you lost?"

Ophelia advanced, her brow pulled together with concern.

The woman tapped her forehead, chest, and nose before dipping her chin to almost touch her chest as she backed away from the door and toward a waiting carriage.

The butler lunged forward and slammed the door shut, collapsing with a groan against the wood. "My many thanks, Lady Ophelia. Bless my mother's soul, but that woman was as mad as a milk maid without a proper pail."

"Who is she?" she hissed as the woman let out another round of obscenities outside. Ophelia's face reddened, and the butler looked away at the crass mention of what the servant could do with his fancy speech and insulting manners.

When the butler shrugged, Ophelia asked, "We should offer assistance, correct?"

His eyes widened, and she sensed the man would not prove to be an ally in this situation. If she meant to confront the mad woman again, it would be on her own.

Ophelia took a deep, fortifying breath and opened the front door to see the woman blindly swinging her cane at the gardenia bush bordering the walk. She couldn't help but wonder what the plant could have done to anger the woman. The sight was both laughable and perplexing at the same time.

Though Ophelia was sure the Atholl gardener would not feel the same.

When the petite woman saw Ophelia exit the door, she held the cane high, clutched something hanging around her neck, and spat.

She actually *spat* on the ground between them.

Ophelia glanced behind the woman to the carriage waiting in the drive. The coachman and footman stared at everything but what was happening fifteen feet from them. It was as if only she saw the mad woman with her cane held high, ready to do battle.

"Ye cannot pass," the woman hissed, nodding to the spittle before tapping her forehead, her chest, and nose. "Your mark of the devil will not be bewitch'n me. Don't ye be come'n any closer, ye fork-tongued beast." She punctuated her words by spitting once more and swinging her cane in the empty space between her and Ophelia.

"I am afraid I am uncertain of what you speak, madam." Ophelia held her hands before her, but did not dare take a step toward the woman.

"Ye, with your hair like the devil, that be exactly what I be expect'n you ta say."

"My hair?" Ophelia touched the long, wavy lock that hung over her shoulder. What did her hair color signify? "If you find exception with my hair, why are you trying to gain entrance to a home full to brimming with fair-skinned, auburn-haired people?"

"I knew me senses be correct, ye cursed sorcerer." She swung her cane once more to keep Ophelia back. "Me grandson be in there, and likely be'n hauled straight to Beelzebub himself."

Ophelia must have appeared as confused as she felt because the woman laughed, a high-pitched, uncontrollable cackle.

"Yes, most certainly the look of a witch confronted with ye own misdeeds."

"I assure you, Lord Hawke is perfectly safe within."

"Ye be a crone, a hag, disguised by the Prince of Darkness himself with yer fair skin and heavenly glow. An enchantress is what ye be."

"Why I never—"

The woman spat once more, cutting off Ophelia's words as the spittle landed close to the hem of Ophelia's morning gown.

"Do stop this dramatic display, madam." Ophelia cocked her hip, her hand settling there. "I demand to know your name."

The woman's eyes narrowed to slits. "So ye can put a hex on me? I not be stand'n for it."

"Do calm yourself before you suffer apoplexy."

"Is that what your curse be?" The woman faltered back a step, and Ophelia feared she had suffered a malady; however, she continued. "Release me Colin from your evil charms, give us the book, and we be on our way, sure as the day is long."

"Molly!" The stern voice had the older woman cocking her head to the side and her eyes widening as she glanced around Ophelia. "Put your cane down and return to the carriage this instant."

The woman's glare returned to Ophelia, and she spat again, her hand clutching her pendant once more as her cane lowered. However, she made no move to follow through with the last order.

"Now," the man seethed, and Ophelia recognized the desperation she'd heard in his voice when he was at Oliver's Book Shoppe. "Please, return to the carriage and cease with your superstitious ramblings."

Ophelia kept her eyes trained on the older woman as she placed one foot behind the other, slowly backing toward the waiting coach, the cane at her side. It wasn't until Ophelia backed up and bumped against something solid—and the elderly woman allowed another curse to slip out—Ophelia realized she stood pressed against the chest of Lord Hawke.

CHAPTER 5

COLIN STOOD RIGID as the woman's soft curves molded to him from his chest to his knees. Her crown of wildly unrestrained auburn hair created a halo above her head and partly blocked his view of Molly. Everything about her made him want to take a half step forward and press more soundly to her back, maybe slip his arm around her waist to hold her close. The scent of lavender mixed with a hint of vanilla drifted between them, distracting him for a brief moment from the spectacle happening before him—in the Duke of Atholl's drive, in the most fashionable part of London.

Bloody well fantastic.

He glanced over his shoulder to see several Atholl servants gawking from the open front door.

Blessedly, Molly reached the coach, and a footman assisted her in.

The woman pressed against him took a step forward with a sigh of relief.

"Colin, ye hurry along, lest this fork-tongued heathen with her devil's curse drag ye straight ta the fiery pits of—" Molly spat out the carriage window without finishing her words and tapped her forehead.

However, Colin couldn't continue watching as she perpetuated her usual ritual.

"Miss," he said, ducking his chin in shame at his grandmama's outrageous accusations. "I am truly sorry for Molly's—err, my grandmama's—behavior."

When the woman made no move to accept or acknowledge Colin's apology, he brought his eyes to her as she turned to face him.

The first thing he noticed was the sprinkling of freckles across the bridge of her nose. So delicately spaced, as if the hand of a great artist had placed each in the exact spot they would reside forevermore.

"It is you…" The girl from the framed painting behind Atholl's desk. She was older, more woman than girl, but he was certain it was the duke's eldest daughter. The painter had captured her cobalt eyes perfectly with their slight upturn at the corners, though he'd flawed unforgivingly at catching the plump curve of her smirk.

"Pardon, my lord?" She swallowed, and her clasped hands quivered.

A tingle of embarrassment swept up his spine at her nervous stare.

Colin cleared his throat and glanced over the woman's shoulder as renewed humiliation filled him.

"Me lad!" Molly slapped her cane against the side of the carriage as she hung out the open window. "Don't be fooled by her sinful smile. She is naught but a mermaid responsible for take'n ships ta watery graves at the bottom of the ocean."

"Your grandmother certainly has a vivid imagination, Lord Hawke."

The only thing he heard was his name from her lips, not Molly's continued harassing comments.

The only thing he *saw* was the slight upturn of her lips, not Molly attempting to depart the carriage again, all the while his footman and coachman kept her blocked.

Certainly, he was aware of everything, but he could not take his attention off the woman before him.

"You know my name?" his brow rose in question,

and her face flared the most attractive shade of pink.

"She be a siren if'n I ever saw one!" Molly yelled. "Let me depart this blasted coach, ye addlepate."

"My butler informed me my father was meeting with a 'Lord Hawke.' It only stands to reason that you are he." She glanced at the ground, her pink cheeks deepening to red.

"You look much like your portrait in the duke's study." Blast it all, but he hadn't meant to say anything regarding that, and neither should it have been uttered on a sigh. Colin straightened his shoulders and adjusted his neckcloth. "What I meant to say is that your father speaks highly of you."

The man hadn't said a word about any particular offspring, yet Colin would not admit to any such thing.

"That is kind of you to say, my lord; however—" Her chin rose, and he suspected the woman knew he lied. "I would not be surprised to hear my father entirely forgot about his children."

"Sometimes, I wish my family would fail to recall me," he replied.

Sure to form, Molly started her beating on the ducal carriage once again. His father would be enraged to find his prized landau battered. There was no avoiding it. Colin was loath to take his leave before finding out the woman's name.

"You cannot mean that." Her stare widened as she fidgeted with the seam of her gown.

How to explain to a perfect stranger he, in fact, *would* relish that exact thing?

The continuous war between Colin's parents and his grandmama was utterly draining. The trio never failed to place him in the middle, forced to choose between the woman who was far more than merely his grandmama and the pair who had given him life, a proper upbringing, and an adequate education.

"Don't be believe'n that witch's banbury tale of cock and bull. Don't be purblind, Colin."

He held up his finger to silence Molly; however, his grandmama had never been deft at listening to others—or remaining silent when bidden.

With a weak smile, he said, "Allow me a moment to calm her. Please, do not go anywhere, I will be back momentarily." When she only nodded, he continued, "And I swear on all I possess, she is not as addlebrained as she appears."

"We rarely are."

Colin wanted nothing more than to question her further on her peculiar comment, but Molly began howling his name again.

"One moment is all I need," he promised. "I will return."

"Of course." Her flushed cheeks had returned to their normal coloring, and her smile suggested she was just as interested in him and he was in her.

Colin hurried to the carriage, his frown deepening the closer he came to Molly. Perhaps his father was correct in his decree that the old woman was better off at Tintinhull Court in Somerset, surrounded by Coventry servants who were both loyal and discreet. At least there, she could practice whatever superstitions she fancied useful, and would not cause Colin embarrassment, especially before an utterly bewitching woman. And that was exactly the wording he should not use when describing Atholl's daughter, especially not in front of his grandmama, lest Molly redouble her accusations of witchcraft and sorcery.

"What in all that is holy are you doing?" he demanded.

His anger caused Molly to lean back into the carriage, her mouth gaping.

"Have ye gone mad, me lad?" she hissed. "What charm has that fiery-haired siren thrown at ye?"

"She has done nothing, Molly." Colin took a moment for his breathing to slow, and his pulse to stop racing. "You, on the other hand, are jeopardizing everything."

"Did that thief in duke's garb give ye the book?"

"No, he did not, and he is not a thief."

"Then he told ye where ta find it?" she prodded, her brow pulling together as her voice lifted with hope. "Let us be off ta collect Fair Wind's book."

"Duke Atholl has promised to look for the book amongst his collection"—he paused, pinching the bridge of his nose—"however, your treatment of his daughter might very well alter his cooperative nature."

Molly peeked around him, and Colin feared she'd begin yet another tirade. Thankfully, she kept her mouth closed and leaned back into her seat, crossing her arms. She appeared the sulking, petulant child, which suited Colin perfectly, at least until he could make his amends with the woman and seek his leave.

"Now, stay out of sight and remain silent until I can apologize for your outlandish behavior."

"I not be sorry for any of it…" she huffed.

"That I know well, Molly; however, I *am* sorry for the mortification you caused the woman—outside her own home, no less."

Molly waved her hand as if to dismiss him, but did not meet his eye. "Do as ye must, lad, but I caution ye against put'n any trust in a woman so clearly marked by the devil himself."

"Am I to believe you to be deranged, as Father would have me believe?"

"*Humphf.*"

"Very well, sulk all you want." He glanced over his shoulder to see the woman had inched forward a few feet and listened intently to his conversation, even though her stare was trained on a row of shrubs bordering the drive. "Besides, I have no need or want to trust this woman, only make certain she does not tell her father of your deplorable accusations."

When Molly didn't argue further, Colin returned to the woman to offer his apologies for Molly's words and also anything she may have overhead while he'd conversed with his grandmama.

Thankfully, the servants had gone about their chores and closed the front door.

He stopped before her, at a loss for what to say. He owed her an apology and needs must beg her forgiveness even though Molly showed no contrition.

"My grandmama has always been a bit rattle-pated," he tried his hand at explaining Molly's off-key nature.

"Rattle-pated?" she asked, tugging at her ear.

"Oh, it seems when I spend too much time in her company, I adopt her seafaring jargon." Colin shook his head. "She has always been a whimsical woman, taken by notions of fancy and steeped in superstition. It is the reason my grandpapa fell in love with her, if my father is to be believed. But that is neither here nor there. Her accusations were unfounded and uncalled for, and I owe you an apology, Lady…"

"Lady Ophelia Fletcher." She curtseyed, her hair falling over her shoulders when she bowed her head slightly. "And as we've established, you are Lord Hawke."

"Colin."

Her cheeks blossomed once more when she straightened.

"It is nice to make your acquaintance, Lord Hawke," she replied. "Do not let me keep you from your grandmother."

"I will depart only if you accept my remorseful apology, Lady Ophelia."

"If you insist." She smiled and pressed her gloved hand to her mouth to cover her toothy grin. "Now, I must return inside or risk displeasing my father."

"Farewell, Lady Ophelia." He gave a simple wave. With one last smile, she twirled and rushed back in the house, the door opening for her as she reached the landing. "Until we meet again…"

Colin had no doubt they would meet again, but under what circumstances, he was uncertain.

CHAPTER 6

OPHELIA GLANCED OVER her shoulder at her waiting carriage and back again through the murky front window of Oliver's Book Shoppe, all while people pushed past her on the crowded walk. The swoosh of skirts, the brush of a man's shoulder against hers, the idle chitchat buzzing in her ears…it was all too much.

Overwhelming.

Daunting.

It had her face heating, her breath coming in shallow, labored gulps, and every instinct telling her to flee. She should return to the safety of her home. Await Edith's and Luci's return from Gretna Green.

What had possessed her to journey to Bond Street with only her maid as a companion?

She pulled the note from her cloak pocket.

Luci's looping script, upon her newly arrived cream stationery with silver trim, glared at her. She didn't need to open the letter to know exactly what it said. Or, more appropriately, what it demanded of Ophelia during Luci's absence from London.

Sliding her finger over the thick paper, Ophelia's eyes drifted closed for a brief second.

Ophelia was not to write a piece for the *Mayfair Confidential*.

Ophelia was not to investigate, follow, or snoop around Abercorn.

Ophelia was not to put herself in harm's way.

Ophelia *was* to remain close to home and away from any harmful activities until Luci and Edith returned.

And her dear friends expected her to do just that.

Remain the timid, reserved, quiet girl she'd always been; happy to tag along on their adventures but never seeking any of her own. Overjoyed even, to remain in the shadows as Edith and Luci found love. And content to be their scribe for the *Mayfair Confidential*.

"M'lady?" her maid's concerned call came from the waiting carriage where Ophelia had insisted she remain while Ophelia questioned Oliver.

She gave the girl a quick smile and shoved the note back into her pocket.

The time had come to seek her own adventure—no more hanging on to the coattails of her friends nor simply reading about thrilling escapades in her books.

Her chin tilted up a notch, and she squared her shoulders, pasting a confident smile upon her lips.

Surely, if she presented confidence outwardly, it would also take hold within her.

For not the first time, Ophelia realized she was not the great poised beauty Luci was, nor the witty and intelligent woman Edith was.

But that did not make her any less capable.

She would find the book Lord Hawke sought and return it to him.

Despite the man's grandmother and her peculiar accusations, Ophelia was determined to help him.

That he was handsome, intelligent, and had kind eyes impacted nothing.

That she'd had a difficult time concentrating on anything since she met the man several days before also did not signify anything.

That every book she selected somehow had the

hero resembling Lord Hawke—Colin—with his fair hair and piercing green eyes was far more disconcerting. Every tale she read, whether it was swashbuckling pirates or Arabian princes took on the sun-kissed complexion of a certain baron.

Ophelia could not stall any longer. Her family would worry about her whereabouts if she did not return home before afternoon social calls began.

The bell sounded overhead as she pushed through the door. The familiar smell of grass with a hint of vanilla filled her nose, along with the overpowering stench of burning wax. Beeswax to be precise, not the far more affordable tallow used by many merchants. It spoke to Oliver's prestige as one of the finest booksellers in London proper. Perhaps that was where her next adventure lay—where does Oliver gain his funds for beeswax candles with proper wicks?

That was a mystery for another time. This day, Ophelia had one goal: find out what Oliver had told Lord Hawke, and how that corresponded with the man's visit with her father.

It was a simple enough inquiry.

Harmless on all accounts.

"My lady, it is good to see you!" Oliver's greeting usually never varied, but the thin, wiry man stared over Ophelia's shoulder as if he were expecting other clientele. "But where are your friends?"

Ophelia allowed a hesitant laugh to escape her. Of course. Ophelia normally shopped with at least one of her friends in tow. "I am afraid they are otherwise occupied today; however, there is something I have need to ask you, and I did not wish to wait for their return."

"Certainly, my lady. Though I do hope this has nothing to do with your last visit to my shop," he nodded with a grave smile. "May I help you locate a book, perchance? Might I recommend a new set of Colonial adventure novels I received just this morn?"

Any other time, Ophelia would have been thrilled at the opportunity to possess such a rare collection. "Unfortunately, I am not in the market to purchase any new books today."

The shopkeeper's brow rose. "Oh?"

Ophelia journeyed farther into the shop, stopping before the tall desk Oliver stood behind. "I am here about a book—"

"But I thought you said you were not here about purchasing a book."

"I am not. You see, I believe this book has already been purchased."

He tilted his head slightly and pursed his lips, tapping his cheek with his forefinger. "Then you are looking to hire me for an acquisition?"

"Not ex—"

"There is a man, Lord Cartwright, who does a fine job of locating books."

"No, no," Ophelia sighed. "I believe you were in possession of this book not long ago and know its current owner."

His eyes narrowed behind his wire-rimmed spectacles. "I cannot disclose personal information about my clients, my lady, as I told you before."

Once again, Ophelia was losing the man's willingness to assist her. Drat! She would not allow Luci's assertions to be proven correct.

"I am looking for a book. It is about smuggling in the area of Sheerness."

Recognition dawned quickly in the shopkeeper's eyes, and his welcoming smile returned. "Blast it all, but I do wish I knew what all the fuss was over this book. You are the third person in the past month requesting information on the whereabouts of Fair Wind's book on smuggling."

"So you *do* know of it?"

"Certainly. I sent information round to another lord only a few days past; however, what knowledge an outdated book could provide to anyone is beyond my comprehension." The man turned and retrieved an oversized, leather-bound ledger from the shelf behind him. "Let me give you the information I found on the book. That won't harm anyone, I don't think." His flipped several pages and ran his finger down a list.

A tingle of excitement rushed down Ophelia's back at the thought of what she sought being so easily obtained. Perhaps her detection skills were superior to Luci's and Edith's, after all.

"Ah, here it is," he said, lifting his gaze to her with a triumphant smile. "Written by Fair Wind Parnell during the Seven Years' War."

"That is it!" At least, Ophelia hoped it was. "Can you tell me who purchased the book…and when?"

He dragged his finger across the page before stopping and pointing at a name. "I shouldn't give you the name, but since it's your father, I think it will be fine. Atholl. That's all it says, and is exactly what I told the last man who came sniffing around."

"My fa—" Ophelia clamped her mouth shut.

"Are you certain you do not wish to purchase the Colonial adventure volumes?"

"Not today, Mr. Oliver, though if they are still here on my next visit, I shall be persuaded to make them mine."

"Very good, my lady!"

The shopkeeper closed the ledger with a thump and returned it to its shelf.

All the while, Ophelia's mind swirled.

Lord Hawke had spoken with her father because he had solid information leading him to the duke, but if what she'd heard spoken between Molly and Lord Hawke was correct, the duke had promised to preview his collection for it.

But certainly, her father must know where the book is. He was a meticulous man, a keeper of records, a treasurer of the unique. This would certainly be of distinctive historical significance.

"Good day, Oliver," Ophelia said, not bothering to suppress her excitement over her discovery. "Thank you again for the information."

"I still do not understand the import of…"

The man's voice trailed off when Ophelia pushed through the door into the bright afternoon sun, the bell overhead chiming once more. Her step was lighter than it had been since before Tilda's death. The shame of admitting she'd been so engrossed in her book that if someone *had* pushed her dear friend down the stairs, Ophelia had been too preoccupied to see the culprit was suffocating. It was nice to have some relief.

"GOOD DAY, ANDREW!" Ophelia chimed, removing her gloves as she came through the front door. "Is Father in his study?"

The entire carriage ride home, she'd debated how to address the situation. There were no grounds for assuming her father had done anything wrong or had come into ownership of the book in any unsavory way.

"No, my lady." The butler took her gloves and helped her with her cloak. "He is out for the afternoon with the duchess and your siblings.

Odd, her father rarely traveled around London with his horde of children and wife, and surely not during what he considered *prime business hours.*

"However, you have guests."

"Guests?" Ophelia didn't get many visitors, unless you counted those who came to see her mother and were polite enough to request an audience with her, as well. And Lucianna and Edith had long ago stopped being considered guests in the Atholl household; besides, they were safely on their way to Gretna Green at present. "They are in Mother's salon?"

"Yes, Lady Ophelia." Andrew gave a low bow.

"They were served refreshments a few moments ago."

Tea, already? "How long have they been waiting?"

He glanced at the tall clock before wincing. "Going on an hour, my lady."

"I best see to them," she replied with a quick smile. Heavens, but who would wait that long to meet with Ophelia? She hurried to the salon, the door cracked enough to hear giggling from within. She'd know that laughter anywhere. "Lady Prudence and Lady Chastity!"

Ophelia entered the room with a genuine smile.

"Lady Ophelia," both called in unison, popping off the lounge, causing the pastry Lady Chastity held aloft to bounce to the floor.

"Oh, dear, I have soiled your rug." Chastity's face flamed with embarrassment, and she scrambled to her knees to retrieve the sweet treat. "I will make certain—"

"Do not fret," Ophelia said with a light laugh. Lord Torrington's younger sisters were quite persistent when they set their minds to something, and they'd settled on making Ophelia and Lucianna their bosom friends. Edith had escaped the girls' tireless pursuit, for when she wed Torrington, they'd be more than mere friends, they would be sisters. "I shall tell no one."

Chastity regained her seat with a grateful nod.

"To what do I owe this visit?" Ophelia couldn't help but ask. She'd arrived home with a plan; however, until Chastity and Prudence took their leave, she could not see it through.

The pair exchanged a quick glance before Prudence, the dominant of the pair, turned a pitying look on Ophelia. "We presumed since the trio of us were not included in Lady Lucianna and Lord Montrose's trip, we would take the opportunity to keep you company."

Keep her company, or had Edith requested the girls keep watch on her?

It galled Ophelia to think her friends thought she needed someone to keep an eye on her in their absence.

"What Pru means is that with Lady Lucianna away, you must be in need of a friend—or two."

She was hard-pressed to deny a friend would be appreciated, especially with everything circling Lord Hawke and her father. The time to think through everything and gather her thoughts hadn't presented itself. Perhaps, Lady Pru and Chastity were willing to lend an ear.

They may not be as versed in observation as Luci and Edith, but they looked willing as they sat on the edge of the lounge across the table from her.

"Well, there has been a bit of excitement to be had since Luci and Montrose left town—"

"Oh!" they chimed at once. These were the type of females she aimed her *Mayfair Confidential* columns toward—young, innocent women who were susceptible to influence. Both girls perched their chins on her hands, their elbows balanced on their knees. "Do tell us."

With Luci and Edith, Ophelia wouldn't hesitant to share what she'd discovered. She trusted them implicitly. However, sharing Lord Hawke's family tale seemed a breach of some unspoken pact between Ophelia and the handsome lord. Perhaps she could share a bit about the man without breaking his confidence.

"I met a lord." Ophelia paused as both women's eyes widened. Did they think her incapable of meeting a man, or were they only sharing in her excitement? It didn't matter. Ophelia hadn't anyone to confide in when she'd first spotted Lord Hawke at the bookseller's. "He is very dashing with hair the color of sunshine and eyes as green as Sherwood Forest."

When Prudence's brow furrowed, Ophelia realized she hadn't thought to consider if they'd read the tales of Robin Hood.

They recovered quickly and nodded, their wide-eyed stares begging Ophelia to continue.

"I first saw him at Oliver's Book Shoppe—a

bookseller I frequent often—" she clarified before continuing. "He was there demanding a book that belonged to his family."

She was close to crossing a line, but she could not help herself.

"He did not notice me then, but he appeared at my home several days later to meet with my father." Lady Chastity's mouth hung open, and Pru clutched her sister's hand in anticipation. "His name is Lord Hawke. Very fitting, I dare say."

"Very fitting, indeed," Chastity murmured. She retrieved her tea from the table and took a cautious sip, never taking her eyes off Ophelia. "What did he come to Atholl Townhouse for?"

"The same book." The words were out of her mouth before she could stop herself. "I mean, I do not know much about it, only that it is old and has to do with Sheerness in Kent. But, you came to visit me, and here I am, prattling on and on about nothing."

Ophelia sat a bit straighter when the clock chimed the top of the hour. Her father, with the rest of the Atholl clan in tow, would be home shortly. It would effectively cut her off from any further searching, at least until the morrow.

The women must have noticed that she made no move to pour herself tea, nor did she offer to freshen theirs because Chastity took one last sip and set her cup and saucer back on the serving tray at the same time Lady Prudence cleared her throat.

"We very much enjoyed our visit, Lady Ophelia." The pair stood, issuing the proper curtseys. "We do hope you will visit us when you are about on social calls."

A measure of guilt ran through Ophelia at her unladylike manners. These poor girls had been through much in the last several months, losing their stepmother to an illness of the mind and now their brother wedding Lady Edith in a few short months. They were looking for a friend, and Ophelia desperately wanted to be that to them; however, this moment was inopportune to further their kinship.

"Father is taking us for a ride in Hyde Park this afternoon," Pru ventured to say. "Mayhap we will see you there?"

"I'm afraid I have several prior engagements today; however, I will call on you shortly." Ophelia gave the pair a reassuring smile as they all stood. "Do give my best to your father."

"Of course." Lady Prudence nodded.

"I shall walk you to the door." Ophelia ushered the ladies back to the foyer, attempting to keep her pace leisurely and not rushed. "Again, it was lovely to see the pair of you. I do hope your time at Hyde Park is pleasurable."

The Atholl butler opened the foyer door, and the women hurried out to their waiting carriage. Glancing beyond, Ophelia saw no other conveyances in the drive. There was still time.

"Father is still not home?" She smiled, determined not to let this delay set her back in any way or diminish her buoyant countenance.

"No, my lady." Andrew closed the door behind Lady Prudence and Lady Chastity. "Is there something I can assist you with?"

"No, Andrew. I was going to query father about a…" She needed to keep her wits about her and devise a new plan if she hoped to locate and return Lord Hawke's book. "About a new collection of Colonial volumes at Oliver's Book Shoppe; however, it is not so important that it cannot wait until supper."

The servant eyed her, his gaze narrowing. "I can inform him of the matter when he arrives home."

That would be too late, certainly, and it worked best for her if he never found out what she was about to do.

"No, thank you, Andrew." Ophelia did not trust

her father to be completely honest with her anyways, as he hadn't been with Lord Hawke. "I believe I will retire to Mother's sitting room to read."

"I will have Ms. Paulson prepare fresh tea."

"That is kind," Ophelia said, touching the servant's arm before turning back toward her mother's sitting room, which was directly across the hall from her father's study.

She was in search of her own adventures, and while snooping in her father's study was not the most exciting of activities, it was something she'd never dreamt of doing before.

And, if she were being honest, her pulse increased at the mere thought of doing something so outlandish.

Ophelia paused outside her mother's blessedly empty sitting room and glanced toward her father's closed study. No one would question her if she were found in his private room as she'd regularly gained access to collect a new book or debate a subject with her father.

But the duke could arrive home at any moment, putting an end to the opportunity. Ophelia darted across the hall. The latch released without a sound, and the door swung open on well-oiled hinges, revealing her father's most private domain.

It likely appeared cluttered and disorganized to those who did not know the Duke of Atholl, but to Ophelia, it epitomized her father. Every nook and cranny was filled with objects of worth, though some appeared to be little more than rubbish to an outsider.

The sheer size of the collection seemed daunting.

It could take her weeks to search each shelf, open the many drawers, and examine the cupboards lining the far wall.

Ophelia could only assume her father was aware of the book's location and had been taken by surprise by the baron's appearance. The duke prided himself on cataloguing every item in his study…

Scrutinizing the room as a whole, Ophelia looked for any item out of place, but everything appeared as it should be—exactly as she'd witnessed since her childhood.

Ophelia tapped her chin, debating the wisest place to begin her search.

Certainly, the only logical place was her father's desk.

It was where Ophelia kept *her* most prized possessions—in her writing desk. At least it had been before Luci had invaded her personal chambers and displaced all of Ophelia's things.

Hurrying behind the desk, she began pulling drawers open. Riffling through each with an eye for only what she sought before re-organizing the contents. There were no books, only folders with paperwork, maps, quills and ink, and her father's seal.

Next, Ophelia pulled on a knob to a small cupboard below the desk drawers. When the door did not open easily, her fingers slipped from the knob, her nail digging into the dark wood.

Locked!

If Ophelia had something she wanted to hide, she would surely place it in a locked cabinet.

Using her fingernails, she pried at the edge of the door, hoping to shift the lock out of place, but the thing would not budge. She leaned close, trying to ascertain what exactly held the door closed. Blast it all, but Edith would know how to fuss with the lock and have it open in no time, or Luci would simply slam the thing with her elbow and it would give way out of fear.

But it was only Ophelia here. She needed to figure out a way to open the door on her own without assistance from her friends.

"I need something flat." Ophelia popped to her feet and surveyed her father's desk, her eyes alighting on the sharp, short blade of her father's penknife. It would fit perfectly between the door and the side of the desk—and with any luck, it would be sturdy enough to pop the latch holding the door closed. Returning to her kneeling position, Ophelia slipped the knife into the slot and lifted.

Sure enough, the latch opened, and she pulled the door wide as she stared into the deep, cavernous cabinet. Reaching inside, she retrieved a stack of books; one on trade winds off the Kent coast, another detailing the journey past Denmark to Prussia, a small pocket volume detailing the landscape of Russia, and finally, the book Lord Hawke had come looking for.

Smuggling: A Journey from Kent to Denmark by Fair Wind Parnell.

She turned the book over in her hands, running her finger down the worn, brown leather binding. Someone had spent much time with this tome, judging from the deep creases in the cover. Leaning down, Ophelia took in the scent of a fresh ocean breeze, as if the book had never left its place at sea. The pages were yellowed by many years in the elements.

The sound of a door closing echoed down the hall and through the study's open door, followed by the clomp of booted feet as her siblings hurried up the stairs.

Her father was home!

Ophelia haphazardly placed the books back in the cabinet, minus Lord Hawke's book, and closed the door. There was no way for her to re-latch the cabinet without the key, which she most certainly could not locate before her father caught her in his study. There was naught she could do but pray that her father did not remember locking the door.

She leapt to her feet, clutching the book, and placed the penknife back on the desk before jetting around to the front. Her skirt caught on a drawer she'd absentmindedly left ajar. Pivoting, she tugged at the fabric with her free hand and was rewarded with the telltale sound of her seam ripping.

"Bollocks," she hissed, grasping her skirt tighter and giving it one final pull as her mother's voice floated down the hall on her way to her sitting room.

The fabric tore completely to the hem, but at least Ophelia was free.

She dashed to the room's entrance and peeked out, just as Lady Atholl closed the door to her sitting room, giving Ophelia the opportunity to slip from the study and make her way to the servants' stairs. Her breath left her on a loud exhale as she fled to safety.

CHAPTER 7

LADY SISSY CASSEL glared at her brother across the table as he speared a boiled egg and popped it into his mouth. His jaw worked to chew the large bite, pieces falling from his parted lips as he swallowed. It was a fact that Franny, or Lord Abercorn as he was rightfully addressed by the *ton*, was most agreeable—and pliable—with his belly full. She'd learned this when he was a young child—and she already near adulthood.

"My dear brother," she cooed, setting her knife aside. "Have you heard from that bookseller as yet?"

His stare snapped from his meal of roasted pheasant, his utensil scratching against the delicate silver plate. Sissy knew the importance of being subtle with the man. A woman—especially an unwed, older, spinster sister of a duke—was not free to speak her mind or question their brother's handling of their estate and title; however, she was used to taking such liberties with Franny. At least when they were in a private setting.

"No, I have not, dear sister." He returned his focus to his meal as if the subject at hand were nothing more important than discussing the weather. "Do collect me another plate of eggs."

At her brother's demand, a servant set a small dish

containing three boiled eggs at his elbow.

"Do you know who I saw again today?" Sissy asked.

"I must say, I haven't the faintest notion." He cut one egg in half, speared it and a piece of meat before bringing it to his mouth. "However, I am certain you will tell me," he mumbled around his mouthful of food.

She had absolutely no desire to correct his manners while dining—if it kept away other money-hungry maidens and black-haired sirens, it was all the more pleasing to Sissy.

"The Dowager Lady Coventry," Sissy seethed. There was no tamping down her fury at seeing the woman again. "Can you believe she thinks to return to London as if she *belongs* among the *ton*? She is naught more than a status seeker—born at the docks, no less. The wife of a—"

"Sissy, watch yourself," her brother warned, but his words lacked any backbone. "She is a widow, and your quarrel with her was decades ago. I am certain the entire family has long forgotten what transpired between the pair of you—I think it best you do the same."

"My…quarrel… Forget?" Sissy's blood boiled as she stammered. "You know well and true what that family stole from me—from us! And it is all that woman's fault."

Franny shook his head but kept his stare trained on his plate as he spoke. "I know only that the king did what was in his right to do. Besides, I have little use for what Coventry now possesses."

Sissy pushed her chair back to stand. "You are infuriating, Francis."

"So you've told me day in and day out since I was old enough to know the meaning of the words."

"You know that land was to be my dowry. They took it from me."

"It was at least thirty years ago, not too many years after my birth," he argued. "It had nothing to do with me."

"Yes, but you have not followed through with your promise."

"I am searching for the bloody book, Sissy!" He slammed his knife down and stood, glaring across the table at her. His anger fled quickly as it always did when it concerned his only living family member. "Leave us." He motioned to the footman to depart.

When the door closed silently, and they were alone, Sissy said, "Franny, you promised me I'd have my inheritance back; however, you have not been doing enough to see it done."

"Did I not agree to entertain your fancy and look for this book that is only fabled to exist?"

"It *does* exist," Sissy whined.

"Yes, yes, but now you ask that we scurry off to the coast of Kent in search of this or that." He pinched the bridge of his nose. "And, of course, my love for my only sister is great enough to have me leaving London during the height of the Season just to make you happy. I should remain here, in search of a wife, or have you forgotten the Abercorn name could very well pass to some distant, far-removed cousin if I do not produce an heir?"

"That is why this is far more important."

"Returning your dowry?" he sighed. "That helps me in no way whatsoever."

"At least you will not have to worry about me if something should happen to you." She spoke softly, knowing this was always the one thing that solidified his cooperation. "This distant cousin would have no qualms about casting an old spinster out. I would have no recourse but to seek employment in a workhouse."

Abercorn chuckled. "As if they'd keep you for long, Sissy."

"But you do not deny I could have no home to speak of if we do not find a way to gain back the estate we lost to that shrew of a woman?"

Her brother sighed and sank back into his chair. "No, sister. I do not deny that fact. I agreed to assist you. That is all I can do."

"Then I suggest you pack your things," she commanded. "We have a long journey ahead of us."

Without another word, Sissy turned and exited the room. It may be a fool's errand, but she had to see if the dowager's childhood home held anything that could help her gain back her long-lost legacy—and put the bloody Scrooge in her place for good.

COLIN INSPECTED THE report from his steward at Hawke Manor, his small holding near his father's country estate in Somerset. The crops were thriving this year, no doubt due to the rotation schedule he'd devised two summers prior, which allowed the soil's nutrients to naturally replenish themselves by the growing of dissimilar crops. His three-field rotation system, while seen as a fool's waste of viable land by some, was already reaping its benefits, his land's farmers seeing more food than they had in decades.

Most assuredly, leaving an entire field fallow for a season was unconventional, but it was proving successful, even as the winter wheat field thrived and the lentils in field two were producing adequately for the spring weather they'd had thus far.

Bloody hell, he longed to rush into his father's office and shove the report in the earl's face. He'd been Colin's number one naysayer since he'd spoke of the plan nearly three years ago. It was a success. If only Colin could convince his father to allow him to make similar changes at Tintinhull. If he did, both Colin's Barony and his father's Earldom would fill their coffers ten-fold in the coming years.

Colin chuckled. Even with the proof right under his nose, the earl would refuse the plan solely on principle. He knew best…and Colin's "whimsical project" at his own estate, no matter the proof of success, would not sway his father.

Not that the Coventry Earldom was in need of funds…no, the first earl—Colin's grandfather—had made certain his son and grandson would want for nothing in the years after his death.

Colin ran his hand through his hair and massaged the back of his head.

This was astounding news, yet it would mean less than nothing to his father.

A muffled shout followed by stomping sounded through the closed door of the room Colin had converted into his study while in London.

His workspace was next to his father's private office.

A door slammed, and the shouting began once more.

"What in the blazes?" Colin mumbled, pushing to his feet and dropping the report back to his desk. Now was not the time to show his father the latest yield reports if he was already angry.

Colin strode from behind his desk and pulled his door open.

His mother stood in the hall, her arms crossed, and her head shaking from side to side.

"What is it, Mother?" he asked.

Her pinched expression made her normally pale, smooth skin appear wrinkled and aged, and it should have been Colin's first clue as to what had infuriated his father.

She threw her arms wide, in her usual helpless gesture. "Molly, of course. What else could have your father so up in arms?"

Molly.

Colin had gone a full four hours without thinking of his grandmama and the promise he'd made to her.

"You best join them. It is you they are arguing

over."

"Me?" Colin asked.

His mother turned to leave but paused, glancing over her shoulder. "Yes, he discovered you and Molly have been asking about London in search of a certain book."

"How is he aware?"

"Does it matter?" She shrugged and moved down the hall toward the stairs.

His mother was correct. It didn't matter how the earl had learned of their activities over the past week. Molly had been warned, hell, even Colin had been warned, but they'd both ignored his father demands.

With heavy footsteps, Colin moved to the office door. His cold fingers clenched into a fist, and he knocked.

The irate voices inside immediately halted, and his father shouted for him to enter.

How the earl knew it was Colin, he didn't know.

Colin pushed the door wide to see his father and grandmama standing before the hearth, each with hands on their hips, feet planted wide, and scowls on their faces.

Except for their varying heights, the pair was identical…and not only in their appearances, but also their stubbornness, determination, and sense of righteousness.

The most peculiar thing was, neither realized it.

They'd been at odds for so many years, each on their own side of this argument, they'd forgotten their bond—a connection that had started at his father's birth, or likely, before.

"What do the pair of you think to accomplish with this scheme of yours?" his father hissed, clearly demanding Colin's response but never taking his glare off Molly.

"Ye damn well know—"

"Watch your words!" the earl shouted, cutting

Molly's retort short. "Colin?"

"Molly asked a favor, and I was merely appeasing an infirmed woman." The answer was rubbish, and everyone in the room knew it.

"Are you even sick and in need of a London physician?"

Molly's shoulders stiffened, as much as a woman with her hunched stature could. "Ramsey, ye know damned—no, do not interrupt me," she seethed when the earl opened his mouth to chastise her once more about her language. "Ye know I'm ill. I not be have'n much time left."

"Then why are you spending it on this lark?" his father questioned. "You know as well as I that Porter sold that book. He wanted it gone. Why do you want it returned so badly?"

"Because ye be determined ta prove that your father was an unsavory, dishonorable man!"

"He was a common smuggler, a free trader with no respect for the laws governing this great country! He wanted the book gone. If he'd wanted any of us to possess it, he wouldn't have sold it for a mere few shillings."

It was the same argument, the same hurtful words hurled back and forth, and the same subject that never found a resolution or a truce between the mother and son. Colin's heart ached for the pair, who should be spending their time loving one another, but only fought every opportunity they got.

"Enough," Colin said, slashing his hand through the air and moving closer to the pair. "Father, you believe grandpapa was a no-good thieving smuggler?" His father nodded. "And Molly, you are determined to prove he was not only a smuggler but also a valuable ally of King George II?"

"Ye know exactly what I be say'n all these years." She turned her pleading stare on her only grandson. "I won't be go'n ta me grave with anyone think'n otherwise."

"Father." Colin turned his own pleading look on the earl. "What is the harm of asking about London for Fair Wind's book?"

"His name is Porter Parnell, the first Earl of Coventry, not *Fair Wind*." The earl shook his head, running his hand through his soft brown hair. "I have no intention of reminding all of England of our less than noble past, and you should not either. You will need a wife before long, and the grandson of a smuggler is not an attribute most London misses want in a husband."

"Your pretty, senseless wife did not mind wed'n the son of a bar wench," Molly retorted. "If'n me and my Porter's past in Sheerness makes ye feel less of a nobleman, then I have other concerns for ye. It be because of Fair Wind that ye have this fancy house, your hoity-toity society friends, and the title ye use."

The earl sighed and turned to stare into the hearth. "I have worked tirelessly to ensure that my Earldom— Colin's legacy, might I remind you—is not tarnished by our family's scandalous past."

The mention of Colin's future was the one thing that softened Molly's determination—every time— however, his future did not negate Molly's history and ensuring that her dear, beloved husband was not shrouded in dishonor for all eternity. While Colin was still unsure what to believe, he believed *in* his grandmama.

"Father, if we are discreet and draw no attention, what is the harm of searching for the book?"

The earl twisted around to face Colin, Molly now at his side.

His face was a mixture of unease and anguish. "What if you find exactly as I've proclaimed for years?"

"Then that is what we find," Colin conceded. "However, I think we owe it to Porter to at least try and prove what Molly asserts is correct. Imagine how the

Coventry Earldom will rise if it is proven Porter *was* an ally to the king."

The earl glared between his son and his mother, obviously torn. No matter how much they argued and fussed, Ramsey loved his mother—and his son. "You have seven days—and Mother remains close to home in case she is in need of a physician."

Colin and Molly nodded their agreement to the terms.

"And when Mother's treatment is complete and the doctor gives her a clean health record, she returns to Tintinhull—no more debating, and no more sneaking behind my back."

His father's brow rose when neither Colin nor Molly answered.

Molly clutched at Colin's arm. "We have seven days?"

"Yes."

"And you will not stand in our way?" Colin confirmed.

"As long as you are discreet, I will allow you your foolish quest."

"Thank you, Father." It was more than the earl had ever compromised on before, and Colin damn well didn't plan to squander the time. "We will keep to your terms."

"See that you do." The earl strode to his desk and sat heavily in his chair. "Now, if you will both excuse me, I have actual work to accomplish today."

Molly's back stiffened, and Colin feared she would lash out and ruin what little truce they'd agreed to only moments before.

"We will not keep you any longer." Colin tugged at Molly's arm, signaling it was their time to depart. "Also, I received word from my steward in regards to the crop rotation plan. I will have the report brought to you."

The earl had already begun riffling through the many files on his desk, his attention elsewhere. "Fine,

fine."

Colin had little hope his father would actually read the reports, but at least the earl hadn't outright refused him.

Molly took up her cane that leaned by the door as they departed.

He pulled the door shut behind him and paused, his lips turning up in a satisfied grin.

"We did it, Molly."

"We ain't done nothin' yet, me lad," she clucked, shaking her head. "We still need ta find that blasted book."

"I will visit the Duke of Atholl again. See if he remembers anything further about the tome and its whereabouts."

"See that ye do, but stay clear of that fiery-haired sorceress."

Colin chuckled as Molly tapped her forehead, chin, chest, and back to her nose.

He swore her superstitious ritual was becoming more and more complex by the day; luckily, she made no move to spit on the rug-covered floor.

CHAPTER 8

TO SAY THAT Ophelia was pleased with herself, at least thus far today, would be an understatement. She'd located the information she sought, found Lord Hawke's book, and escaped her family's townhouse without notice. After fleeing up the servant's stairs, she'd located her maid, and they'd slipped out the front door to find the Atholl coach still in the drive.

It had all been simple.

On any other day, Ophelia would have been convinced it was *too* easy.

But she hadn't time to dwell on the subject.

Perhaps she could convince Edith and Luci to allow her to take a more active role in the *Mayfair Confidential*, more than simply taking the information they gave her and writing the posts.

Even her friends would admit she'd done a marvelous job in their absence. She needs must dampen her jovial mood before exiting her carriage, though, lest the man suspect she'd gone to nefarious lengths to return his book and thus cast Ophelia in a less than proper light.

She glanced out the coach window at the massive townhouse. A plaque mounted to the stone exterior proclaimed the house *Knightsbridge*. A noble property situated across from Hyde Park in a most elite area.

Lord Hawke, while only a baron, must have a wealthy, prestigious family, indeed.

Even her father, a duke in a long line of Atholl dukes, did not possess the sheer wealth needed to obtain such a grand residence in London proper.

"I will remain here, my lady?" her lady's maid inquired.

"Yes." Ophelia gave her a confident smile. "I should be but a moment. I need return something that belongs to Lord Hawke."

"Very well." The girl didn't question her further, and Ophelia was happy for it.

Daring to arrive at a gentleman's home unannounced was highly inappropriate. However, besides having the book delivered by a servant, there was no other way.

...and this was the only way she'd be able to see the handsome man again. Maybe then he would be banished from her dreams, thus casting her back into reality.

Her footman opened the carriage door, set down the steps, and assisted her departure.

She hid the book in the folds of her skirts. The last thing she wanted was to make it necessary for the servants to lie for her if her father discovered the book missing—or, Heaven help her, he found out she'd called on a gentleman without his consent or her mother's accompaniment.

There was little chance Ophelia would allow such a trivial detail to stop her.

However, that did not stop her pulse from racing or her face from flushing as she walked toward the door. Blast it all, but she'd forgotten her fan in her haste to depart, and there was little she could do as her skin reddened to a shade similar to a ripe tomato.

Taking a calming breath, Ophelia raised her gloved hand to knock, making certain the book was still hidden in the folds of her skirts.

Her knuckles hadn't even rapped against the door when it swung open, causing Ophelia to yelp in surprise and hop backwards.

Likewise, the butler stared back at her with rounded eyes, his mouth gaping. He hadn't expected to see her standing on the stoop any more than she had predicted the door to open with such gusto.

"Miss," he said, his manners righting themselves quickly. "I do apologize. Lady Coventry is not receiving guests. Would you like to leave your card?"

Bollocks!

She'd forgotten her fan…and her calling card.

Her pride from a few moments before dimmed quickly.

Ophelia was not giving up, no matter if she made a cake of herself before Lord Hawke. "Actually, I am here to see Lord Hawke, and…Molly," she said, pasting her most sincere smile on her face. At the butler's furrowed brow, she continued, "If Lord Hawke is not at home, I can return at another time…"

"The dowager and Lord Hawke are in residence."

It was good news, but the butler still appeared puzzled by her request to see the pair. He did not show her in, nor turn her away, but stood staring as if she certainly must have more to say.

"Ah, yes, the dowager, please forgive my informal request." Her smile faltered slightly when the man continued to glare. "When I met the dowager, she was…"

Ophelia clamped her mouth shut. She was rambling, and just about announced Molly's harebrained antics in the Atholl drive. It would not do to inform the butler that the first time she'd met the older woman had been with her cane aimed at Ophelia's head.

Swallowing hard, Ophelia kept her stare on the servant, refusing to look away or show any weakness. "…she was waiting in Lord Hawke's coach." It would have been wise to refrain from mentioning Molly at all, but it was too late for that now.

"May I inform Lord Hawke and the dowager who is calling?"

A name…her name. Her missteps were adding up too fast for Ophelia to keep track of; no fan, no calling card, and utterly dismal manners.

"Lady Ophelia Fletcher, daughter of the Duke of Atholl," she added as an afterthought, in case the man did not remember her name.

Finally, the butler stepped aside, opening the door wide enough for Ophelia to enter. "Do come in, my lady."

She stepped into the foyer and was instantly surprised by the grandness. A silver chandelier hung from the vaulted ceiling, holding what must be over a hundred tiny candles. Matching sconces adorned the walls in every direction. Three shelves stood proudly, each arranged precisely with trinkets, books, and objects Ophelia could only assume were of great historical value, though she recognized none of them. The floor beneath her shone as if it had been polished only moments before she arrived, and the balustrade was crafted of the darkest wood she'd ever beheld. A rug covered the floor in the center of the foyer and was certainly worth more than all of the carpeting in the Atholl Townhouse combined.

Lord Hawke lived a life of luxury Ophelia could only dream of.

But then why was he desperately searching for an old book on smuggling in Kent?

Footfalls sounded, drawing her attention to a corridor leading to the left of the stairs, though the hallway was too dim to see anyone.

The butler gestured in the opposite direction. "My lady, this way to the dowager's receiving room. I will inform my lady of your arrival."

"Actually, it is Lord Hawke I am here to see," she

replied. It would not do to have Molly causing a scene the likes of which her servants would be unable to stop. It had been one thing to raise her cane at Ophelia in her own driveway with Lord Hawke coming to her rescue, but who would prevent the old woman from bashing her over the head at Knightsbridge? "I have something that belongs to him."

"Lady Ophelia?" She glanced over the butler's arm to see Lord Hawke striding her way. "What in heaven's name are you doing here?"

She glanced at the floor as a heaviness settled in her arms. Had it been unwise to come?

Belatedly, Ophelia remembered she had proper business here, she hadn't come out of some foolish fancy or on a whim.

Ophelia turned to face the lord, her chin notching up and a grin overtaking her lips. "I found the book you were searching for." With the volume, about the size of her adventure novels, proudly displayed before her, she took a step in his direction.

Her sense of accomplishment soared once more when he hurried toward her and snatched the tome from her hand then grabbed her arm with the other before pulling her toward a room off the foyer.

Lord Hawke pushed into the room, all but dragging Ophelia behind him, then kicked the door shut.

He released his hold on her at the same moment, and Ophelia stumbled a few steps before he reached out and steadied her.

Lord Hawke turned the book over and over in his hands, touching the binding, running his finger along the embossed cover, and he even bent forward to smell the thing. She wondered if he caught the scent of the ocean in its leather-bound exterior, too.

"Where did you get this?" His glare refocused on her. The words were a breathless whisper as if she'd presented him with a map of Atlantis or the fabled Trojan horse. "Your father said…"

Ophelia clasped her hands behind her back and rocked on her heels. "I went and saw Oliver. He told me my father had purchased the book. With that information, it was easy enough to locate the book in my father's study."

Lord Hawke glanced down at the book once more and shook his head, returning his narrow-eyed stare to her. "But Atholl said he hadn't any—"

"Yes, I thought that was odd, too, especially after I inquired as to what you'd visited Oliver's Book Shoppe for and learned my father was the last known person to be in possession of the book."

"Oliver's?" Lord Hawke stammered, his hand dropping to his side, the book forgotten. "How did you know I sought out the bookseller?"

"I—well—" Ophelia hadn't thought about how to explain her presence at Oliver's Book Shoppe, but a measure of honesty could be shared without mentioning Abercorn. "My father and I went there several times when I was growing up. I still frequent the shop. I was there when you came in and demanded the book. I did not think anything of it that day, but when you appeared at my home several days later, I decided to lend my help."

"Even after Molly nearly clubbed you with her cane?" He pinched the bridge of his nose and lifted the book once more. "It doesn't matter. Molly and I thought this book gone forever. It disappeared shortly after my grandfather passed and my father took his place as the Earl of Coventry."

The man's shoulders sagged as if a long-time weight had fallen away. His brow smoothed, and if Ophelia weren't mistaken, a slight grin settled on his face as he began once more to turn the book over and over in his hands.

"Where did you find it?" he asked, finally opening the cover.

"In a locked cabinet in my father's desk." She

couldn't help her triumph smile.

"I am surprised he handed it over to you so easily."

"Oh, he did not," she replied, gaining a sharp look from him. "I searched his office until I found the locked cabinet then I sprang the lock with a penknife and found your book." She took a deep breath before continuing. "I brought it straight here."

"You stole it from your father's study?"

His eyes narrowed on her, and his shoulders stiffened much like they had at both Oliver's and her family townhouse when he'd come searching. However, he had the book back. She'd returned it. Why did he appear so...irritated?

"Do remove your frown, or I will assume you are unhappy I returned the book."

"You took this from your father's study...without his knowledge. You must return it immediately before he discovers it missing."

"I will do nothing of the sort, my lord."

"Yes, you will!" he demanded.

CHAPTER 9

COLIN GLARED AT the woman, who despite his evident fury, did not back down or admit any wrongdoing. Lady Ophelia Fletcher was maddening, brazen, and in complete denial about the trouble she was in—and the discord she'd unwittingly brought to his doorstep. He need convince her to return the book immediately, or Colin would have little choice but to return it himself.

It was far too much of a coincidence for him to have come around inquiring about the book only to have it disappear from Atholl's study only days later. Plus, he'd gained information from Oliver… And now this?

If Lord Atholl discovered his desk had been tampered with, the magistrate would be at Colin's father's doorstep before Colin could get the woman out.

"Lady Ophelia, while I am overjoyed to see this book, it was not wise of you to steal it from your father." He gave her his most pointed glare, and her eyes brimmed with tears. Bloody bollocks, but he couldn't have the woman running from his home in tears, that would cause a scandal just as easily as the stolen book being found in Colin's possession. "Please, do not cry."

Her lower lip trembled, and a single tear escaped.

"I am a cad, my lady." He brushed the tear from her cheek before it could make its way down her face and off her chin. When she glanced up at him, her blue eyes were as clear as a cloudless London sky, as fresh as the air after a solid rainstorm, and as injured as a rabbit in a snare. "I did not intend to sound so gruff."

And it was all Colin's doing.

She glanced around the room, a most innocent blossom staining her cheeks, but her tears dried. "I guess I should have thought things through a bit more before…"

It would be ungentlemanly to allow her to take all the blame. "Truly, I thank you for your bravery and cunning in locating and returning my family's book; however, I cannot allow you to suffer any adverse consequences on my behalf."

She pressed her fist to her mouth, and her shoulders fell.

"Perhaps I can have a tiny look before you return it."

Her gaze snapped to his, and he felt rather than saw her spirits rise.

Colin turned his attention to the book once more. *Smuggling: A Journey from Kent to Denmark* by Fair Wind Parnell. He traced his grandfather's name, hardly able to believe the book actually existed—or, more accurately, *still* existed. He and Molly had spoken of it for so many years, it was like a mythological object, always spoken of in lore but never presenting itself in actuality. It was smaller than he'd imagined it to be—less than fifty pages. The binding, several decades old, should be tattered and cracking, yet it appeared unblemished.

That alone spoke to the book's worth.

Not a value in shillings or pounds, much like his father assumed was the measure of a man, a title, or an estate, but a worth measured in honor, integrity, and bravery. It was what Fair Wind said made a man, or at least that is what Molly had told Colin on hundreds of occasions. Property, possessions, and the extent of a man's coffers meant little if a man did not hold honor, loyalty, and love in his heart.

This was everything Molly proclaimed would elevate the first Earl of Coventry, Porter "Fair Wind" Parnell, from a known Sheerness smuggler to an ally and confidante of King George II. Within these pages, Colin could find indisputable proof his grandpapa was one of England's most trusted men during the Seven Years' War, taking missives between George and his nephew, Frederick II, in Prussia.

Colin could hardly draw breath.

His airway was constricted, and his body laced with tension.

Here, now, Molly would find her vindication.

Colin would be allowed to celebrate his grandpapa openly without his father's naysaying condemnation.

All he need do was open the book and read the pages added after Fair Wind's time serving the king was done, those that detailed his harrowing journeys from Sheerness to Prussia. Not from Kent to Denmark as the cover displayed.

Bloody hell, but excitement should be coursing through him, demanding he call for Molly, his parents…and anyone who'd disparaged his grandpapa in the past.

Yet Colin was unable to open the book, though he demanded his fingers do exactly that.

Instead, he brought the small volume to his nose and breathed in deeply. It was almost as if he could smell Fair Wind's many adventures at sea; the scent of a salty breeze cascading over the white caps of the open ocean.

Would it be in his power to give the book back once he opened it, or would he forever claim possession of his great family legacy?

He had to risk it, to know for certain whether all Molly had said throughout his life was true. That all the hate and unsavory comments his father hurled at both Colin and his grandmama over their belief in Fair Wind and his accounting of the past could be thrown to the wayside and forgotten.

Their family could be mended.

Their future one of solidarity, not strife.

It was almost too much to hope for, but it was exactly what he'd wished for his entire adult life.

He held within his hands the means to solve every problem the Coventry family had, debunk every revolting story about his heritage, and solidify his family name for generations to come.

"My lord?" Lady Ophelia laid her hand on his arm. The warmth of her touch quickly seeped through her gloved fingers, down through his coat sleeve, and heated his skin. "Is all as it should be?"

"It is, thank you," he choked out, his head swimming from lack of breath.

"Are you not going to open it?" she asked, her voice that of a melodic temptress. Undoubtedly, she was the siren Molly had accused her of being because with her question came the irrevocable need to do as she said. "I know I am quite interested to see what is so special about this particular book."

He glanced at her, inwardly praying she would take the volume from him and run—hide it where it would never tempt him again. But instead, her cerulean crystal eyes begged him to open the cover and show her what secrets the book held.

Colin was helpless to let the book go, just as he was powerless to look away from Lady Ophelia.

"Go ahead," she coaxed.

Reluctantly, and with a sense of great loss that burrowed deep within him, Colin removed his stare from her and focused on the book. He flipped the cover open to see his grandpapa's handwriting for the very first time. It was heavy on the page, the quill tip obviously having placed far more pressure to the paper than necessary—strong, bold, and unwavering, just as Colin envisioned Fair Wind to be.

He turned the next page...

And was greeted by the torn edges of several missing sheets.

His heart beat frantically, and he flipped several more pages only to find an accounting for Fair Wind's first journey out of the Sheerness port and the wilds of the North Sea.

Erratically, he turned page after page, determined to find what his grandmama claimed should be written within. But no detailed explanation of Fair Wind's true purpose at sea appeared.

Not even a scrap of evidence or a mere sentence to contradict his father's assertion that Porter Parnell was anything but a no-good, unscrupulous smuggler.

"How can this be?" he groaned. "Is this the condition in which you found the book?"

His penetrating stare landed on Lady Ophelia, and she shrank back in fright at the venom that could be heard in his words.

"Y-y-yes," she stammered. Her eyes showed nothing but innocence, not an ounce of guilt to be found. "I opened the cabinet and took the book, that is all. I brought it directly here."

"There were no other papers with it? Possibly a small stack of torn pages?"

She shook her head, her auburn curls falling over her shoulder. "The drawer held no papers, only a few other books on trade winds and the landscape of other lands, some assorted writing instruments, and an ink pot...oh, and an old accounting ledger."

"I think it best you return the book with all due haste." He worked hard to hide his disappointment from Lady Ophelia. It was no good to him, and would only serve to harm Molly further. Without Fair Wind's personal accounts of his travels for the king, the book was worth more as kindling in the Coventry hearth. Colin would not cause his grandmama any more pain.

"But you went to great lengths to find it." She refused to take the book even as he attempted to place it back in her hands. "You must need it far more than my father."

"It belongs to the duke. He purchased it from Oliver's Book Shoppe." Colin shook his head as she tried to hand the book back to him. "I think it is time you depart, Lady Ophelia. Your family must certainly be worried about your whereabouts."

Her brow furrowed, and she frowned. It was something that normally transformed a person's face into a less inviting version of their usual expression, but with Lady Ophelia, he found himself longing to smooth her brow, turn her frown into a smile once more, and tell her everything about…everything. His family, their strife, their scandalous past, and even his promise to Molly. Colin refused to admit his failure…especially to the divine creature before him. She was a lady, the daughter of a duke, and there was little chance she'd ever witnessed a scandal or had ever been touched by the less savory aspects of the human nature.

No, Lady Ophelia, with her fiery hair, fair skin, and eyes the color of a clear sea did not deserve to be drawn into his flawed and broken family.

"I suppose you are correct, my lord," she sighed, crossing her arms, the book clutched tightly to her chest. "The book belongs to my father. I will simply return it since you are no longer interested in it, and we shall continue as if this never occurred. Unless…"

Unease settled on Colin. "Unless?"

"Unless you are willing to tell me what this is all about and who Fair Wind Parnell is."

To tell her anything would lead to telling her everything. One certainly could not leave the conversation at: Fair Wind was my grandpapa and a famed smuggler.

There would be further questions, and the wanderings of Lady Ophelia's mind would likely end far worse than the actual circumstances behind it all.

"I guess I will be going." She paused for a brief moment, giving Colin the opportunity to speak, but he remained close-lipped. "Very well. It was a pleasure meeting you. I will see myself out."

She pivoted to quit the room, and Colin's chest tightened.

If she left without any further explanation, he suspected he'd never set eyes upon her again.

He should be satisfied to see her go, taking the blasted, no-good volume with her.

Neither she nor the book would bring him anything but trouble.

Then why did he feel a hollowness overtake him the more she moved toward the door—and out of his life?

LORD HAWKE WAS insufferable. Did he think her dim enough not to notice the light in his eyes when he spied the book? The way he'd held it with such reverence as he smoothed his hands over the binding. The innate rightness she'd felt when the book was in his possession.

Only to have him shove the thing back at her and demand she return it to her father's desk as if it weren't of great import to him.

Well, Ophelia would show the man. She would return the title to her father and make certain Lord Hawke never set eyes upon the book again. As far as she was concerned, the lord could jump into the Thames, and she would not bat an eye or assist him.

She placed her hand on the door latch, prepared to open it and flee. He had been correct, at least in part, her family would be worrying over her whereabouts at any moment.

"Lady Ophelia," he groaned. "Wait."

She froze, her hand on the handle, and waited for him to continue. After the embarrassment he'd caused her, Ophelia would not *wait* around for more. She'd risked much taking the book and journeying to Hyde Park in her father's carriage to see the title returned to its rightful owner.

"Fair Wind is a relation of mine," he said. "My family is originally from Sheerness, Kent, or at least my father's family is."

Ophelia turned back to face Lord Hawke. "Why is the book so important to you?"

His jaw was clamped shut, and she feared he'd said all he planned to say on the matter. Rubbing his hand across his face, Lord Hawke visibly relaxed.

"Fair Wind was my grandpapa."

Ophelia attempted to hide her shock at this information, but when he shook his head, his frame stiffening once more, she knew she'd done a poor job of it.

"If Fair Wind is your grandfather, then he was Molly's husband?"

Behind Ophelia, the door slammed against its hinges, sending a draft of wind billowing her skirts about her ankles.

"Ye better believe it!" Molly cackled, thumping her cane heavily into the bare wooden floor as she entered the room. "Fair Wind was the best bloody seamen there ever was—and an even finer husband."

"Molly!" Lord Hawke stalked past Ophelia and Molly, closing the door soundlessly before rounding to glare at the older woman. "Have you been listening to my private conversation with Lady Ophelia?"

"Sure have, ye foolish lad. Seems a boon I was, too, or ye woulda let Fair Wind's book leave this house without me have'n a look." The woman took a step toward her grandson, her skirts pressing against his legs. They would have been nose-to-nose had the woman been two feet taller. "You thought ta keep this from me, Colin, me boy?"

Her voice cracked, and Ophelia momentarily felt an immense amount of compassion. "Lady Coventry—"

The woman rounded on her, pointing her cane straight at Ophelia's heart. "Me name be Molly, none of this Lady Coventry nonsense."

"I was only going to say…" Ophelia gulped when the woman slammed her cane back to the ground and turned back to face Lord Hawke. Colin. "Molly, please—"

Suddenly, the room grew uncomfortably warm, and Ophelia's head began to swim. She cursed her forgetfulness once more and settled for fanning her heated face with her gloved hand.

"Don't just stand there, Colin," Molly chastised. But the woman's voice sounded far away. "The lady be about ta faint dead away."

Just as swiftly as it had started, her face cooled as a breeze cascaded over her scorching skin and her eyes refocused. Colin was waving his handkerchief before her as Molly dragged a straight-back chair in her direction.

"I don't mind if the devil-haired woman faints, but not in me receive'n room. Imagine the horrors if she conked her head soundly and bled out on me freshly polished floor."

Ophelia sat heavily in the chair with a mumbled thank you and leaned forward, hoping it would help her to breathe.

"Pull her hair forward."

"Great idea, Molly." Hands ran across the back of her neck, pushing her hair forward. "This should cool her quickly."

"Let me have a look."

Another set of hands touched her skin, these were

rougher with callouses, as Ophelia breathed in deeply. She hadn't succumbed to a case of the vapors in ages—since they'd rescued Lady Edith from the evil clutches of Lady Downshire.

"What are you looking for?" Colin said close to her ear.

"The mark of the devil. Ye be certain I'll find it, too."

"The what?" Ophelia squeaked, throwing her head back, at the same time Colin pulled Molly's hands away from her.

As Ophelia stood, Colin had hold of Molly and was slowly inching her away from Ophelia.

The old woman grabbed her pendant with one hand and tapped her forehead, chin, and chest before turning her head to the side.

"Don't you dare!" Colin warned. "You know mother does not favor having the rugs cleaned and the floors scrubbed due to your spittle."

"A pox on your mum," Molly grumbled, but allowed Colin to lead her to the chaise lounge closest to the hearth. "Don't see the harm in have'n a peek at the chit's neck—just ta confirm one way or the other."

"Confirm what?" Ophelia asked.

"If'n ye be in cahoots with the devil."

"That is preposterous, Molly," Colin sighed, giving Ophelia an apologetic smile. "If she were working with the devil—as you claim—why would she risk so much to bring us Fair Wind's book?"

Molly appeared to mull over her grandson's question as she rested her chin on the head of her cane. "I s'pose it could all be a ploy ta snare a husband…"

"My lady!" Ophelia glanced between Molly and Lord Hawke. He could not believe she'd done all this in a vain hope that Colin would be so grateful he'd pursue a courtship with her. "That is more preposterous than your assertion I am marked by the devil because of my red hair."

"Oh, is it now?" Molly's gaze narrowed on her, and Ophelia wondered for a quick second if she could be a carrier for the devil before shaking her head in denial. "Well, I had ta be certain. If'n ye aren't here on the devil's errand ta lay a curse on me grandson, then what be your reason?"

"Enough." Lord Hawke slashed his hand through the air, silencing Molly and bringing all attention to him. "Molly, she brought us the title we sought, there is no reason to question her motives."

"If'n ye say so, me lad." Molly let out an unladylike snort. "Now, hand over me damned book."

Both Molly and Lord Hawke turned their attention to her once more, and Ophelia noticed she still clutched the volume to her chest. She hadn't so much as dropped it during her near faint.

"I wasn't going to bother you with it because the pages are missing."

Ophelia handed the book to Molly and stepped back, hoping Lord Hawke would keep talking and she would remain unnoticed, lest he demand she return home again.

"Pages…miss'n? That cannot be."

"Are you certain that Fair Wind added the pages and had the book rebound after the king's death?"

Molly vigorously nodded, her tightly coiled hair at risk of toppling into her face. "Oiled the leather meself and watched him scribe late inta the night ta make certain he wrote everythin' down."

Opening the book, Molly ran her finger down the inside of the spine, and Ophelia could not help moving closer. Indeed, there were at least a dozen pages ripped from their place, leaving only the jagged edges where the paper had attempted to hold its place.

A great sob filled the room as the tears began slipping down Molly's cheeks to land on the open book, her shoulders shaking with each outcry.

"There is no way I'll prove me Porter an honorable

man," Molly choked out as her sobs turned to ragged sniffles.

Colin knelt before her, taking the older woman's hands into his, his thumbs gently rubbing the backs of her ungloved fingers.

Ophelia abruptly stepped back, fearing she was partaking in a private moment between the pair. One she had no right to witness. However, she could not wrench her stare away as Colin embraced his grandmama, pulling her close and murmuring in her ear. The older woman nodded, so slightly Ophelia nearly missed it, before Colin pulled back and stood.

Pushing off her cane, Molly gained her feet as Colin placed a hand under her elbow for support. Molly shook off his assistance and moved toward Ophelia, her cane in one hand and her late husband's book in the other.

Her eyes still brimmed with tears but they no longer fell.

"This book, it belongs ta your father," Molly sighed, holding it out for Ophelia to take. "Thank ye for bring'n it ta me—us—but, sadly, it is of no use ta us now."

"But Fair Wind still wrote it," Ophelia challenged. "Would you not like to keep it?"

"Not if'n it means bring'n trouble down on your head, foolish girl." Molly thrust the book at Ophelia once more, and she had no option but to take it or watch it fall to the floor. "Now, the pair of ye, be gone. I'm need'n some privacy."

Molly's shoulders stooped more than Ophelia had noted before as the woman shuffled back to the lounge.

"I will return, grandmama," Colin said, nodding at Ophelia as he moved toward the door. "I will send Beth in with tea."

Ophelia followed, unsure what else to do. Any offer of condolence might push the older woman into hysterics, yet if she said nothing and simply departed the room, it would be a blemish to Ophelia's place as a lady. One did not run away when another was hurting.

She paused at the threshold as the woman collapsed onto the lounge, her cane falling to the floor with a clatter. "Molly," Ophelia said. "I am abundantly sorry for causing you any pain. If I had known, I wouldn't have—"

Colin grasped her elbow and steered her from the room.

"My lord." She tugged at his hold. "I owe your grandmother at least a few words of…" A few words of what? Condolences, positive thinking, hope?

"She is not listening," he whispered as he once again urged her forward and they made their way to the front door. "I have known her all my life—many say I know her best, besides her dearly departed—and I can assure you, she is hearing nothing at this moment."

"I should have left when you bid me take my leave," Ophelia huffed. "Or better yet, I should not have come at all."

"But I am happy you did."

"Truly?" she asked, her chest fluttering at his overly kind—yet impossible—words.

He nodded as they entered the deserted foyer.

"But I upset her terribly." She'd given the woman the worst news possible, besides never locating the book in the first place. The volume was so light in her hands, ever so unassuming. How could it cause so much heartache? "It is not right to leave her wallowing in such sorrow."

"I will walk you to your carriage, see you safely on your way, and be back at her side in a few moments. You have my promise."

His word should not fill her with such faith, but it did.

The same servant who'd shown her in stepped into the foyer and opened the door, allowing Colin and Ophelia to make their way outside. Her carriage waited only thirty paces away, but he pulled her to a stop, and the door closed not far behind them.

No one could be listening from the house, and they were too far from her coach to be overheard by her maid or driver. They were alone in every sense but the visible one. The thought sent a shiver of expectation down Ophelia's spine. Colin placed his hand on the small of her back, causing her stomach to flutter with nervousness. Certainly, this was not normal—for Ophelia had never known the touch or kindness of a man beyond the normal interaction with her father and brothers.

"Lady Ophelia?"

At his soft words, she turned toward him, not caring that the front door could open at any time or that her maid was likely watching her. They stood so close she had to crane her neck back to see his face properly or be forced to stare at his muscular chest. The mere thought of his chest sent a rush of heat through her that pooled between her legs.

There was little doubt something was wrong with her. Could it be she was coming down with a sudden illness? Overheating, shivers, a fluttering belly—these were not at all common things to her.

He was waiting for her to speak, and Ophelia was mortified to realize she hadn't a coherent thought in her mind beyond the splendor of his form, the wayward fall of his pale hair, and the depth of his moss-green eyes. If he sought to discuss his physical attributes, she might well find her tongue. Beyond that, Ophelia only wanted to feel his hand on her lower back once more, hear her name whispered on his gravely exhale.

Bollocks, but she had the overwhelming urge to call him "Prince Amir," as if he were a character from one of her treasured adventure novels.

"Yes, Lord Hawke?" The words were spoken nearly too low for even her to hear.

But then, he smiled. "Thank you for bringing the

book. You did not need take such a risk, but I am happy you did."

"But, what now?"

"What do you mean, what now?"

"How will you prove your grandfather an honorable man?" Ophelia suspected the story of Fair Wind was not over yet, there was still much to tell—or in this case, discover—about the famed smuggler and his purported association with royalty. If this had all been a book, she would be helpless to put it down until she finished it. Certainly, Lord Hawke realized this was not over. "There must be another way."

A sorrowful note lit his eyes. "What is next is something I do not know, nor will I wager to guess at this moment." He sighed, and Ophelia couldn't help but wonder if he were giving up. "For now, I will console my grandmama and pray this does not further break her heart."

She stared up at him, her eyes silently begging him—for what, she did not know.

Lord Hawke took a step back, putting distance between them, and grasped her free hand. "With that, I will bid you ado." He leaned forward and placed a kiss on her glove-covered hand.

Just as quickly, he released her, turned back toward his front door, and disappeared inside.

Her coachman cleared his throat behind Ophelia, and she turned to see the steps down and the carriage door open, awaiting her.

The flutter, much like a horde of butterfly wings, in her stomach did not recede with Lord Hawke out of sight—neither did the tingle traveling through her ebb as she made her way to her waiting conveyance.

Peculiar, indeed.

CHAPTER 10

WHERE WAS THE blasted man?

Sissy paced back and forth in Francis's study. She'd been waiting for nearly two hours for him to arrive home from his afternoon social calls and for them to be on their way. There were important matters to be dealt with, yet, it seemed her brother was far more interested in finding his next ladylove than keeping his word to his sister.

Picking up the small bookend from Franny's desk, Sissy tossed the weighted object shaped like a goose from one hand to the other. The distraction did nothing to reduce her ire at her brother, nor her all-consuming need to be on their way. Time was running short...not for her, but for Francis. It would only be so long before he found another woman who caught his eye and Sissy would be relegated to the shadows once again.

If there was one thing Sissy despised, it was the men in her life—the males who ruled her very existence—putting her second to their whims. First, her father had gambled away her dowry. Then her betrothed had absconded with another when it'd become common knowledge she held not a farthing to her name. And lastly, and possibly the most enraging, was when her dear brother promised her he'd right the situation but could not keep his shaft in his trousers for long enough to secure Sissy's future and ensure her legacy returned. Oh, Francis never admitted it was lust that led him astray time and time again. No, the silly imbecile actually believed himself in love—on five separate occasions.

Yet, his actions made it impossible for Sissy to find love even once.

There was little need to address Franny's assertions that one did not need money, land, or title to find love. They both knew that was the biggest lie of all. One only need explore Sissy's past to know the folly of that thought. Without a dowry, men of the *ton* had passed Sissy up at every turn. Even the daughter—and then sister—of a duke could not find a suitable match without a certain amount of financial assurance.

Not that Sissy would ever find love now, especially at her advanced age—no, it was more about taking from that shrew, causing her family the embarrassment she'd caused Sissy in their youth, and taking back something that rightfully belonged to her.

She would have it back—at any cost.

Not that the stakes hadn't increased as the years passed.

Sissy had found it increasingly difficult to keep her brother focused on the matter. Did he not see that once Sissy had what she wanted, he would be free to pursue his own wants and needs?

"Mrs. Carnes!" Sissy shouted, setting the bookend back on Francis's desk.

The study door opened on well-oiled hinges, and the Abercorn housekeeper curtseyed to Sissy. "Yes, m'lady?"

"Have the coach readied," she instructed. "If my brother thinks to keep me waiting all day, he is sadly mistaken. Have my things loaded for the journey."

"M'lady, I will send word to the stables."

Sissy waved her hand in dismissal, and the housekeeper closed the door as quietly as she had opened it.

Franny may think her single-minded focus was out of place and misguided, but Sissy knew better than most what was due her.

She placed her hands on the smooth, wooden surface of her father's desk—the same one Francis had taken over after the duke's death all those years ago. Their father could have rested peacefully had Sissy been born a man and the Abercorn heir. Never would she have allowed such shameful acts heaped upon her family's name to continue unresolved.

The fact of the matter was: the Dowager Lady Coventry had taken something from her, and Sissy would have it back.

The door opened behind her. "Is the carriage ready, Mrs. Carnes?"

"Sissy." Abercorn huffed. "I made it very clear I would accompany you to Sheerness, but I had things to attend to first. I am a busy lord, sister. I cannot drop things every time you fancy a trip to the coast."

That the man still believed himself in command—in control of *her*—was comical. Francis was oblivious to many things happening around him…and Sissy had no urge to correct him.

"Oh, brother, I am so thankful you are home." She turned and hurried across the room to wrap him in a tight embrace. "I desperately wanted to make certain everything was handled and ready. I certainly know you are in much demand, and I owe you greatly for agreeing to accompany me to Sheerness."

It only took a few words and a tight hug for Francis's irritation to subside.

He pulled from her embrace and straightened his coat. "Well, I am pleased to know you understand the magnitude of calling me away from London at such a time."

"I promise, we will be gone but two days, at most."

He glanced about the room and moved to his desk,

straightening the bookend Sissy had handled a few minutes prior. "Do speak with Mrs. Carnes about the servants moving my belongings."

"Yes, Franny, I certainly will."

"Very well, let us be off," he replied with a nod. "If we hurry, we can be to the coast by nightfall."

…and be back in London by midday tomorrow with all the proof Sissy needed to take back what rightfully belonged to her.

With a confident smile, she followed her brother from the room.

COLIN STOOD IN the empty foyer, fighting the urge to turn and watch Lady Ophelia's carriage pull from the drive onto Hyde Street. There was naught for him to do but let both Lady Ophelia and his grandpapa's book go and return to Molly with all due haste.

It was better this way.

His father would never suspect the proof of Porter's past was forever lost.

Nor would Molly have him continue on this fool's errand.

He only prayed Lady Ophelia was skilled enough to slip the book back in its place before Atholl noticed it had gone missing.

Taking a deep breath, Colin shook off the feeling he had somehow disappointed Lady Ophelia. Which was a ludicrous thought. If anyone should be disappointed in him, it was Molly. He'd made her a promise to find the book and show his father proof of Fair Wind's true activities at sea.

He'd failed, and now he dreaded facing his grandmama.

However, there was naught to do but get on with it.

Perhaps with this concluded, Molly would take the

time to rest, see the physician, and then return to the country. She was happier there. She must be. Away from the watchful, doubting eyes of her son and daughter-in-law. Free to wander the country manor and its surrounding property.

In a way, Colin envied her freedom there.

He needs must put that thought from his mind. Colin belonged in London, learning all he could from his father in preparation for taking over the Coventry Earldom in the future. His days of frolicking about the country with his grandmama were a thing of the past.

Colin strode back to Molly's salon, fearing he'd find the older woman a sobbing, hunched form when he returned. No wails of sorrow or deep cries of misery greeted him as he approached the room, its door open as he'd left it.

Hurrying into the space, he found Molly not on the lounge where he'd left her but standing close to the hearth, her side profile facing him.

A smile played upon his grandmama's lips, creating creases of joy along her cheeks and at the corners of her eyes.

"Molly, how are you getting on?" He stepped fully into the room, and she turned toward him with more pluck than she'd exhibit in years. Her smiled faded to a frown. "I am sorry for the disappointment."

"It cannot be helped, me lad."

"That does not mean I do not believe every word you've ever told me about Fair Wind."

Colin moved to her side, and she raised her wrinkled, age-spotted hand to his cheek, patting it softly. "That I know well, Colin. It only be a burden ta know others do not have faith in Porter."

"Others do not matter, Grandmama."

"Tsk-tsk." She patted his cheek with more force. "Don't I wish that be true."

"I can continue searching for the missing pages." Colin hadn't any notion what made him volunteer to forge on with their quest; however, he knew for certain that it would break his heart if his grandmama didn't see her final wish to fruition. "There are more places I can look. Revisit Atholl and see if he was the one responsible for removing the pages…"

Molly laughed, which quickly turned into a ragged cough as she clutched her pendant and attempted to catch her breath. It happened more and more frequently in recent years, and it worried Colin to no end. The physicians were helpless to find what ailed her, the apothecary could not concoct a remedy to keep the hacking coughs at bay for longer than a few hours, and with it all, Molly became increasingly exhausted from the sudden fits.

"No, me lad, it is simply another bit of me beloved that will remain out of reach—much like this wasteful pendant he be give'n me when we journeyed ta Eton the first time ta secure your father a place at University." She flipped the jewel-encrusted necklace over in her hand to show Colin the back engraving, though they both had committed the inscription to memory long ago.

If'n it be answers ye seek, look ta where it all began, and ye shall be rewarded.

"I will keep Sheerness and our time there in me heart forever," she sighed, a rattle in her chest making it hard for her to inhale again. "Just as ye cannot allow your father's wicked thoughts ta invade and take root in your mind. Never will ye forget the work'n men who gave their all for ye ta live in this fancy house."

"Yes, yes," he reassured her. "I will never allow Ramsey's beliefs to corrupt my sensible mind."

"He was such a nob, your father. Still is." She lowered herself to the lounge once more. "Always go'n on and on about his da, the unscrupulous smuggler who sailed the seas, all while pose'n as a right fancy bloke and use'n my Porter's hard-earned coin to pay for everythin'."

"What…when did Grandpapa give you the necklace?"

Her brow furrowed at his question as she thought, rubbing the pendant between her fingers as she did. "Well, it be that time we sent Ramsey off ta school. He'd become a rebellious lad who sought ta lash out with harsh words at every turn. Porter and I came ta London for our first—and only—proper town stay— think'n it be benefit'n Ramsey when he graduated if we be accustomed ta town life and could introduce him ta society all proper like. Your grandpapa went out after, deposit'n me in this monstrosity of a house, and was gone for what seemed like days but was only mere hours. When he returned, he gave me this. Said for me ta hold it when all hope seemed lost."

But all hope was not gone, Colin would not allow it.

"Mayhap we should do exactly as Fair Wind bid?" he suggested.

"Whatever do ye mean, lad?" Molly sat forward on the lounge, her brow rising.

"We are looking for answers, and it only seems reasonable that we must go back to 'where it all began'." The thought was clear despite its impulsiveness. It was a wonder neither of them had thought of it before this moment; however, until a short while ago, they'd been convinced the proof lay in London, not along the rocky coast of Kent. "Grandpapa must have left some evidence of his work for the king in Sheerness. That is what this is all about, reminding not only us but also Father of our family's past."

She tapped her chin. "And that be in Sheerness," Molly said with agonizing slowness.

"Exactly, though I am uncertain if it is his writings on the travels for the king he wants us to find. Or something else." Colin's heart lifted, and then soared when he saw the light return to his grandmama's gaze. "We should leave today. Now, even. I will have the carriage summoned, and our bags readied." He paced toward the hearth and flipped around, moving back in Molly's direction. His sure, solid steps were muffled by the rug underfoot. "We will arrive after supper, but I am certain we can find lodging. They would never turn away the famed widow of Fair Wind Parnell. Oh, but you worked as a barkeep in your youth. They will know you as surely as they knew Grandpapa."

Molly stared at the head of her cane as Colin rambled. She seemed as overwhelmed by it all as he. Which meant, there was still hope.

Colin chuckled and started for the door. "You wait here while I make the arrangements."

"Me lad, ye know I can't be go'n with ye."

Nothing could have halted him in his tracks faster than those words. "What?"

"I am old, Colin…and sick."

"But the journey is only six hours, at most, and I will have Father's well-sprung traveling coach prepared. It will be as if you are here or in your private chambers." This was a task they'd begun together, and bloody hell, Colin was determined to finish it with Molly by his side. "We will be away from London for only a short time, and your next appointment with the physician isn't for several days."

Molly only shook her head. "I can't be travel'n ta Sheerness, lad, though I'd much enjoy see'n me old home—the first Porter and I shared after wed'n. Or that old tavern I earned me keep at before meet'n your grandpapa." Her gaze darted out the windows to the garden below, but Colin sensed she saw none of it. "If'n I ever make it back home, it not be today. Take the fiery-haired devil with ye."

"What?" Colin's entire body tensed as he attempted to hide his shock at her declaration. "Absolutely not. That is an absurd notion."

The time had come…Molly had lost all common sense.

"She possesses the book." Molly glared across the room at him from her seat on the lounge.

"We no longer need the book," he retorted.

"Well, the people of Sheerness are a loyal bunch." Molly nodded with pride. "They'll not be help'n ye, if'n ye trample into their town ask'n pointed questions. You will learn noth'n. But with the book and the woman at your side, the townsfolk might be more forthright with their information."

"One moment, you think the woman possessed by the devil—"

"I did not say I do not still think she—"

"And the next, you tell me to take the woman to Sheerness." He groaned at the severe consequences of such a thing. "How do you expect me to travel out of London with an innocent, unmarried woman and not find myself either shackled to her or at the end of her father's dueling pistol?"

Molly only shrugged in response.

His grandmama *shrugged*. The beat of his heart thrashed in his ears as his mind swirled around the possibilities...

No, there was no chance in hell that he would take Lady Ophelia with him.

"The book belongs ta her."

"It belongs to her *father*," Colin huffed. "I will simply call on her and say we have changed our minds. That we wish to keep the book. If I am in possession of the volume—and with my striking resemblance to Fair Wind—I should have no issues gaining the townspeople's cooperation."

"It seems ye have everythin' figured out," Molly sighed. It was the same sound she'd made when Colin had built his own boat to sail across the pond at his family's country estate. She'd said it would not hold for the time it would take him to paddle across, but in Colin's ten-year-old mind it was sturdy enough to cross the English Channel. Of course, he'd been only twenty feet out when the raft began taking on water. He'd ended up swimming to shore—and there Molly was, a feline-like grin upon her face. "Ye are a wise lad."

In other words, Molly was sure he had nothing figured out and that he was as unwise as he'd been in his youth.

"I am certain you know more than an old wench like me," Molly mumbled. "I am noth'n but a weak, frail woman with a mind not as solid as it was."

Frail? Weak?

Two words Colin would never dream of using when talking about or *to* his grandmama. Proof of her strength had been witnessed by his coachman, footman, and the duke's butler as Molly had swung her cane at Lady Ophelia in the Atholl drive.

"You are positive it is Lady Ophelia I should take with me?"

"I see no other choice, me lad."

Bloody hell. It seemed he was taking Lady Ophelia to Sheerness with him, he only need convince the auburn-haired beauty to make the journey.

But hadn't she already offered to help him continue his search for the truth?

CHAPTER 11

OPHELIA TILTED HER head back against the wicker chair, allowing the midday breeze to push her long tresses from her face, and the warm sun to kiss her lips. Pulling the blanket tighter about her shoulders, she sighed. The day had grown breezy after she left Lord Hawke's townhouse and returned to Mayfair—to an empty home.

Normally, especially since Lucianna had taken up residence with her family, Ophelia would enjoy the blissful silence of a deserted townhouse; her father meeting with his man of business, her mother paying social calls with Sarah, Elizabeth, and Jennifer in tow, and her brother, Jacob, at his weekly fencing lesson. Today, however, the silence only carried the weight of loneliness.

Luci and Edith were safely on their way to Gretna Green with the fine men they loved.

And she was left in London, alone.

Perhaps that was why Ophelia hadn't returned the book to her father's cabinet as planned but instead retired to the garden outside her mother's salon to read it.

At first, she'd hesitated, thinking she was crossing the line of propriety in some fashion, reading the private writings of Lord Hawke's grandpapa. When she'd stared at the book in her lap, her resistance hadn't lasted long as her interest grew and anticipation built.

Without a doubt, Ophelia knew the book held an adventure, even with the missing pages.

And so, she'd nestled herself in a wool blanket, perched on her mother's favored wicker chair, and read.

Page after handwritten page was filled with harrowing days at sea, stops at foreign and exotic ports, and logs of exports loaded upon the ship. And in between all that—a rare, shining light—were tales of Molly, written by the man who'd loved her above all else.

It was these brief asides that captured Ophelia's attention and kept her reading. Much like the one she'd just finished:

M'love, m'life, m'lady
It is for she and she alone I be at sea.
It is ta prove me love and devotion ta she that I continue.
Me Molly girl, ye be all I need.
Yur pretty curling hair, yer cunning, yer kind eyes.
They all bring me ta heel, but it be the way ye
smile that keeps me head above water.

These passages were utterly enchanting, powerfully moving, and made Ophelia long to find a man who would feel such immense feelings of love for her.

She'd read such novels for years—possibly longer—but they'd never affected her, reached to her very core, and left her wanting for things she'd never thought to be hers as this did. A love similar to that which Edith shared with Torrington and Luci had found with Montrose.

But that love had been denied, or rather cut short, for Tilda. How was Ophelia more deserving of a happy, content future filled with love and companionship than her dear friend?

Her eyes drifted shut, and she allowed her mind to

wander to things they had no business envisioning; a small cottage in the middle of a meadow, the bright, warm sun blazing above, the slight wind carrying the scent of lavender from the flowers that had been planted with love along the a small, fenced-in yard. And a small child, a boy with fair hair and tanned skin, playing with a set of brightly painted blocks. He stacked them high, toddled back to admire his handiwork, and then giggled as he knocked his tower down and began anew. In her mind, Ophelia laughed along with the boy, not at his purposeful action of destroying what he'd so painstakingly built, but at the merriment in the child's blue eyes when he waved her over to help.

Blue eyes…

They were mirror images of Ophelia's, but no other trace of her existed in the child, yet the boy was familiar to her in every way. From the fall of his tawny hair that covered his brow to the determined glint in his eyes when he set about constructing a tower taller than the last.

Yes, in her daydream, she was content and happy, wanting for nothing.

A chuckle sounded behind her, and Ophelia took her careful watch off the boy to see where the sound had come from. It was also particularly familiar and comforting; however, the laugh must have reached her on the breeze because no one stood there.

A deep hollowness filled her, taking over her lovely dream and causing the clouds overhead to roll in, threatening rain.

Ophelia glanced about, but the boy had also disappeared.

She was utterly, terrifyingly, unmistakably alone.

Her chest felt empty, a great hollow void.

She inhaled air, but nothing seemed to appease her lungs as they burned, demanding but never satisfied by the warm, lavender-scented air she drew in.

Her body weakened and crumbled as she

suffocated.

"Lady Ophelia?"

That voice…

Swiftly, she drew in a deep breath, and the emptiness grew less daunting. The panic of a moment before subsided as the clouds overhead drifted to the horizon to reveal the welcoming sun once more.

A hand brushed her cheek, and her eyes snapped open.

The blanket had fallen from her shoulder to rest on the arm of chair. A quick glance up told Ophelia no more than an hour had passed since she'd allowed her eyes to close and her mind to wander.

Squinting, Ophelia sat up straight and glanced around her. Someone had said her name—touched her cheek?—but the bright sun kept her momentarily blinded. Her panic returned, and Ophelia leapt up, the book sliding from her lap to the dirt at her feet.

"My lady," Lord Hawke said, as if mere inches from her ear. "It is only I."

"How, I mean, when…" she stammered, her stare finally coming into focus to see Lord Hawke leaning unflappably against the garden gate, his boots crossed at the ankles, and not close to her at all.

"My apologies for frightening you." He pushed away and strode toward her, a lock of hair falling to cover one eye…so familiar. "I arrived in the drive"—he gestured behind him to his waiting coach—"and saw you sitting here, so peaceful I almost didn't have the heart to wake you."

"I—well—" She shook her head, attempting to collect her thoughts and banish her daydream. Her cheeks heated at the thought, and Ophelia ducked to collect the book to hide her embarrassment. "I was reading, and I must have closed my eyes for a brief moment."

"I've been watching you in slumber for nearly an hour."

"You have?" The shrill edge to her voice was nearly as mortifying as her blush from being caught in her silly daydream.

He nodded solemnly, and his brow pulled low. "I must say, you have a snore men three times your size would envy." Her mouth gaped open, and he chuckled, just as he'd laughed in her dream. "Come, Lady Ophelia, I am a man most noble."

"Certainly," she sighed. "You would never do something so wicked as watch a woman sleep without alerting her to your presence."

"Errr, no," he said. "I would never be so dense as to mention a woman's snoring in polite company."

Lord Hawke was utterly perplexing. Had he been watching her but didn't witness her snore, or had he just walked up and did?

He laughed again, the sound breaking through her unease. "I arrived only a moment ago, and you were completely silent—so quiet I stilled myself from checking for your breath."

Quiet was good. That meant she hadn't spoken aloud in her dream.

"Well, thank you for waking me." She smiled, hoping to change the topic. "If you hadn't, I fear to think how I might have become burnt by the noonday sun…my complexion ruined and my freckles spreading from my nose to my cheeks and forehead."

"What are you reading—"

"Why are you here—"

Ophelia dipped her chin and grinned as they both spoke at the same time.

He cleared his throat. "I came because Molly and I had an idea for finding confirmation of my grandpapa's true intentions at sea."

"And I was reading your grandpapa's book." She held it out to him.

His brow rose. "I do hope it is a compelling read."

"You haven't read it?" she asked.

"I saw it for the first—and only—time when you arrived with it earlier."

"Well, while I highly recommend you at least skim the book, it is a lot about daily life at sea and more than a dozen logs and lists of imports he brought back to England—oh, and the occasional verse about Molly." The blasted shiver traveled down her back once more, and Ophelia adjusted the blanket she held around her shoulders. "He also wrote of Sheerness. It sounds like a lovely town. It's a shame the book lacked the adventure I normally favor in a read."

"Real life is rarely as grand as Robinson Crusoe."

"You know Crusoe?" Her breath hitched.

"Certainly." He cocked his head and shook it. "I may not be as worldly as Fair Wind, but I have read a novel or two."

"I did not think—" His chuckle halted her words, and they both smiled. "Besides, I know life is not always a grand adventure; however, it does not harm the soul to escape into fantasy every now and again."

Ophelia feared she'd said something wrong when he glanced around the small garden, crossing his arms. "I am happy to hear you think Sheerness a lovely town because," he paused, his stare narrowing on her as if his next words and her response meant much, "that is where I—we—are headed. Molly and I believe answers reside in the town she and my grandpapa both loved so much."

"Thank you for letting me know. I truly cannot wait to hear what you find—"

"No." He held up his hand to stop her.

He hadn't come to say goodbye or inform her of their change in direction. "Oh, you came for the book!"

She pushed his family heirloom toward him, once again feeling she'd stepped over some invisible boundary when she'd chosen to open and read Fair Wind's writings. How could she have ever been so foolish to think the baron had come to see her?

Lord Hawke had come for his family's legacy, that was all. Not out of any lasting responsibility to her.

"I suppose it is a good thing I haven't returned the book to my father as yet."

She gave him no choice but to take the title from her or leave her looking ridiculous with her arm outstretched, holding it toward him, her other hand clutching the blanket about her shoulders.

"There was actually something else I came to ask you." His stare focused on something over her left shoulder, clearly avoiding eye contact with her. "It is…ah…"

"Yes, my lord?" They shared no other entanglements or associations. Would he request she ask her father about the missing pages, see if he was aware that they'd been torn out?

Lord Hawke rubbed the back of his neck and swallowed. "Molly thinks it best you accompany me to Sheerness."

"Me?" There was no way to mask her surprise. "But she thinks me a marriage-hungry maiden with the mark of the devil."

It was nearly impossible not to laugh at the woman's assertions, though Ophelia feared it would make her appear all the more deranged if she broke out in unbridled mirth.

"Yes, but, as she wisely pointed out, the book belongs to you." They both glanced down at it, firmly in his grasp. "And beyond that, she believes we will be better received and locate the information we seek far easier together."

It sounded as if he still endeavored to convince himself of her usefulness.

"I cannot simply collect my bag and disappear with you to Sheerness." She pressed her hand to her chest, concentrating on slowing her erratic heartbeat—and the notion of adventure set before her. "What would I tell my parents? What would society think of a proper lady gallivanting about England alone…with a man?"

CHAPTER 12

HE SIGHED; THE weight that had settled earlier lifting from his shoulders. "This was the exact concern I spoke to Molly of. It is not proper at all. It is imposs—"

She tapped her chin in thought. "Though, if I collected my things quickly and we left now, no one would be the wiser, and we would be long out of London before anyone even came searching for me."

Every instinct in him flared with alarm. "You are actually considering this?"

"When did you plan to depart for Kent?" she answered with her own question.

"Today, actually," he stammered. "Now, in fact. I have my traveling coach at the ready in your drive."

"Then I request but a few moments—ten at the very most—and I will be ready."

"But—but—I only came to request the book, not convince you to risk your reputation only to prove correct my grandmama's long-held belief about Fair Wind."

"It is clearly important to you—and Molly," Ophelia said, her chin notching higher. "And if Molly thinks I can be of assistance, it would be unkind of me to refuse."

It was absurd of her to agree. Possibly the most

foolish errand his grandmama had ever requested of him—and she had sent him with her pendant, as well. This was important to the old woman, more than Colin had ever suspected, and deep down, it was just as vital to him. Once this mess was behind him, Colin would either have the proof necessary to convince his father, or he would be relegated to asking for his father's forgiveness for the years spent arguing over their family past. Either way, Molly would be banished back to the country, and Colin would continue as Lord Hawke, heir apparent to the Coventry Earldom.

"You will wait for me?" she inquired, her voice so melodic and…innocent, as if she were asking him to wait for her to hand her glass off at a ball so they could dance, not climb into his coach and travel hours from her family with no protection but that which Colin provided.

He hadn't thought about leaving without her. "Of course, my lady."

The brilliant smile she turned on him was worth the risk they were taking.

"Oh, thank you for taking me with you on this adventure! I will meet you at the coach." She turned quickly, the blanket falling forgotten to the ground as she raced toward the house, entering through a side door that opened into the small garden in which he stood. "I will only be a moment."

The door closed behind Lady Ophelia, and despite the rock that had settled in the pit of his stomach, he was smiling on the inside and certainly looking forward to their carriage ride. If for no other reason than to find out why a lady would jeopardize her reputation and future to help a man she barely knew.

Colin made his way back to the coach, nodding to his driver as he held the book at his side.

An adventure?

He snorted and mumbled, "Not bloody likely."

This trip would be more of a disaster—of epic

proportions—than an adventure. At the very least, Colin was seriously compromising Lady Ophelia's reputation, even if no one found out that they journeyed alone together to Sheerness.

His head pounded, and he massaged his temples. He could only image the story she'd concoct to keep the magistrate from chasing them down. It would be Colin's blasted luck that he'd find himself in trouble for this entire debacle. And this was all due to Molly's whim— well, that and his insistence that information could be found in Sheerness. But there was no reason he couldn't have outright refused to even consider including Lady Ophelia in this adventure…far more aptly called a *misadventure*. The book was not explicitly necessary for the journey. She was not integral to discovering the information he needed. Nor should he be listening to a woman who truly lived by the superstition red hair was a mark of the devil.

Yet, here he was.

And here came Lady Ophelia around the side of the house, a satchel held securely under her arm and a thick woolen cloak over her shoulder. The wide brim of her bonnet did not hide her feverish grin as she rounded the corner and glanced to make certain the front door was closed before hurrying to the coach, tossing her traveling bag inside, and leaping in after it.

He peeked in the conveyance as Lady Ophelia climbed onto the rear-facing seat and began arranging her skirts after her mad dash.

"Shall we be off, my lord?" she called, a bit too excitedly for Colin. "It would not suit either of us to have my father stumble upon us in the drive."

"We would not want anything of the sort to happen, especially not before we've even begun our journey." He slowly climbed into the carriage, and his footman lifted the steps and shut the door, the only light within from a single pulled drape casting a shadow across Lady Ophelia's face. "Ready?"

"More than ready, my lord," she said, arranging her cloak and satchel on the seat next to her.

For the first time, Colin noticed her change in attire. She had switched from a sage-green walking gown to a deep blue riding habit, the neckline cut daringly low and offering him an ample view of her heaving bosom as she continued to breathe hard from her run to the coach.

She riffled through her bag, giving Colin a moment to inspect her further without alerting her to his task. The traveling habit highlighted her fair complexion and complemented her already crystal eyes. The sleeves were tight about her arms, the bodice stretched tightly in a most alluring manner, and the skirts flowed to the carriage floor where they pooled, hiding her boots. She'd also pinned her hair at the back of her neck in a prim knot suitable for traveling, yet her hat was far grander than was needed in an enclosed conveyance.

A knot lodged at the back of his throat as his stare landed on her low neckline once more. He'd only met the woman on three occasions, this being the third, but in their short acquaintance, she'd always favored gowns of a far more modest cut and color. There was little chance they'd successfully travel to Sheerness and back without notice with her dressed in such a captivating habit; even now, Colin was incapable of taking his stare off her.

"My lord?" She waved a small paper-wrapped parcel in front of him. "I asked if you were hungry."

Blinking several times, Colin hoped his smile was not as sheepish as he felt being caught lavishing over her bosom. "My apologies. I was pondering our plan once we arrive in Kent."

"Oh?" Lady Ophelia set the parcel in her lap and untied the twine holding the paper closed to reveal a loaf of flat bread and a wedge of cheese—and even a large portion of plump, purple grapes.

"When did you have time to collect a meal?" The

woman was full of surprises—though this was a welcome one, as he hadn't eaten since early that morning. "You were not inside for more than ten minutes."

She unhurriedly retrieved a cloth napkin from her bag and smoothed it over her lap before answering. Her chin lifted as she spoke. "I find the best way to accomplish something with all due haste is to enlist the help of a trusted servant. In this case,"—she paused to arrange the food on the cloth and presented the feast to him—"it was my maid, who was more than willing to pack our meal while I collected my things and changed."

"Are you not worried she will tell your father where you've run off to?"

She waved her hand before popping a grape into her mouth, the translucent juice marring her lips as she chewed. "Heavens no," she commented around her food.

Colin shrugged as he accepted a portion of the bread and a sliver of cheese as they hurried through the crowded afternoon streets of London toward the country.

"Where did you tell your maid you were going?" He could not believe she'd speak the truth of the matter, or risk them being stopped long before they reached Kent.

"To Gretna Green." She placed a hunk of bread between her lips, her eyes drifting closed as a sigh escaped her. "Have you ever tasted anything as heavenly as fresh bread, Lord Hawke?"

"Gretna Green?" he groaned.

Her eyes opened, and her stare narrowed on his look of shock. "Of course," she sighed heavily. "They wouldn't believe if I said I was running off to any other destination, and they would worry. It was the only way to assure they would not send someone after me."

Her satisfied grin only confused him more. "How is the Scottish border meant to keep them from coming after you? I would think it would be all the more reason to stop you from doing anything foolish." Perhaps Lady Ophelia *was* looking to ensnare a husband, though he'd be loath to admit that Molly was correct.

"Foolish, my lord?" Her brow rose, and her cheeks blossomed with pink. "I can assure you, I have never done anything even the slightest bit foolish, with the exception of this trip to Sheerness."

"There is traditionally only one reason a woman travels to Gretna Green…"

"I am aware. To wed."

"And this would not concern Lord and Lady Atholl?"

"Well, they very pointedly forbid me from going; however, they will know I am not in harm's way." She spoke slowly as if he were the one dull of mind and not the other way around. "How long did you say the trip to Kent would be?"

"Ummm, well…" Everything about the woman threw him off course. Perhaps Molly had actually spotted a kindred spirit in Lady Ophelia but had misinterpreted her has a crux. "Six hours at most, with a stop for fresh horses in Dartford. But can we not return to the topic of Gretna Green?"

She handed the remaining foodstuffs to him and returned to her bag, ignoring his question. "Six hours…in a carriage…with naught to occupy my time— " She pulled a small red leather-bound book from her pack and held it aloft. "I suppose I will get much reading done. You do not mind turning up the lamp, do you? Reading without proper light is known to cause significant harm to a person's eyes."

Colin could do nothing but stare, wide-eyed, as she reached over and increased the wick on the lamp and settled her book in her hands. She flipped it open, her mouth moving as she read silently, leaving Colin to finish the meal she'd brought.

The bread was tasteless, and the cheese unsatisfying

as he watched Lady Ophelia settle in across from him; her posture at ease and her brow furrowing as she read.

Her complete repose and ease with their inappropriate situation did nothing to diminish his apprehension.

TO COLIN'S GREAT surprise, Lady Ophelia did let slip a slight wheeze as she slept, many would call it a deep, labored breath, though it was entirely at odds with her soft, angelic beauty. It hadn't taken long for her lids to droop and the book to slip to her lap as her chest rose and fell in peaceful slumber.

It was not so easy for him. He'd inspected the road behind them on more than a dozen occasions, fearful that Atholl had sent someone to chase them down, but the road behind them remained deserted. They stopped in Dartford for a fresh pair of matching greys and continued their journey, all without waking the woman across from him.

He marveled at her serene nature, unlike the tortured slumber he'd interrupted in the garden earlier. When he'd happened upon her in Atholl's yard, she'd appeared restless; her brow pulled low, her jaw clenched shut, and her fists balled tightly. It was perhaps the reason he'd started their conversation off lightly and had, against his better judgment, asked her to accompany him.

It had been Molly's doing—all of it.

If his grandmama hadn't raised her cane at Lady Ophelia and created such a spectacle, would Colin even remember the woman?

Yes, he would remember her. There was no chance he'd forget the woman before him.

Her long hair had escaped from its knot sometime during their travels and fell down around her shoulders, nearly reaching the seat beneath her. He wondered if it would slip like silk through his fingers or perhaps have a sturdier, thicker texture.

Shortly after they'd departed Dartford, the sun had set, and Colin had turned the lamp to low to avoid disrupting Ophelia's sleep. The gentle sway of the carriage had nearly tempted him into slumber, as well, but he needed to remain vigilant during their journey. With only his footman and driver, they were an optimal target for highwaymen. His father's lavish traveling coach spoke of immense wealth, though Colin's barony barely brought him enough funds to make repairs in the village and maintain the small manor house, which was truly little more than a cottage.

Lady Ophelia was his responsibility as long as she was in his care.

And he would bloody well not allow any harm to come to her.

A sharp rap from his driver signaled that they'd arrived in Sheerness.

Ophelia shifted on her seat, her eyelids fluttering as she woke. Her back arched, and her boots poked out from beneath her gown, much like a feline stirring from a long slumber in the stables. The hint of a smile touched her lips, as if she remembered a dream from her hours of rest, but it disappeared quickly when her eyes fully opened.

"Have we arrived in Sheerness?" she asked, her voice rough with sleep.

"Yes." He pulled the drape back to reveal an empty yet well-kept inn yard. The thatched-roof building bordering the property must be the inn. Proving his suspicions accurate, a young lad ran out and spoke with his driver before hurrying back into the building. "It is late, but I will request a meal be sent to your room as soon as you are settled."

"That is not necessary, I can—" But her stomach betrayed her with a loud growl. "Well, very well, a meal would be welcome, however…" She grasped her satchel and slipped her hand into each pocket, feeling around before moving to the large main pouch.

"What is it?" he asked when her gaze darted to the discarded paper from the meal they'd shared earlier, and her shoulders slumped.

Concern knitted her brow, and a sheen appeared in her eyes. "I—I—forgot my pin money."

Bloody, rotting bollocks but the woman was going to cry.

Her bottom lip trembled as his footman swung the door open.

In an instant, and before thinking better of his actions, he knelt before her, his hands on the seat cushion on either side of her legs. "Do not fret," he soothed. "I will handle the room fee and your meals. You are on this harebrained journey because of me, after all."

"But—but—but—that is far too much, my lord!"

"Come now, it is the least I can do, especially if we are found out and your reputation is compromised."

She released a huge breath, and her clenched hands stopped trembling in her lap.

"That is better," he coaxed. "Gather your things, and we will inquire about rooms and a meal. Tomorrow, the true adventure begins." He almost choked on the word *adventure*, though he suspected it was what she needed to hear to collect herself.

Colin grasped her satchel and held it out for her to fill with the few possessions she'd removed in her frantic search.

With her bag in hand, he assisted her from the coach, and they made their way into the inn.

As he'd feared, the ale room was vacant and closed for the evening; however, the proprietor stood at the ready when they followed the hall down to the main staircase.

Short, with tufts of uneven grey hair and a rounded belly, the innkeeper looked upon them with a welcoming smile and a greeting to match. "Welcome ta Sheerness, m'lord." He bobbed his head. "And welcome ta ye, m'lady. I be Caruthers. Will ye be need'n a room?"

"Two rooms, kind sir." Colin glanced at Ophelia from the corner of his eye as the innkeeper scrutinized them. "And a hot meal, if that is not too much trouble. We have been travelling for many hours and are famished."

Caruthers turned away with a grimace. "We don't be have'n two rooms, m'lord," he curtly replied. "Only inn around, and this be a busy night, a busy night indeed."

"One room will do, I suppose." Ophelia tensed on his arm at his words. "How about a hot meal?"

"Will a warm one do?" He came around the desk and took Ophelia's satchel from Colin's shoulder. "Me wife already gone ta bed."

"One room and a warm meal sounds heavenly, Mr. Caruthers," Ophelia said with a wary laugh. "Thank you for accommodating us this late into the night."

"'Tis me job, lass," he huffed and started up the stairs.

Colin gestured for Ophelia to start up before him as he took his bag from his footman and followed Ophelia and the innkeeper up the stairs—to their single room. Now was not the time to ponder how he'd gone from searching for a fabled book to sharing bedchambers with Lady Ophelia.

One thing he knew for certain, Molly would find endless amusement from her grandson's predicament.

Would his grandmama have sent him on this quest if she'd known he would be forced to sleep in the stables with his footman or share a bedchamber with the fiery-haired sorceress?

CHAPTER 13

THEY'D ARRIVED IN Sheerness a couple of hours before the sun set after a quiet journey across the breathtaking English countryside. While Kent was a lovely enough part of England, Sissy much preferred the Southwest shire of Somerset—her true home. Her quaint dwelling, a mere manor house compared to many country estates she'd visited, had been named for her after her birth, Sissiela Hall. Her father, the previous Duke of Abercorn, had been so proud of his first child that he'd purchased the land and manor home to bequeath to her and her bridegroom when she wed.

She'd visited the home, not far from Tintinhull, many times in her youth. It was absolutely perfect.

Yet, Sissy's piece of happiness had been stolen from her before her fifteenth birthday.

Heavy in debt, her father had lost the property and the land surrounding it. She'd even heard the Earl of Coventry had renamed her home, Hawke Manor.

But she was very close to having it returned to her.

And Sissy would relish Sissiela Hall being hers once more.

Currently, she pushed around her evening meal at the only Inn in Sheerness; a drab establishment not suited for noble guests. They'd spent an hour questioning shop owners and residents to find the best place to search for what she sought. She'd allowed Francis to do most of the talking as she played the innocent female relation. It had been unnerving to stand by and allow her brother to blunder through his half-hearted inquiries. However, she bit her tongue and permitted him to speak for her.

"Are you not satisfied with your sole?" Francis asked, his own plate emptied of the savory fish. "London severely lacks fresh sea fare."

Sissy kept her eyes trained on the room around them. Any of the customers—or even the servants—could be a relation of Molly or Porter Parnell. They need be careful what they spoke of and who they spoke to.

"Do stop sulking, dear sister." He pushed his plate away, waving to a servant to remove the dish. "You pleaded for me to bring you to Sheerness, and we are here. We will continue our search tomorrow, though it baffles me what you think to find after all these years."

Of course, he had no clue as to what resided in Sheerness. The bloody man did not realize the many things that occurred under his *own* roof—the acts Sissy had undertaken to keep her brother safe from his own bleeding heart. And if all worked as she'd planned, he'd never have need to know.

"I am only anxious for the morrow, Franny." She looked up at him from beneath lowered lashes to gauge his mood. "My entire life may very well change drastically with our return to London."

"And if all remains as it has been my whole life, we will not be the worse for it. You will always have me, by your side, to protect and take care of you." His tenor was calm and reassuring. It was the voice of the brother who'd pledge to Sissy that he would seek vengeance from all those who'd harmed her. Yet, that promise had been made by a fifteen-year-old boy…and forgotten not long after the words were spoken. "You trust me to care for you, right, Sissy?"

She eyed him from across the table. He'd aged in the last year since his wife's death, his hair had greyed, and his face had wrinkled from strain. His once smooth, golden skin was now marred by age spots—matching her own. His eyes, once alight with mischief and excitement, were now dulled by loss. She wondered if hers mirrored his...

"Of course, I trust you, Franny," she insisted.

However, Sissy saw nothing wrong with working herself to ensure her future—and the downfall of the Dowager Lady Coventry.

OPHELIA GRASPED HER travel bag where it sat upon the single bed as Colin moved into the hallway to settle the account for the room. The bed was barely large enough for one person but was neatly made with a light green coverlet. The chamber was sparsely furnished with a washstand, armoire, and two straight-back chairs with a small round table between them. Only a glimpse of Sheerness could be seen through the tiny window set high in the wall above the table.

Unfortunately, it was black outside, which halted her from climbing upon a chair to gain a view of the seafront town.

What the room lacked in furniture, it made up for in charm; the coverlet was hand-sewn with a landscape of the coastline about the edges, a glass vase full to brimming with sea shells on a side table, and a ceramic washbowl with ships sailing from port painted inside on the washstand.

Tiny but spotless, the room would do for one night.

She exhaled softly. The journey had been tiring, made even more exhausting as she'd feigned sleep for nearly the last three hours. Her neck ached from the impossible angle she'd held it, with her head against the side of the carriage. She hadn't taken a decent breath since she'd slipped—rather, tugged, squirmed, and shimmied—into Luci's daringly low-cut traveling habit. She glanced down at the swell of her breasts over the top of the bodice, and a flush overtook her. The sight of her was utterly indecent. It was a wonder Lord Hawke had agreed to bring her along with her dressed in such a provocative manner; however, Ophelia had reveled in his gaze upon her the entire journey.

It had been her belief that he'd have settled on the ride and read Fair Wind's journal, but he hadn't taken his eyes off her except to glance out the window every hour or so. He'd thought they'd be followed—and hadn't she been responsible for giving him that exact impression?

She'd known full well what she was doing when she told him that she'd left word that she was off to Gretna Green. What she'd kept to herself was that her two dear friends were headed there.

It had been great fun to see him twist with worry. For those scarce moments, Ophelia knew what if felt like to possess Luci's and Edith's great beauty and wit. It had been an exhilarating start to their adventure together.

Until she'd misguidedly agreed to share a room with Lord Hawke.

She'd sought adventure, not complete ruination.

She inhaled as deeply as her gown would allow and placed her hand on her lower back where a twinge of pain had started when she alighted from the traveling coach. If there were any night she needed a restful, rejuvenating sleep, it was this one.

The thought of sleeping in the same room as Lord Hawke banished all thoughts of deep slumber from her mind.

"Well, Lady Ophelia," he said, entering the room behind her. "Caruthers promised our meal would be brought up shortly. I will dine with you—if that is agreeable—and then find lodging in the stables with my men."

His decision should have brought her relief. "You cannot sleep in the stables, my lord." She turned to face him, the door open at his back.

"It is only one night," he replied. "Tomorrow, we will set out early to find what we came for and, with any luck, be on our way back toward London by midday."

"As you said, it is only one night." Why was she arguing with his decision to keep her reputation intact? "There are plenty of blankets. I shall sleep on the floor, and you may have the bed."

"I would never allow a lady to sleep upon the ground," he scoffed, shaking his head.

"All right, I will sleep in the bed, and you can take the floor. Is that more agreeable?"

"Certainly, but—"

"Then it is settled." Ophelia gave him a curt nod. She hadn't given him the opportunity to renew his efforts to sleep in the stables. "Besides, we may very well have a tiring day tomorrow, and we need to be rested with our minds ready. Otherwise, we may be forced to spend another night in Sheerness."

He avoided her stare as he looked about the room, and she knew she'd won this battle.

They would share the room.

Why did Ophelia suspect this was the first step to her losing the war?

A light tap at the door signaled their meal had arrived. "Good evening, m'lady, m'lord." The maid, a young woman, likely a relation of the proprietor, hurried into the room, balancing a tray with two covered plates. "The cook here be one of the finest for miles. We be have'n fish caught this morn with plum rice and bread."

She quickly set the meal out on their tiny table and bobbed a slight curtsey before she departed the room, closing the door behind her.

The click of the latch and the girl's footfalls down the hallway echoed through the space.

Ophelia had never been alone in a room with a man. Why did the mere presence of a bed make this seem bolder than the previous six hours in the coach together?

"The table does not appear large enough for us both to dine," he said, as if the size of the table were the only thing to focus on—and not the fact that Ophelia had made a huge mistake by thinking they could share the room without lasting consequences. "I will remove my plate and eat on the bed."

"Then I will join you." Ophelia collected both plates and returned to the small circular rug between the door and the bed. She eyed the neatly made cot as Lord Hawke took his seat. "Besides, we have yet to discuss how we plan to go about finding information on your grandpapa."

She sat beside him on the bed, each of them perched on the edge with their plates nestled on their laps. The fish, a translucent white piece of meat, smelled divine, and the rice appeared well seasoned. The bread was not as fresh as the chunk her maid had packed for her, but neither was it stale.

They sat in silence, picking at their meals, and Ophelia feared she'd set out on this adventure with him without so much as questioning their actual course of action. She was unfamiliar with the area, she hadn't the slightest clue where to begin looking, nor did she know what Lord Hawke and Molly thought to find in Sheerness.

Her positive outlook thus far became somewhat diminished. If Edith were here, she'd know what to do and where to look for answers. Lucianna could question someone without them even suspecting they were being questioned.

"Lady Ophelia," Colin said, looking up from his plate. "I realized I do not know much about you. Why did you so readily agree to come with me? Do you seek to anger your father? If we are discovered, you would be compromised."

This was the exact topic Ophelia had tried her best to not think about since she'd hurried into her townhouse and gathered her belongings. She hadn't thought of the consequences if they were caught alone together, nor had she meant to incite her father's wrath. If she admitted any of this to Lord Hawke, she'd appear the senseless girl everyone thought her to be.

However, if she avoided acknowledging at least a bit of the truth to him, she would be abandoning her own integrity. Perhaps a compromise—just enough to satisfy his question without baring her soul about her friends leaving her behind when they traveled to the Scottish border. Odd that she hadn't thought of Tilda or the muddled, unresolved mess with Abercorn all afternoon. She had lived with the events of that night, they'd weighed upon her every day since her friend died; however, a few hours with Lord Hawke had drawn her thoughts in a completely different direction.

"I truly did not consider my father or my reputation when I agreed to accompany you," she admitted. "It seems I am always the woman to wait around for directions, to be present but still go unnoticed, always part of another's exciting moment but never feeling like I fully belong. So, I saw an opportunity and grasped at the chance to embark on my own adventure."

"You left word that you were departing for Gretna Green?" When she nodded, he continued. "How did you expect to get there?"

"Stagecoach." Her tone held too much bite. It wasn't Lord Hawke's fault that while Ophelia craved adventure and excitement, she hadn't taken any time to think though…well, anything.

But he nodded politely as if silently agreeing to overlook her less than ingenious plot or his earlier mention of the most common reason for traveling to Gretna Green.

"Well, it appears your adventure has turned into a misadventure of sorts."

"How so?" Ophelia knew exactly how but was unaware why he'd think things had gone awry.

"Well, you speak of wanting your own adventure, but alas, we have departed London on an excursion that has little—or nothing—to do with you." His brow rose in challenge.

"Not so. Not so at all." Bother! Lord Hawke was correct, but Ophelia would rather stuff her entire rice portion into her mouth and swallow than admit it. "The book you need belongs to me."

"What do you think of Fair Wind and his past as a smuggler?" At any other time, she would have felt the question was offensive and insensitive.

Lord Hawke's lips pressed into a straight line as he pondered the question. "He died before I was born, and since my father insists on acting like grandpapa never existed, I have only heard tales from Molly." He paused to take a bite of bread, and swallowed before continuing. "As you can assume, her stories of Fair Wind's heroics have only become grander as the years passed, but I do believe there is a measure of truth hidden within each story. The fact that my father rebuffs everything, tells me Molly's stories are far closer to the truth than the current earl would ever want to admit."

"But if your grandfather *had* assisted the king, it would be a great honor for your family."

Lord Hawke nodded. "Yes, that has always been my view, as well, but my father believes the harm to our family name would be irreparable if it were determined Fair Wind had been nothing more than a smuggler who'd been granted a title and lands for no purpose."

They fell into a companionable silence as they finished their meal, and she pondered what he'd said.

Ophelia was aware of the risks involved, better than most young women. She, Luci, and Edith had been tarnished by their accusations against Abercorn the year before, and even now, with both her friends betrothed and in love, there were scarce invitations bestowed upon the trio.

Her family had been like Luci's and blamed Ophelia for speaking out against Abercorn, yet she knew they all suffered. Ophelia had four siblings whose futures were affected, and she hadn't considered that at all.

Much as she had impulsively absconded from London with Lord Hawke.

"Lady Ophelia," he whispered, taking her empty plate with his and returning them to the table. He stood tall and glanced out the high window. He stared for so long, she wondered what could have captured his notice no fully that he seemed almost in a different place entirely. "We do not know much about one another, do we?"

His inquiry took her by surprise.

"I suppose we do not." Yet, his loyalty to Molly showed him to be a man brimming with heart. His defense of Ophelia, despite Molly's claims to the contrary, showed he was a champion of the unjustly accused. He was above reproach, and not a speck of her felt the least bit hesitant in his company. What more did she need to know? "What will you do if we find no proof of Fair Wind's honorable dealings?"

The mettle of a man was not found in their successes but in their failures.

Ophelia had never understood the deep-rooted meaning of that until now, though her father used the phrase often.

Many men, her father explained, gave up, or worse yet, they pushed their failures off on others. They blamed everyone and anything besides themselves.

"I will keep searching," Lord Hawke sighed as he

turned to face her. Sorrow was etched on his downcast expression. "If it gives Molly any measure of happiness and continues to be important to her, I will search until the end of my days."

"That is a long time."

"Not so long as an eternity endured with a shadow cast over oneself." He returned to sit next to Ophelia on the bed. "What will you do if we return to London and our adventure together is exposed?"

She shrugged, clenching her hands in her lap to stop herself from reaching out for him. "It will not matter overmuch."

"A woman who so easily disregards her reputation." It was Lord Hawke who reached out first, laying his hand upon hers. "I would be most aggrieved if our adventures caused you any hardship."

CHAPTER 14

HE STROKED HER clasped hands lightly, afraid his slight movements might frighten her. The way she leaned toward him, her head bowed a fraction of an inch, spoke volumes. He'd been wrong about her—wholly incorrect. She was not the innocent debutante he'd believed her to be since their first meeting, nor was she worldly. Her nature hinted at something darker, however—more than the modest and demure figure he'd known thus far.

It had struck him as a whimsical flight of fancy when she'd so readily agreed to accompany him to Sheerness.

But now, he wondered if she sought more than just adventure.

Or, more accurately, if she ran from something.

"As the daughter of a duke, I would think your reputation would matter greatly—especially to you." There must be something he was unaware of, some information that, had he been one to dabble in societal gossip, he would know. "Has your marriage been arranged already?"

Her stare finally left her lap and settled on his as he held his breath, not at all prepared for her answer. He would be a thousand times a scoundrel if he'd been fool enough to not only leave London with an innocent woman but also another man's betrothed.

She had spoken of Gretna Green earlier. Would her parents assume she'd run off with another man?

Colin cursed Molly's outlandish demand that Ophelia—*Lady* Ophelia—accompany him. He should have dismissed the entire thing completely in that moment.

"Of course, I am not betrothed." She pulled her hands out of reach. "It is just that not all debutantes, even the daughters of dukes, are vigorously sought after. And you, the son of an earl and a baron in your own right, why are you not wed?"

Her face flushed, and Colin chuckled when she covered her mouth.

"Do not be embarrassed," he said. "That is by far the easiest question to answer."

She looked up at him from under lowered lashes, and he was reminded how angelic she'd appeared in the carriage. Even now, with the candle on the washstand behind her, a soft glow surrounded her. The pale expanse of skin revealed by her low-cut gown was not as enchanting as the guarded look in her eyes, or the way she clutched her skirt with nervousness.

He was uncertain why, but he needed her to understand the severe consequences if he returned to London empty-handed. "My family has been in turmoil for years—longer than years, decades." Colin sighed. He'd never spoken of his family's discord with anyone, least of all a woman he barely knew. "Once he was old enough to know not all families came from small sea towns and accumulated their wealth by means other than inheritance and savvy business investments, my father only spoke ill of Fair Wind. When Molly and my grandpapa decided to send their son for a proper education, he became exactly what my grandparents had fought against becoming when they were bestowed the Earldom by King George."

Thankfully, Lady Ophelia remained quiet, allowing him to speak.

"My father became entitled and condemned Molly and Fair Wind for their less than noble past. He grew bitter and angry when reminded of his own meager upbringing in Kent. Ramsey, my father, erased all traces of the Parnell family past as soon as Fair Wind died. He expelled Molly to the country, banishing her from his home in London."

"Poor Molly," Ophelia whispered. "Your father does not sound like a kind man."

"You misunderstand, he is not an *unkind* man, he is just a lord who embraced his arrogance and his right to his title." Colin shook his head at his father's folly. "He thinks of what's to come but forgets the past. One has no future when there is no history to build on."

"And you plan to show him the error of his ways?"

He couldn't tell if she meant the question as a jest or asked with seriousness. "No, above all else, I want to end the war within my family." The struggle seemed insurmountable in that moment. "I want the strife over. Whether Fair Wind was an ally of the king or a mere common smuggler from Kent, I want the truth known. Either way, I am not ashamed."

"I think that is most noble of you, Lord Hawke."

"Colin. Lord Hawke is too formal," he said with a smile. He'd never truly realized how alone he felt wedged between his father's disapproval and Molly's adamant, never-ending insistence. "And I do not do this thing out of any noble intent, I assure you. It is quite unbearable being placed in the middle of my father and Molly. They are so very similar in many ways: stubborn, determined, and neither is ever wrong."

They both laughed at his unplanned jest.

Colin sober quickly, though. "Molly adores me because I am a mirror image of Fair Wind, and I think my father remains detached from me for the same reason."

"That must be hard." She sighed, picking at the seam of her gown. "However, if people are willing to fight, then does that not mean they care enough about the other to put forth the effort to quarrel?"

"You are a wise woman, Ophelia." Her eyes dipped to her lap once more when he used her given name. "Has no one ever praised your intellect?"

"It is hard for one to notice most of the time."

"How so?" he asked. "Every time we speak, I am reminded yet again how brilliantly insightful you are."

"My lord. Colin"—she corrected quickly—"that is very kind of you to say."

"It is also true."

She was still, in many ways, a mystery to him. There was something about her that spoke of heartache and loss, yet she blushed like the innocent debutante she was. She shared astute perspectives on issues a woman of her standing should know naught about.

The glow from the single candle behind her cast a shadow across her face at the same time her hair surrounded her much like a fiery halo. She appeared the temptress Molly suspected her to be; however, if Lady Ophelia were casting a spell on him, Colin was glad of it.

Her cerulean eyes lifted to meet his. It was more of a collision than any innocent meeting.

She pulled him in, and he was desperate to follow wherever she led.

Straight to Hell? Colin was prepared for the burn.

To the deep depths of the ocean? Water had never felt so welcoming.

As high as the clouds above? He would revel in the fall back to solid ground.

Colin was incapable of moving away, standing, or departing the room—as he bloody well knew he should.

Walking away was no longer an option. Every instinct told Colin he should run...away from Lady Ophelia, back to London, hell, he should flee to Hawke

Manor.

Instead, he closed the distance between them, bringing their lips within a breath of one another…and he waited. She need only move a fraction of an inch, and their mouths would meet.

Ophelia had the choice to pull away. Seconds passed, but she didn't move, her breaths fanning against his heated face as their eyes held. Holding himself back from wrapping her in his arms nearly broke Colin.

As time continued, and their breathing slowed, something far more intense traveled between them—filling the inch separating them and decreasing the abyss unraveling them. He could almost feel her warm, soft lips against his—their touch, their texture. Could imagine how she'd settle against him in his arms—all womanly curves against his solid body. Colin committed to memory the scent of her—like spring blossoms on a rainy London morning.

Lady Ophelia was greater than any woman he'd had the pleasure of meeting. She was Heaven on Earth, a beacon of light in a dark fog, and a woman Colin could never hope to make his.

Just as the night with the coming morn, he would be powerless to grasp hold of her and keep her near.

Thud. Thud. Thud.

They leapt apart when a barrage of fist falls hit their door.

"Water for ye, m'lord!" a man called.

She stood, glancing at the dwindling candle on the washstand and then back to him. The blush he expected to see did not creep up her neck, nor did she shrink from him in shame.

"Enter," she commanded, her voice raspy, unlike her usual light, melodic tone.

The inn servant bustled into the room with a large, copper basin. The water steamed and sloshed over the edge onto the wooden floor as he set it close to the washstand.

Colin barely took his stare off Ophelia to thank the servant as he departed the room.

"You must be exhausted." Colin leapt from the bed, his gaze darting about the room. "I will bid you good night, my lady."

Her brow pulled low. "Where are you going?"

"To sleep."

"Where?"

Could it be that she did not want him to leave?

"I will find my rest in the stables with my men as mentioned." There was only so far Colin would push the boundaries of propriety. Many would say he already crossed the line when asking Lady Ophelia to travel to Sheerness—alone—with him. However, Colin suspected he'd traversed across long before that…when he'd agreed to Molly's outlandish plan. Now that they were here, Colin could not, in good conscience, stay in such close proximity to her, especially after what had transpired between them only moments before. He shuddered to think what might have happened had the servant not interrupted them. "It is improper for me to stay here." *With you*, he added silently.

The increased rise and fall of her bosom as she inhaled and exhaled made Colin think Ophelia was also pondering what could have transpired if they hadn't been disturbed.

He shook his head, refusing to let the notion gain purchase in his mind.

Lady Ophelia, while openly seeking an adventure, had not agreed to be ruined.

Nor did Colin seek to take advantage of her.

"The room is large enough for us both." She spread her arms wide as if to convince him that remaining, overnight, in the same private room was in any way a sensible idea. "Please. The journey was long for the both of us. At least stay here where it is warm."

He frowned, scrutinizing the room.

Ophelia took a step toward him. "Come now," she

said, gesturing to the bed. "There are sufficient enough pillows and bedding for you to make a proper sleeping area close to the hearth."

He released his held breath in a loud exhale, relieved she hadn't suggested the actual bed to be large enough for the pair of them.

"Please." She clasped her hands before her, turning her widened, imploring stare on him, freezing him in place. "I would never forgive myself if you were made to sleep in the stables, especially knowing you funded the coin for this room."

Colin looked from the bed, to the floor, to the closed door.

No one would know, except for them.

And he would never breathe a word to anyone.

"Fine," he grumbled. "Under one condition…"

Her lips turned up in a victorious grin. "Anything."

"I will only use one blanket from the bed." His brow rose as he begged her to argue or deny his condition. It would make everything simpler; however, she nodded with all seriousness. "I will use my coat under my head."

"If you wish." She turned and removed her satchel from the end of the bed, depositing it on the floor before collecting the thickest blanket. "Here you are, my lord."

"Good night, Lady Ophelia."

"Sleep tight, Lord Hawke."

Why did Colin suspect he'd lost some greater battle that had been going on without him noticing?

With a sigh, he turned his back to her and spread his blanket on the floor—the cold, hard floor.

The rustle of fabric sounded behind him, and Colin imagined her undressing, slipping into a nightshift before crawling into bed.

However, when he turned, she was merely removing her cloak and gloves. He hadn't even noticed she'd worn them throughout their meal and conversation.

"I will step outside so you can change in private."

Her cheeks did blossom with color at that, giving Colin the urge to step close and continue what they'd started earlier.

"There is no need," she replied. His breath hitched at her meaning. "I will sleep in my gown for warmth"—they both glanced to the paltry fire in the hearth—"and change into a fresh dress on the morrow."

After one final, searching stare, Ophelia looked away and blew out the candle. She pulled the covers down before crawling onto the bed. She snuggled in deep and shifted to face the wall.

Had he mistaken the longing in her eyes? It was far more likely that it was regret he saw in their blue depths, a churning turmoil that was a result of their combined making.

It was difficult to ignore the interest she'd taken in him—and his family. And she hadn't latched on to his words because of their sordid nature or his family's unsavory past.

Certainly not. Lady Ophelia had been genuinely concerned and had gone so far as to offer her own words of wisdom on the situation.

Colin moved his coat and lay on his makeshift bed, the hard, wooden floorboards pressed into his hip. The pain would be worth it to remain close to Ophelia. If he'd retired to the stables, he would have fretted so much over her being alone in the inn he'd have journeyed back and slept outside her door to make certain she remained safe.

Listening, her breathing became slow and shallow as she found sleep.

Something Colin envied greatly.

No measure of relaxation would bring him rest with the fiery-haired temptress so close at hand. Molly held her beliefs that Ophelia's auburn hair marked her as a sorceress—luring men to their demise—however, the woman asleep in the bed behind him was pure light and goodness, with a caring, compassionate side he'd never seen in another.

Colin shifted to his back to relieve the ache in his shoulder and hip from the floor, entwining his fingers and placing his hands under his head as he focused on the ceiling. His gaze traced along the planks of wood above him. If he listened intently, another inn guest could be heard snoring from the room next to theirs. He wondered how that man had come to be in Sheerness, and if he sensed the immense change happening so close to where he slept.

The soft breathing continued, and Colin's own inhales and exhales aligned with Ophelia's until they breathed as one.

Turning, Colin saw she'd also moved to her back, her closed eyes facing the ceiling.

A lump in his coat pocket pushed at the tender area behind his ear when he removed his hands from behind his head. He slipped his fingers into his jumbled coat and pulled out Molly's treasured pendant—her one piece of jewelry, and the only item she'd kept on her person as far back as Colin could remember. As a young boy, he remembered toying with the jewel-encrusted piece as Molly read to him at night. When they'd been out by the lake at Tintinhull, the sun had gleamed off the pendant, and Molly had spoken of the keepsake as his grandpapa's remaining eye on earth.

Colin held the thing above his head, the chain hanging down inches from his face, but it appeared like any other necklace worn by a woman. His grandmama had told him many times that the power of the piece came from the person who wore it, not the object itself—and perhaps that was true. The thing did not glow or sparkle as it did when it was about Molly's neck. The stone did not hold the depth of color he'd beheld all these years.

The treasured pendant had come with Colin as an

omen of good luck to be had.

There was much riding on his journey to Sheerness, and that was without even factoring in the impact it would have on his entire family. Molly would either be vindicated or heartbroken by the information he returned to London with. His father would be forced to make amends with Molly or banish her to Tintinhull in Somerset for as long as she took breath.

Colin clutched the pendant to his chest as his eyes fluttered shut, heavy with sleep.

As he drifted into a restless slumber, his mind conjured the most startling image—Lady Ophelia, with his grandmama's treasured stone securely fastened about her neck.

CHAPTER 15

OPHELIA WOKE WITH a start—everything wasn't as it should be. The bed she lay upon was lumpy, the coverlet was coarse where it was gathered by her cheek, and her entire body ached. Unable to move, she raised her head slightly to note that the bedding and her gown had become unbearably tangled during her fitful rest.

Breathing…someone was breathing soundly very close by.

The labored inhale and exhale was rhythmic and deep. Part of her prayed the noise would lull her back to sleep.

Unfortunately, the scent of stale air, smoke, and meat cooking made escape impossible.

Ophelia pushed the coverlet down and struggled to sit up—blast it all, but she'd been foolish enough to sleep in her riding habit. Not even her dress, but Luci's low-cut, curve-clinging traveling outfit. No wonder she couldn't move her legs. The skirting was sturdy and thick to keep her protected from traveling dirt and grime. She hadn't dreamed it could also be used as a solid means of restraint.

Glancing over the side of the bed, she saw Colin lying sprawled on the floor, also in his clothes from the day before, his coat securely tucked under his head.

The high window only allowed a fraction of early morning light to touch her, but it was enough to see the room was as it had been when she'd rolled toward the wall and concentrated on slumber.

She'd been a fool not to change into her nightshift when he'd offered her privacy the evening before, but she'd been afraid he'd change his mind and not return, departing in favor of a night in the stables. Added to that, Ophelia would not have been able to unfasten and shimmy from Luci's constricting gown without assistance—and so, she'd spent nearly a day now in a dress that prevented her from gaining a deep breath. She'd more than noticed the way Colin had observed her in the carriage.

Again, she was in the same precarious position as the evening before.

How was she to unfasten Luci's gown without her maid to change into a new one?

She could request Lord Hawke's help, but after last night, Ophelia did not trust herself to keep him at arm's length. She'd barely been able to keep him a breath away the previous night...and she'd had all her clothes firmly fastened, including the buttons on her cloak.

Would she be able to resist leaning into him if the promise was much more than a kiss?

Ophelia had fallen asleep with dreams of his lips against hers—demanding, yet tender. He'd guide her as to how to execute a proper kiss, and she would allow him to teach her all. Willingly, she would have accepted his gift without rebuff. Yet, something had held her back as they'd sat on the bed, knees nearly touching with his mouth so close she could almost taste the meal they'd shared.

If Colin had been disappointed that she hadn't leaned the final inch toward him to bring their lips together, he hadn't shown it.

Ophelia wondered if they'd been given a few more moments, if the servant hadn't interrupted them, would she have pressed her lips to his?

She'd been so befuddled by it all, she'd forgotten to wash up with the water the servant had delivered. A quick look at the full water bowl on the washstand confirmed that Colin hadn't cleaned up after their long day of travel either.

Could it be that he'd been as taken aback by their moment of intimacy as she? Certainly not. He was a man of wealth and title; surely such things would not affect him. It was more likely he was shocked by her forthright nature and thought her a woman of low morals and no decorum. Add this to her preposterous and imprudent decision to accompany him to Sheerness, and Colin had every right to think poorly of her.

Even more damning, she'd all but begged him to sleep in the same room as she.

What had she been thinking?

She hadn't been, at least not with her normal, rational mind.

Luci had been justified in warning Ophelia against looking into Abercorn in her absence. Neither of her friends would be shocked by the muck she'd gotten herself into since they left for the Scottish border.

Colin shifted, his foot kicking out and knocking against the leg of the small, round table, rattling their dinner dishes.

She held her breath, waiting for him to rouse.

When his breathing continued, unperturbed, she relaxed once more, taking advantage of the time to inspect him without his notice as he'd done when he thought her asleep in the carriage.

It should strike her as an invasion of his privacy; however, this seemed less personal than reading Fair Wind's book. She wasn't merely an outsider delving into his past any longer.

In a way, Ophelia was now part of Fair Wind's legacy, be it good or bad.

Colin had said he resembled his grandfather with

his fair hair and sun-kissed complexion. This morning, a lock of silky blond hair lay across his face, tousled from sleep. One hand was balled into a tight fist at his chest, and the other was at his side. She could imagine him at the helm of a ship, the waves crashing against the portside bow as he commanded his men. He was reserved, though she suspected he took charge when the time called for it.

Lord Hawke's compassion and caring for Molly and her wishes spoke volumes about the man he was. He was not concerned about tarnishing his family name if he did find proof that Fair Wind was merely a smuggler with a jaded past.

Even now, he seemed at ease sprawled on the floor, a confidence about him Ophelia was hard-pressed to understand. It wasn't arrogance or entitlement, but more of an understanding of one's self and an acceptance that was far more than just skin-deep.

She trusted him enough to flee London by his side without knowing so much as a single detail about their plan, except the town they were headed to. She'd never been one to blindly follow another without cause. Certainly, her faith in Luci and Edith was grounded in years of unconditional friendship, only solidified by Tilda's tragic death, but what had Colin done to gain such unquestioned trust?

Ophelia had no answer for that.

Far more startling was why *he'd* trusted her on this journey.

There was no doubt that Ophelia knew far more about Colin than he did about her—and still, he hadn't hesitated, beyond a brief moment, to include her in everything. His excuse—her being the rightful owner of Fair Wind's book—had been a ruse. One only need half a brain to see that much. She'd offered to return the book, but he'd turned her away.

The heady aroma of frying meat, fresh bread, and coffee filtered into the room from the tavern below.

Boots sounded in the hallway as other guests roused and went in search of a meal to break their fast. Voices floating up from the gathering crowd below finally had Colin stirring.

"Good morn," she called from above as his eyes opened, and he smiled. "Sleep well?"

He pushed to sit as something tumbled from his chest into his lap. The small amount of sun entering the room gleamed off the object, reflecting an array of dancing colors and light across the far wall.

"Is that Molly's pendant?"

Colin cleared his throat and grasped the necklace, holding it high for her to see. "Good morning, and yes, it is." His voice was deep and raspy from sleep, but he rubbed his eyes with his free hand and slipped the pendant into the pocket of his wrinkled coat. "Have you been awake long?"

At least an hour, she thought, but her words betrayed her with a fib. "Only a few moments, my lord."

"Very well." He pushed to his bare feet and stretched, his hands nearly touching the low ceiling. "I am famished. Shall we dress and break our fast?"

Ophelia was hungry, that much was true, but a meal was not the most prevalent thing on her mind at the moment. There was little doubt she could have attained all the nourishment she'd need if only she were allowed to observe the confident, handsome Lord Hawke for another hour or so.

CHAPTER 16

COLIN PACED AT the bottom of the stairs, awaiting Lady Ophelia so they could find their meal and be on their way. He looked into the tavern once more to see the crowd had further thinned as guests ate and departed. The room had been teeming with people when he'd first arrived downstairs.

What was taking her so dreadfully long?

He'd given her privacy to dress, but now he wondered if that had been a mistake and something had gone wrong above stairs. Colin wasn't versed in women's attire; however, it should not take this bloody long to change one's gown.

Convinced there was something keeping her, Colin started up the steps toward their shared room. The hairs on the back of his neck stood on end in warning. He passed an older couple as he hurried down the hall toward their closed door.

"Good day," he said by way of greeting as he slipped past them.

Coming to a halt outside their room, he raised his hand to open the door but thought better of it. She could possibly be indecent on the other side. Instead of reaching for the latch, he knocked.

"Lady Ophelia?" he called, but no answer came.

He placed his ear to the door, hoping to block out the sound of the people in the tavern below. He heard the rustling of fabric and a low curse. She was inside, but then why not answer his knock?

"Lady Ophelia, it is Lord Hawke—" Bloody hell, she knew damn well who he was. "May I come in?"

There was a flurry of sounds; more footfalls, the scraping of the chair, and finally, the sagging of the bed ties."

"Do answer me, or I will be forced to enter in fear you are in danger, my lady."

"Come in," she said in a trembling voice that barely penetrated the wood.

Colin took hold of the handle, uncertain what he'd find on the other side of the door when he entered.

He pushed the portal wide, the interior of the room lit only by the light coming in through the small window and the single candle from the night before. Their empty dishes still sat on the table, and the blanket he'd used was folded neatly on the end of the bed with Lady Ophelia's satchel on top.

She sat beside her traveling bag, her head in her hands, partially gowned in a dark blue dress with one side hanging loosely down her arm. Her shoulders shook, and she did not look up when he entered, closing the door behind him.

"Ophelia?" He took the three steps to her and kneeled, lightly pulling her hands from her face. "What is wrong?"

She glanced up at that moment, and his heart plummeted from his chest as tears pooled in her eyes and streamed down her cheeks. The blue was no longer the color of the ocean several feet off shore, but the deep cobalt of a growing storm.

A quiet sob escaped her on a hiccup.

"Shhhh," Colin murmured. His leg weakened beneath him as he continued to crouch. "Do not cry."

Never would anyone consider Molly a woman

prone to fits of tears—and not on one occasion had Colin witnessed his mother in any state as vulnerable as Ophelia appeared at present.

"Please, allow me to fix whatever has upset you." His attempt to soothe her was met by yet another sob, this one not as quiet. "Do you wish to return to London? We can leave now, this very moment." When she only shook her head in refusal, he continued, "Did someone come to your door after I left?"

He shouldn't have left her alone, no matter how secure and protected the inn had felt to him.

"No, no one," she stammered. "I—I—I—"

"What, Lady Ophelia?" he demanded softly. "Tell me what has upset you, and I will do my best to fix it."

Her lower lip trembled as he searched her face for any sort of answer as to what could have possible transpired while he'd waited at the bottom of the main stairs.

"I—I cannot—I cannot fasten my gown." Though her words were shaky, Ophelia lifted her chin and stared him directly in the eyes as if she were imparting her only grave flaw or admitting a serious transgression. "Can you assist me, my lord?"

Colin pushed to his feet and held his hand out to her. "Come, my lady. I would be honored to offer my skills as a lady's maid."

Her chin tilted up as she met his stare, a small smile touched her lips, and she placed her hand in his...her blessedly bare hand. Wrapping his fingers around hers tightly, he helped her to her feet, and she turned to face away from him. Her corset was still tied and her undergarments in place—it was only the back of her gown that remained unfastened, a long row of pearl beads serving as buttons.

"Do not chastise me if I am not overly adept at fastenings, Lady Ophelia." He reached forward, starting with the bottom button and began the arduous task. It was little wonder women were in need of maids. Colin was able to adequately dress himself and tie a cravat without his valet's assistance, but these…these tiny, nearly ungraspable buttons would prove him worthless if he were not a determined man. She shifted slightly, her hands wringing before her. "I am nearly halfway done. I promise not to miss a single one."

"Thank you, Colin."

His aching fingers faltered, stumbling over the next button before he could focus and continue.

An eternity later, that also struck him as only a few hurried moments, he pushed the final pearl button into the top hole, allowing his hand to graze the back of her neck where her hair was already secured in place with several metal pins.

"Finished." He stepped back and admired the long row of pearls, each slipped into the correct slot. There must have been fifty of them in total. "Are you ready to depart? The public room was nearly empty below. We should be able to eat quickly and be on our way."

"I will collect my things." Taking hold of her satchel, Ophelia turned.

No longer were her eyes moist with tears, nor did her chin tremble.

He now faced the woman who'd climbed into his carriage the day before; reserved, poised, and with an almost undetectable glow in her stare.

The midnight blue gown hugged her body in a more modest fit than the low-cut habit from the previous day—and Colin had to admit, at least to himself, it suited her far better. This was the woman he'd saved from Molly's uplifted cane. This was the proper miss who'd thought to do him a kindness by returning his grandpapa's book. It was this demure, serene female nervously worrying her hands and standing before him who he'd happened upon in the Atholl gardens the day before.

She needn't attire herself in risqué gowns to capture Colin's unwavering attention.

No, Lady Ophelia need only concentrate on presenting herself to others.

They left the room and made their way down to the public area; all the while, Colin kept her pulled close to his side.

Several stares turned in their direction when they entered the room and selected an empty table. There was little doubt every eye was focused on Ophelia, and not Colin with his rumpled coat and unpolished Hessians.

Bloody hell if Colin didn't stand a bit taller as he escorted her to their table. A servant hurried over, pulled their chairs, and assisted Lady Ophelia to her seat.

"The meal be boiled eggs, bread, cheese, and ham…coffee or ale ta drink." The servant didn't waste any time scurrying back toward the kitchen and returning with heaping plates.

Their meal was eaten in silence, giving Colin time to think through where they'd begin their search. Molly had been kind enough to send him with a list of places she thought they'd find things left by his grandpapa. He'd nearly forgotten that he'd slipped the envelope into his coat's inside pocket for safekeeping.

He retrieved the paper and broke the seal while Ophelia's head remained lowered over her plate. She ate slowly, her table manners everything he'd expect from a woman of elevated refinement. Her movements as she sliced an egg in half, speared a section, and brought it to her lips fascinated him in an unfamiliar way. He dined across the table from many people—beautiful, intelligent, and witty women included—but something about Ophelia's delicate nature had him disregarding their purpose in Sheerness and the limited time they possessed to achieve it before departing for the return trip to London.

"What have you there?" she asked, wiping the corners of her mouth with her napkin.

Glancing down, he realized he'd been clutching the slip of paper in his hand.

Colin pushed his plate to the side and smoothed the letter on the table between them, reading it for the first time. "It is a list of places Molly suggested we visit for information."

Ophelia's brow rose in question, but she made no move to ask anything further as she took her last bite, giving Colin a moment to inspect the list. The places appeared easy enough to find if he spoke with the innkeeper and collected directions. Sheerness was not a large town and was inhabited by mostly seafaring men and their families. If Fair Wind had chosen to call the town home, even decades after taking his place in London, then the people here must be as kind as he.

A man chuckled at a nearby table, and Colin looked over to see it was the lord and lady from upstairs, also having their morning meal. The gentleman appeared oddly familiar, but there was little chance Colin would be acquainted with another person in Sheerness.

Colin turned back to the note before him, folding it to slip it back into the envelope as Ophelia continued watching the pair at the next table. When he made to return the paper to the envelope, it caught on something and would not slip farther in. Turning the envelope upside down, Colin shook it and another paper fell out, as small as a calling card, but with his grandmama's hurried script across the front. He flipped the page over, and the back was blank.

Strangely peculiar.

It must be something that hadn't fit on the other paper—or perhaps an afterthought Molly had added after jotting down her list.

Colin, me dear lad.
I had no option but ta send ye where it all began for
Porter and meself. I hope ye find what ye seek, just as we
did.

Take care of Lady Ophelia.
Molly

He blinked a few times, thinking he must have read the note incorrectly before glancing around the room. Colin sensed that all eyes were on him—that Molly had somehow tricked him and would, at any moment, leap from her hiding spot with her cane held high and a thunderous laugh.

But no one paid him any mind, even Lady Ophelia continued to scrutinize the older pair at the table across the room.

Molly was no doubt up to something, and it had naught to do with Fair Wind.

Hastily, he returned her note to the envelope, but kept Molly's list at the ready. He would ask the innkeeper where they could find their first location.

If they hurried, they could be on their way before the sun crested.

Colin remained silent when he noted Ophelia's lips pressed into a grimace and her frozen appearance. She hadn't moved, but still kept watch on the couple.

"Are you acquainted with the pair?" he asked. A chill ran down his back at the thought that Lady Ophelia would be ruined long before they returned to London if they encountered someone she knew.

Instead of answering, she pushed back her chair and stood. "Shall we be off? An adventure awaits, my lord."

Her posture was straight, and her chin held high, but her smile wavered slightly, belying her eagerness. For not the first time since they had departed London, he wondered what she hid from him. Though, if Colin pushed her for answers, she'd likely ask him questions he was uncomfortable with answering, as well.

Tucking the envelope with Molly's note into his pocket beside the pendant, he stood. "I think it is time our day began. I have Molly's list ready and thought the best place to start would be to ask the proprietor for directions."

He searched the dim, public room, but the innkeeper was nowhere in sight. The space was nearly vacant at this hour, most travelers having departed with the rising sun and the fare more than the local community could afford.

"If you will wait here, I will find directions and have my driver prepare the carriage."

She hurried around the table, setting her hand at his arm. "I think I will join you. Sheerness cannot be so large that we will need the carriage."

"I think you are correct, my lady." Colin scanned Molly's list once more. "Shall we start at the beginning?"

Stepping into the open inn yard, the sun cast a shadow, and the cool ocean breeze blew about them, ruffling Colin's neckcloth and billowing Ophelia's skirts about her ankles. Two carriages pulled from the inn yard, one heavy with trunks, and the other a well-adorned traveling coach, its wheels throwing dust into the air.

A stable boy trotted up to them, a lopsided grin on his face, his clothes a size too big but clean. "Can I fetch ye coach, m'lord?"

"That will not be necessary." He glanced at Ophelia to confirm their decision, and she nodded. "We will take in Sheerness on foot."

"Fine notion, m'lord." The boy's head bobbed up and down.

"You would not happen to know where we can find a tree where people carve their names?" Colin held the list high, reading Molly's words. "The Tower Tree."

The servant's jovial, helpful nature subsided, and he shook his head from side to side.

"You do not know that place?" Ophelia asked. "Mayhap we should—"

"No, m'lady. I be remember'n that tree. Me pa used Ma's fish knife ta cut their names."

"Can you tell us where to find it?"

"Well, in the inn." The boy pointed toward the public room they'd just exited. "Ol' Bosworth cut the tree down and made tables for the tap room."

They cut down the tree?

Colin swallowed hard, his shoulders slumping as the news sank in.

There was no hallowed tree for them to search. Molly's carefully collected places had been reduced from four to three, and they hadn't so much as left the inn yard.

Lady Ophelia placed her hand on his shoulder and gave a comforting squeeze before plucking the list from his hand. She shielded her eyes and inspected the next place.

"Oh, this should be simple enough to find," she mumbled. "Thank you—"

"I be Owen, m'lady," the boy chimed in when Ophelia paused.

"Well, Owen." She shook the paper before her. "Thank you for your assistance. We are off to the docks."

Colin couldn't help but admire her optimism as they set off toward the water's edge, which could be seen down a long, wide lane from the inn. They passed dock workers and a lady pushing a cart filled with fresh sea fare for the market. The salty sea odor increased the closer they journeyed to the water lapping against the wooden docks and the tiny fishing vessels dotting the coast. It appeared any merchant ships were either not in the port at present or had taken their business elsewhere.

The wind increased as they walked, teasing Lady Ophelia's locks from their pins to dance about her shoulders.

She stared out at the water, not noticing—or at least not commenting on—his stolen sideways glances.

"Have you been to the ocean, Lady Ophelia?"

Colin knew many Londoners who'd never been near open water except when they traveled near the river Thames. He, on the other hand, had grown up on stories told to Molly by Fair Wind and his father's occasional tales of his youthful visits to Sheerness before they'd permanently settled inland.

"Only a few months ago, when Luci and I went to Southend in Essex to rescue—errr, *collect* Edith; however, the trip was not a long one, nor traveled for pleasure." Her hands clasped his arm tighter the more she said. "I fear I was not able to enjoy the sea breeze or the sound of the waves."

Rescue? Yes, he'd heard the word before she'd corrected herself.

"Tell me more about your friends. It sounds like a trip to Essex—no matter the hurried nature—counts as an adventure of sorts."

Her stare fell away from the water in the distance to the ground before them.

She gave her head a soft shake. If he hadn't been watching her from the corner of his eye, he would have missed the subtle gesture.

"Come now, Sheerness hasn't been your only adventure outside London," he prodded, knowing there was more on the topic of Southend he needed to hear. "Tell me, Lady Ophelia."

"Southend was not my adventure, my lord," she sighed. "While I will not deny the daring and exciting aspects of the journey—a trip that would have seen us returning without Edith in tow—I was merely there to aid my friends."

"So, you crave your own quest?" He didn't expect a response, for the answer was obvious. It was a subject Colin could understand. So much of his own life had been written by his father or commanded by Molly, much like the reason they were in Sheerness now. It wasn't one of his choosing, but an obligation of sorts. "My arrival with plans to travel to Sheerness seemed the perfect opportunity, then."

She laughed, a light chuckle captured by the wind and blown inland. "Yes, I am happy to see you agree with my decision."

"I cannot say I agree with your choice to flee London without leaving any true note as to our destination—putting your reputation in jeopardy—and all for my grandmama and a family tale that may not be grounded in fact." He did not add the more preposterous part about being accompanied by a man and insisting on sharing sleeping quarters. Neither of them need be reminded of what had almost occurred during their private hours at the inn. "However, I do fully understand your need for something to call your own."

At least Colin had his small estate, Hawke Manor, near Tintinhull Court in Somerset. It wasn't anything grand, but it belonged solely to him as Baron Hawke. No one could take it from him. Though, women rarely owned land, lived in a home not of their father's or husband's choosing, or traveled unaccompanied.

Freedom, what little he possessed, had always been something he'd taken for granted.

Lady Ophelia—and other society maidens—lived under a staunch set of pre-determined rules of conduct. Any infraction would see the woman publicly shamed— or worse, cast from society altogether.

Would this adventure cause Lady Ophelia lasting ruination and shame?

Colin shuddered to think of the consequences their actions could cause. The mere notion of Lady Ophelia suffering due to him was unthinkable.

"My friends, Lady Lucianna and Lady Edith, are on their way to Gretna Green at the moment," she shared, bringing her stare back to the ocean. "Luci is to wed the Duke of Montrose."

She'd left word with her lady's maid that she was departing for the Scottish border, and now it made sense as to why her parents would not fret overmuch. They would assume she was safely with her friends—and not alone with a stranger on the coast of Kent.

"But you were not invited on their adventure?" he asked.

"It is not so much that I was not invited as I was forbidden to accompany them by my father."

"It is a long journey, especially for a woman not in her family's presence," he mused aloud.

"My father's reasoning exactly, my lord."

"Why do I think you were not all that upset at his refusal to allow you to accompany your friends?"

"You are very perceptive." She glanced at him, the hint of mischief he'd noted in her bearing as they'd left London returned. "While I do so wish to be at Lady Lucianna's side when her vows are spoken, it is always a bit tiresome being surrounded by two couples who openly adore one another. I sometimes gain the impression that I am utterly invisible and useless to the foursome. They have a carriage with four wheels…and a fifth simply has no place."

Every driver was aware that a spare, fifth wheel was always wise to have on hand, but Colin kept that knowledge to himself. "That cannot be the extent of their feelings toward you."

"Oh, heavens no, the girls are so very much in love with Torrington and Montrose I am certain they do not notice my melancholy in the slightest."

Colin had lost track of their progress as he'd been listening so intently to Lady Ophelia. She'd afforded him a glimpse into her world—one Colin was unfamiliar with. While his parents were cordial with one another, he would not label the wedded couple *in love*. He would, however, describe them as indifferent to Colin's comings and goings except how they affected the Coventry Earldom. Molly had been the only person concerned with Colin's upbringing, and mostly she'd remained at Tintinhull Court for his entire life.

To have family—or even close friends—who cared about his well-being and took an interest in his life seemed foreign.

"Why did you not disregard your father's edict and journey with them?" he asked as they turned around a large warehouse building and began walking parallel to the water, making their way toward the docks—and the tiny ale house Molly had written was situated between the fish market and the Sheerness office that kept track of all ingoing and outgoing ships and their cargo. "It seemed easy enough for you to slip away."

"Perhaps I did not truly wish to accompany them. We have spent much time together since our dear friend, Tilda, died. Mayhap it was time for me to find a measure of independence." She halted and looked straight ahead, giving him no opportunity to comment further. "It seems we have arrived…"

Her voice trailed off as her hand slipped into his and their fingers intertwined. The warmth of her skin through her gloved hand warded off the morning ocean breeze—but did nothing to keep the foreboding feeling from settling around him.

"It appears we will not be finding what we seek here."

CHAPTER 17

OPHELIA STOOD BESIDE Colin, their fingers interlocking as they both took in the sight before them. The fish market was a buzz of activity as fishermen brought in their morning catches. The records office, only noted by a wooden shingle hanging above the door, was yet to open for the day.

And between the two businesses—a shell of a building, its burned and decaying walls falling in on themselves with a sign to ward off anyone who might trespass. The single window on the front had been smashed out, no glass remaining.

She squeezed Colin's hand, a silent plea to not lose hope.

To her surprise, he didn't pull his hand back, but held hers tighter.

"Where to next?" she sighed, glancing up at him standing at her side, but he remained staring straight ahead. "We have two more places on the list, correct?"

Colin closed his eyes for a moment, and his chin fell.

She could not imagine the bleakness coursing through him at yet another setback.

"Yes." With his free hand, he retrieved the list from his pocket, unfolding it with one hand and keeping his grip on hers. "My grandpapa's old ship may still be at the dock. Molly says he kept all his important maps and notes aboard."

That the vessel would still be at port after all these years seemed difficult to believe—the notion of his possessions being on board was downright preposterous.

However, Ophelia held her tongue, she was hesitant to further dampen his mood. "Then we should be off to the dock."

"I do not know how to identify the boat if it is there," he said with an exasperated sigh, releasing her to run his hand through his hair. His light locks reflected the sun as they fell to cover one eye. The disheveled look suited him well, and Ophelia thought for not the first time that he would appear at home on a vessel on the open water. "I should have forced Molly to travel with me."

Her stomach clenched. It was absurd, but Ophelia felt as if she'd disappointed him in some way. It wasn't even conceivable she could assist him beyond giving him Fair Wind's book, though that did not halt the feelings of failure and dejection. Luci and Edith would know exactly what to do if they were here. They wouldn't allow defeat to stop them from finding what they sought.

Straightening her shoulders, Ophelia smiled broadly and turned toward Colin, determined to show him she could be useful. She wasn't merely the odd woman out this time, nor the one taking directions from those who "knew better."

"I think we should ask at the records office." She pointed to the building bordering the burned-down ale house. "They will have logs that make note of all the ships coming and going from Sheerness—and, hopefully, have record of Fair Wind's vessel."

She was hard-pressed to tamp down her confidence at finally taking a measure of control in their adventure.

"Very well," he said with a nod. "Let us begin there."

He held his arm out, and she slipped her hand into place. It was as if they'd strolled together for many years, their pace was evenly matched, and his hold on her felt right. She wondered for a brief moment what it would be like to dance with Colin, perhaps a waltz or a lively reel, with an entire ballroom bearing witness. Would other debutantes cast envious stares her way? It was more likely they wouldn't even notice Ophelia in Colin's arms as his handsomeness would certainly be the only thing attracting anyone's notice.

It was odd, this journey with Lord Hawke. She'd never been away from her family—or her friends—for such an extended period of time. It was freeing in a peculiar way. The fact that she hadn't given a second thought to what her parents might think was unsettling—and a bit selfish—but blast it all, Ophelia rarely stood on her own two feet without someone there to support her.

Along those lines, it had been nearly an entire day since she'd thought of Tilda and everything that had happened with her friend. She hadn't been plagued by night terrors as she'd slept, Colin on the floor close by.

The records office appeared closed from afar, but as they moved closer, a light could be seen through the open window, along with a man sitting behind a desk, quill in hand. As they entered, the clerk glanced up, his eyes widening in shock. His chair scraped against the scarred, wooden floor when he stood, glancing about as if they'd entered his private domain and he was uncertain how to proceed.

"Good morn, sir," Ophelia said. "Do you hold the records for Sheerness?"

His head bobbed, and he hurried across the room, his hands clutched before him. "Certainly. Certainly, miss. Births, deaths, land, and sea. I'm Mr. Ackerson."

"Lovely to meet you, Mr. Ackerson." Ophelia remained close to the door. The business office was piled high with crates, trunks, papers, and files, making navigating any farther an unwise decision lest she risk being crushed by falling boxes. "We are looking for a boat."

Ackerson's eyes narrowed, and he glanced over his shoulder to the area at the back of the office. "Sea it is. I keep everything in the back. Come along."

Ophelia glanced at Colin and shrugged before he stepped in front of her and led the way toward Ackerson. The man hurried ahead of them, clearly familiar with the safest and most expedited route to the sea records. Despite the clutter, not a speck of dust had settled on anything. She could not imagine that many people visited the record's office, but everything appeared clean, if not orderly.

Slipping by an upright pile of rolled maps, Ophelia decided her father would greatly enjoy a visit to Sheerness, if only to spend an entire fortnight exploring this room. Maybe she would speak with him about it when she returned home.

"Almost there," Colin whispered over his shoulder. "I do not see how the man can find anything in this mess."

Ophelia crossed her fingers and held them high for him to see, and they both laughed, though she noticed his chuckle was more hesitant than hers. Yet, she was determined to think positively. They needs must find some information to take back to London—and this ship was only one of two leads left. Mr. Ackerson and his impractical sorting methods was possibly their best—maybe their only—option.

"What are you looking for?" Ackerson asked, his hands on his hips as he surveyed the pile of folders and papers haphazardly stacked. "Shipment manifest? Export log? Injury details?"

"Er, we are looking for a ship."

"Name?" he queried.

"Sadly, I do not know," Colin admitted.

Ackerson turned sharply toward them, his stare narrowing as he brushed his palms down the front of his trousers. "No name." He scratched his head. "Type of vessel?"

"I am afraid we do not know that either," Ophelia answered when Colin's shoulders fell. "But we know approximately the year it came and went."

Ackerson pursed his lips and returned his gaze to his files. "That may help. What is the date?"

Ophelia looked to Colin, a bit of hope returning.

"A little over fifty years ago. During the Seven Years' War…"

The man exhaled heavily and shook his head. "That was a busy time for Sheerness to be certain. We had ships coming and going nearly every day for four years. Exports, imports, and even a few ships belonging to the king. Are there any other details you can share? If not, the three of us will be here searching long into next month."

It was a difficult topic, but Ophelia suspected Colin would have to name Fair Wind as the captain they were here about. Was Colin's grandpapa a well-known man in Sheerness, or had his memory faded and disappeared with time?

Certainly, even the tales of a smuggler's adventures would be passed down with the town folklore. Ackerson must be the town historian, as well.

"Would the captain's name help?" Ophelia asked.

"Depends," Ackerson mumbled. "Again, lots of boats coming and going…most not from around here, so I won't have record of them all."

Colin paused, and Ophelia nodded in support. "This man was from Sheerness."

"From Sheerness, you say?"

"Yes," Colin said, clearing his throat, and Ophelia feared it would be all he'd say. "He was born here, wed my grandmama here, and only moved away because he had no other choice."

The man slipped his hands into his trouser pockets and rolled back on his heels. "Not many folks leave Sheerness," he mused. "Suppose I'd have some record of him, or my pa might remember him."

"Porter Parnell," Colin said in a rush, it was as if he waited another moment, he'd lose the nerve to speak his grandpapa's name. "He wed Molly Kirkwise."

Ackerson tilted his head to the side and hummed, narrowing his intense stare on Colin. "Porter Parnell—married to ol' Kirkland Kirkwise's eldest gal?"

Ophelia wasn't certain if Ackerson knew whom he spoke of, or was only stringing together the oddest name he could think of, but Colin nodded confirmation and smiled.

"You're looking for Fair Wind?" Ackerson asked.

"Not Fair Wind, his vessel," Ophelia corrected, but the man didn't take his stare off Colin.

"Afraid you won't have any luck finding his ship in these parts." Ackerson took a step toward Colin, and Lord Hawke moved away until the back of his legs collided with a large trunk. "Well, I must say I am surprised I didn't notice right when you walked in."

Ophelia had the odd urge to step between the men and block Colin from Ackerson's intense scrutiny.

However, Colin spoke before she could move. "Do I look so much like him?"

"I never met him in person, but his portrait hung in the ale house next door until it burned to the ground." Ackerson tapped his forehead, chin, and chest in the same way Ophelia had witnessed Molly doing during one of her tirades. "You must be his son?"

Colin chuckled, and the tension in the room fled. "Grandson, actually. Colin Parnell, Lord Hawke when I'm feeling particularly formal."

"It is a pleasure to meet you, and it is a swell thing that we aren't high in the instep here in Sheerness."

"You said I would not be finding Fair Wind's vessel at the dock?"

"'Fraid not." Ackerson shook his head in apology. "Boat was nearly sinking. Merchant company, some businessman from London, came through a few years ago and bought the ancient thing from Molly's cousin, Jedidiah. I can see what other logs I have, though if I remember my father's tales correctly, Fair Wind kept meticulous notes of his journeys…did not favor leaving them here with the records office."

It was another false trail. Certainly, there would be no proof of Fair Wind's true purposes at sea in such a public office where anyone could request information. Without the boat and what could be hidden within, they had nothing. Colin's grandpapa, whether smuggling goods into England or running missives for the king, would not value his personal information spreading to the townsfolk.

Ophelia could not imagine the time and effort Fair Wind had put into hiding his missions for the king. There was no other explanation than he was a loyal, dedicated servant during his time at sea. It was either that or Colin's father was correct in proclaiming the man a no-good smuggler.

There was no chance she would allow Colin to depart Sheerness without proof, one way or the other.

It meant a great deal to him—and, surprisingly, to Ophelia, too.

"Thank you, Mr. Ackerson," Colin said curtly. "We will not monopolize any more of your time this day."

The man smiled, raising his ink-stained hand and taking hold of Colin's, giving it a healthy shake. Next, he turned to Ophelia and bowed low.

"It was an honor to meet Fair Wind's grandson and wife, I assure you." He nodded, sending his hair back into his eyes. "It was lovely to make your acquaintance, Lady Hawke."

"Oh, no—"

"That is not—"

Ophelia and Colin spoke at the same time, but both laughed at Ackerson's mistake.

She took a step closer to Colin and set her hand on his arm. "It was a pleasure meeting you, Mr. Ackerson. Do have a lovely day."

Tugging lightly on his arm, Ophelia turned Colin toward the door and proceeded back into the morning sun.

They walked only a few steps before Colin pulled her to a halt.

"Why did you allow him to think us wed?" he asked, his brow furrowed.

She couldn't admit that she thought the title "Lady Hawke" sounded appealing, nor would she admit she'd dreamed of just that thing the previous night, though Ophelia hadn't remembered it until a moment before.

Colin stepped in front of her, and she lifted her chin to look him straight in the eyes. Before leaving London, she would have been reduced to a mumbling mess with pink-stained cheeks at such a misspoken comment. But not now, not in Sheerness…and not with Colin.

Something had altered her in the last day or so—truly, she'd noticed it begin the day she eavesdropped on Lord Hawke in Oliver's Book Shoppe.

Ophelia leaned up on her tiptoes, and before she could change her mind, placed her lips against his. He remained still, likely in shock, for only the span of two heartbeats. They were Ophelia's rapid heartbeats, but two nonetheless, before his lips softened and parted, beginning to move against hers.

It was not the private moment from the previous night. It was not the chaste kiss she'd thought to give him to stop his line of questioning or rampant thoughts. And it certainly was not the harmless gesture of a friend.

Before she knew what was happening, her hands clutched his shoulders, and his arms encircled her, pulling her against his muscular chest. The midsection of a man who toiled and knew the hard work of the sea—or perhaps gained his daily exercise in the stables or working the land.

It was the most peculiar thought at such a grand moment.

Her first kiss.

Ophelia's fingers released their grip on his shoulders, and her palms slowly drifted down to his chest, and the mere inch separating them.

She allowed him to set the pace of their kiss, their lips moving together in a slow, sedate rhythm, his hands kneading her lower back in the same movements. It was then that Ophelia remembered Luci's first kiss with Montrose—if one could call it that—and she slipped her tongue across Colin's lower lip.

She was rewarded with a deep moan.

Yes, if she remembered correctly, Montrose had been so lost in pleasure he hadn't realized Luci was about to bite him for his impertinence.

But Ophelia had no such plans.

Actually, she had no plans at all.

Beyond this moment.

Beyond this embrace.

Beyond this kiss.

She did not worry about her parents' wrath at her fleeing London. She was no longer disheartened by her friends leaving for Scotland without her. She was beyond fretting about where they'd next look for Fair Wind's past. And neither did she believe all men were like Lord Abercorn, a danger to women. Colin was most assuredly not a scoundrel or a rake—as her friends had learned about Montrose and Torrington.

Ophelia sighed, pressing herself closer to him and reaching her arms up and around his neck.

In this moment, Tilda was not gone, her first London Season was not shrouded in mourning, and everything about being in Colin's arms was right. She didn't long to expose dangerous men of the *ton*. She felt no urge to be the champion of all young women. She was not living on the outside of Luci's and Edith's friendship.

No, she was with Colin…and he was holding her close, their lips meeting and moving together as if they'd been born for this moment. As long as he was with her, nothing else mattered.

CHAPTER 18

WITH THE SUN beaming on his back and the ocean breeze playing with his hair, Colin pulled Ophelia ever closer. Her petite size melded perfectly against him, her bosom pressing into his chest as his hands explored her backside. He was helpless to do anything else as her tongue slowly slid across his lower lip once more, his moan deeper than the last.

The woman was a temptress, a sorceress, a bewitching nymph in ladies' clothing.

And Colin wanted her enchantments focused solely on him.

Today. Tomorrow. And every day thereafter.

How had he ever lived without this?

Bloody hell, he didn't even know what *this* was.

Without thinking, he reached up and uncoiled her arms from around his neck and stepped back. But he knew it was a mistake when he looked down at her plump, kiss-bruised lips and her wide-eyed stare of desire. At some point, long tendrils of auburn hair had escaped her coiffure and hung about her face and shoulders. Everything about the woman screamed heat…and passion…and utter oblivion.

Her large, blue eyes turned blank, the fire dying quickly as her chin fell to her chest before she looked away from him toward the ocean beyond in the harbor.

He placed his finger under her chin and tried to bring her gaze back to his, but she pulled away and cleared her throat.

"I believe we have one final place to search." Her tone was raspy, as if she'd just woken from a deep slumber—or barely escaped the throes of passion without getting burned. "Shall we request directions?"

Had she been unaffected by it all, or was she hiding pain he'd unwittingly caused?

Bloody hell, but they were only several hundred feet from the fish market where people came and went. Anyone could have seen them. In fact, Mr. Ackerson had a perfect view from his front window. The man would think nothing of a couple kissing, especially since he was under the mistaken impression that they were wed.

Colin glanced around them, rubbing the back of his neck to relieve the sudden tension threatening to take over. No one paid them any mind, no one halted and gawked at the pair of them in a scandalous embrace.

"Mayhap it is best we start back for London," he sighed. It was past time he returned her to her home before he caused her any further harm. If they remained any longer in Sheerness, they might be forced into another night away from London. After their kiss, Colin doubted he'd be able to turn her away—or remain in command of his own longings—for another long night. "It is unlikely we will find anything, or worse, prove Fair Wind merely a common smuggler. Going back without any new information could be a mercy for Molly."

Ophelia swung back toward him, her glare meeting his, and he swore he saw sparks of outrage in their deep blue depths. "Molly would not give up. *We* cannot give up. We, at the very least, need to venture to the final place on Molly's list. If we find nothing there, we return to Mr. Ackerson and request to speak with his father...or mayhap Molly's cousin who sold Fair Wind's ship. This is not over."

He didn't want it to be over, either; although, he was now uncertain of his motivations. Did he still seek answers for Molly and his father, or was he being selfish and only thinking of keeping Ophelia close for as long as possible?

"Lord Hawke," she sighed, taking a step closer. Colin had the urge to recoil at her return to formality, but he held his ground. "Life is not about conquering every problem and obstacle set before you, it is about what you do when the problem is unsolvable or the obstacle seemingly insurmountable. Are you prepared to return to London and tell Molly that we gave up when things became difficult?"

Colin remained stunned, staring at the woman before him. She should be unrecognizable, so at odds with the woman he thought he knew, but for some unexplainable reason, it was as if he were seeing her true self for the first time. She was giving him a gift, one she held close and allowed few others to witness.

Finally, she cast her gaze back toward the sea. "I, for one, will not return to London without something—anything. Molly disapproves of me as it is, and I will give her no other reasons to doubt my steadfast nature."

Her words were said with an edge of steel behind them.

Ophelia believed everything she said.

Colin's hand slipped into his pocket to retrieve the list and find their final stop. He would continue on, if not for Molly, then for Ophelia.

As much as this was his responsibility, a journey he had agreed to venture out on…this was Ophelia's adventure. There was little doubt she needed to solve the mystery surrounding Fair Wind's past, possibly more than even Colin did.

His fingers did not find the notes from Molly but her pendant. The familiar hunk of stone, set in silver with a long chain, was warm in the palm of his hand.

He'd grown up believing his grandmama's favored necklace held powers not of this world but of another altogether. It was pure fancy, and something Colin still believed in no matter that he'd dispelled his youth a long time back.

Colin pulled the pendant from his pocket and held it between them. It dangled in the breeze, the sun casting rays of light off its many facets.

Undoing the clasp, he stepped toward Ophelia and refastened the chain at her nape. The pendant hung low, settling between her breasts. Colin had never noticed how the red hue matched Ophelia's hair perfectly. If he didn't know the pendant had been specifically crafted for his grandmama by the man who loved and cherished her, Colin would believe the stone was cut and placed in its silver setting just for Ophelia.

She glanced down at the necklace. "This is Molly's treasured pendant. I cannot…she would not approve…this is not meant for me."

In that instant, Colin didn't care if they were standing alone in their private chamber at the inn or the middle of a crowded London ballroom.

As she reached up to remove the necklace, Colin stilled her hands, taking them within his. "Upon reflection, I think Molly suspected this would one day belong to you."

"But, I cannot, this is—" she stammered, glancing from him to the pendant and back again.

"I have always been told, by both Molly and my father, that I am similar to Fair Wind in many aspects. My father thought I'd inherited his less than savory ways. My grandmama held close that I was the loyal and undaunted man Fair Wind was." He paused, collecting his thoughts—choosing his words correctly. "Today, I wholeheartedly want to be the man who would have this precious stone cut and set for the woman he loved. I want to be the man who gave up all he loved in life to make a better future for his family—and those yet to come. With that being said, this belongs to you, Ophelia. Another thing I am most certain of is that if it hadn't been for Molly, my grandpapa would not have been the man he was on that day he commissioned this necklace."

Colin was terrified to look too closely at her. Would she be repelled by his words? Would she demand they return to London? Would she think him addlebrained like Molly?

He needs must get it over with, confront her without reservations; good or bad.

When he returned his stare to her, he saw both everything and nothing he'd thought to see. Her eyes were moist with gathering tears. Her cheeks were glowing, but not with embarrassment over his proclamation. The most noteworthy was that she leaned toward him, not away.

"Ophelia!" a female voice shouted over the sound of carriage wheels on the wooden planks underfoot.

"There you are! I thought we'd never find you!" another woman called.

They turned as a carriage, pulled by four large greys, halted beside them. The door flung open, and two women exited, followed closely by a pair of men dressed as if they should be in London making social rounds and only happened upon him and Ophelia while out and about.

Ophelia hurried to embrace the women; one with hair the color of night and the other with pale hair the color of spun sunlight.

Colin fought against the feeling of abandonment that crept through him.

The pair of men, completely at odds with one another in appearance much like the trio of women now exchanging hugs, pinned him with intense stares.

He wanted to demand to know who the foursome was and how in the bloody hell they had found him and Ophelia all the way in Sheerness.

It was only Ophelia's joy at seeing the two women that kept Colin from pulling her back to his side and demanding answers from the group at large. Another pang of what could only be jealousy sparked within him as Ophelia embraced both men. The one as large as a small house slipped his arm around her and squeezed gently as she laughed. Next, the man at his side patted her shoulder before hugging her with one arm, as the tall, midnight-haired woman returned to his side.

Mercifully, Ophelia turned back to him and hurried to his side, grasping his hand and pulling him toward the group. She lifted her chin, and he nodded at her beaming smile. His irritation receded as he took in the utter transformation in her. Certainly, she was nearly always optimistic and happy, but there was something new here now, something that had been missing during their acquaintance thus far. He couldn't look away from her as he noted the new light in her blue eyes. No longer did they appear a shrouded ocean but rather a clear, blue sky on a warm day. Anyone who could bring such sparkle to Ophelia's eyes was worth his notice.

"Lord Hawke, Colin,"—her tone deepened with his name—"may I introduce Lady Lucianna and the Duke of Montrose?" Colin nodded to the couple. "And Lady Edith and Lord Torrington."

"These are the friends you spoke of?" he asked, not realizing he'd said the words aloud. "Lady Lucianna, Lady Edith—it is a pleasure to meet you both."

Colin couldn't be certain, but he thought he heard the large man, Torrington, growl at the word *pleasure* used in conjunction with Lady Edith's name. He was fine with that as he'd been ready to do battle with the two men when they'd embraced Ophelia.

"My lords." Colin bowed stiffly to the pair. "It is also a pleasure"—he paused on the word with a smirk—"to meet you both."

"What are you doing here?" Ophelia breathed. "You should be solidly on your way to Gretna Green."

"We traveled as far as Northampton before Luci realized she could not wed Montrose."

"What?" Ophelia exclaimed.

"…without you present," Lady Edith said with a smirk. "However, when we arrived at Atholl Townhouse, your maid said you'd followed us to Scotland."

Colin couldn't help but allow the good cheer and banter to surround him. This type of easy, close friendship was a thing he'd been denied most of his life.

"Thank the bloody stars for Pru and Chastity." Torrington leaned over and placed a kiss to Lady Edith's forehead. "If they've learned anything from the trio of you women, it is to listen not only to what's being said, but also what's being avoided."

"And that led you here?" Ophelia asked.

"No, it led us to Oliver's Book Shoppe during the dead of night…and then here," Montrose grumbled. "We traveled all night to reach Sheerness only an hour ago."

"Come now, Monty," Torrington slapped the man on the back. "It isn't as if traveling the dark England roads at night is something new."

"Speaking for yourself?" Montrose snapped back. "And do not call me Monty again, or you'll find yourself harnessed to the carriage and pulling us back to London."

"I may be as large as a bison—as you've so kindly called me on occasion—but I can still outrun you if needed."

All three women giggled at the exchange, even though Colin tensed with concern. The men did not appear to get along well enough to travel all the way to the Scottish border without injuring one another—either with words or fists.

"Do not mind them, Lord Hawke," Lady Edith said, turning her kind smile on him. "We feared Ophelia might be in trouble, so we came with all due haste."

Ophelia tensed at his side, her fingers digging into his arm.

"I am afraid it was I who was in trouble and in desperate need of help, which Lady Ophelia so kindly offered to give." He ignored the startled looks from the two women and continued. "She has been instrumental in helping me locate information about my grandpapa's past."

CHAPTER 19

TRIUMPH COURSED THROUGH Sissy as she held the pages securely in her hands. She had the sensation of being young again, the thought of everything that would be hers once more making her entire body hum with anticipation. There was no need to suppress her glee at the discovery so easily found nestled in plain sight. They'd been in the room only a short time before Sissy spotted what she was looking for—and after their near disaster at the inn that morning, she'd almost thought they'd be the ones exposed. Yet, Lady Ophelia had barely given her a moment's glance. The girl's eyes had settled on Sissy with a quick look of possible recognition, but quickly returned to her companion. Sissy had held her breath for what seemed like hours as the auburn-haired woman once again focused on her meal and the man before her.

Thankfully, Franny preferred his back to the room and indulged Sissy in her love for remaining in the shadows—or they would have surely been discovered.

It had taken every ounce of calm she possessed to hurriedly finish her food and spirit herself and Franny from the tavern before the auburn-haired woman made the connection in her mind. Sissy had seen the silly chit in Lady Lucianna's wake only a month prior when they'd come to confront Francis about his offer of marriage.

But still, Sissy would recognize the woman anywhere.

What had surprised her was the gentleman Ophelia was seated across from.

Lord Hawke, Colin Parnell—the dowager's grandson.

Had he found the location of his grandfather's private belongings, too?

She'd rushed poor Franny out the side door of the establishment, convincing him it would cut down on the walking distance to the building she'd learned belonged to Porter Parnell—which, in turn, would have Francis back in London in time to attend a ball or some such other societal engagement.

"Do tell me again what these papers have to do with gaining back my property in Somerset," Francis inquired, still huffing from climbing the flight of stairs to locate the small living quarters.

My property, Sissy thought.

"…and I must insist again, no one will care a whit about the Coventry family's past. We had a notorious gambler and rakehell for a father—certainly, a free trader is not all that scandalous."

But there was so much more—oh, so much more!—to the matter. Things the dowager's son, Ramsey Parnell, didn't want those in London to discover.

"Don't you fret about anything, Franny," Sissy crowed. Coventry was unworthy, even her own brother could use a proper dressing down for his part in Sissy being made to wait so many years to reclaim her home. "With these"—she waved the pages in the air between them nearly swiping at his nose—"I have what I need to return what is mine to our family."

"It only seemed a grand hassle for something so insignificant." He meandered about the dusty room, a bleak expression overtaking his normally jovial demeanor. "And if what you plan to do when we return to London is any indication, the disturbance to our lives will only increase."

It irritated her that Francis thought securing his sister's future was so burdensome—an unnecessary disruption to his daily life. "I am doing this for us. This is our family's due, and it is our responsibility to see it returned to us."

"The land—and the manor house—are likely worth little after all these years." He scoffed. "Why go to such lengths to see it returned to us when we have our townhouse in London, home in Bath, and our country estate?"

He had a London townhouse, a home in Bath, and a country estate—Sissy did not.

And when Francis wed again, all of it would belong to the new Duchess of Abercorn. And the woman would very likely label Sissy an irritation, a relation not worth supporting…and then where would Sissy go?

Sissy was growing older, and she was tired of fighting every day to have something to call hers. The day was fast approaching when she might not be able to handle the next possessive woman who entered her brother's life with her sights set on being a duchess.

"This is something that is all mine and cannot be taken from me." Sissy stuffed the pages into her handbag and pushed past Franny toward the exit. "Now, can we be away from here? This filth is likely to ruin the hem of my gown."

With a smirk of satisfaction, Sissy listened as her brother's footsteps treaded behind her as he was forced into the position of following *her* from the room and down the staircase.

A SHIVER OF anticipation traveled down Ophelia's

back as she watched Edith's and Luci's mirrored expressions of shock transform into knowing sideways glances as they noticed the large necklace nestled between Ophelia's breasts and the way she held Colin's arm as if she'd cease to exist if she let him go. Her chest filled with pride—in herself and the man at her side. Edith and Lucianna hadn't thought Ophelia had been in any real danger, but had needed to feign concern to gain Torrington and Montrose's support in following her to Sheerness. Essentially, they'd duped their betrotheds into making the mad dash to Kent.

Ophelia's only question was: why.

"How can we help?" Montrose asked, glancing at Luci. "I assume we will not be journeying back to London until Lady Ophelia and Lord Hawke have found what they came for."

"You assume right, my love," Luci chimed in. "I don't care what Torrington says about you…you are the brightest man I know."

Montrose threw a narrowed glare at Torrington, who only laughed and slammed him on the back again.

At first, Ophelia had the urge to turn away their help and send them back to London; however, both Edith and Luci turned expectant stares on her. They were her friends. They loved Ophelia, and their journeying all the way to Sheerness only convinced her that she'd been too hard on them. Especially Luci during her stay with Ophelia after her father had cast her out.

"We have discovered nothing of great significance as yet," Colin said, making the decision to accept their help. "We have one last place to visit, and then we will be reduced to questioning the townsfolk about a man who hasn't lived in Sheerness for many years."

"Lead the way." Montrose motioned for Colin to take the lead.

"My grandpapa and Molly rented rooms above the blacksmith's shop," Colin said.

"Oh, we passed the place when we drove through town." Edith smiled, always one to make note of certain things that did not appear important but nevertheless always seemed to be useful. "It was only three doors down from the inn we stopped at."

"You stopped at the inn?" Ophelia gulped.

Luci winked, letting Ophelia know they'd discovered that she and Colin had shared quarters the previous night. "The proprietor pointed us in the direction of the docks. It appears an auburn-haired beauty is difficult to miss in such a small town."

Ophelia's cheeks heated as a blush crept up her neck. She looked up at Colin, but he appeared unaware of her embarrassment or the fact that her friends had discovered their scandalous sleeping arrangements.

Instead, he started off, everyone following behind her and Colin as they made their way back toward the inn and the blacksmith's shop beyond.

It should be an invasion of her privacy, the act of her friends swooping in to take over her adventure, except they trailed her—they didn't push her aside or demand she follow their lead. Colin, with her on his arm, was in charge. The ladies were here because they genuinely wanted to help, and were desperate to learn more about the man Ophelia had fled London with. There had been a time, not many months ago, that Ophelia had been similarly curious about Torrington and Montrose.

They reached the inn quickly, the duke's carriage following them at a distance, and hurried on toward the blacksmith's shop.

"Molly says this building still belongs to her family and no one has lived up top since she and my grandpapa moved to London after accepting his Earldom from the king." Colin spoke aloud, even though Ophelia assumed he was working everything out in his mind. "If there is anything to be found here, it will be the room they shared for the first five years of their marriage."

Ophelia glanced over her shoulder, and Edith's brow rose in question. They hadn't the time to explain everything now. It was a long story, one that could be imparted on their journey back to London.

The blacksmith's shop was deserted, the doors wide open, and the forge lit with various tools lying discarded about the large room. Whoever worked within mustn't be far.

"Hello?" Ophelia called into the dim interior. They all waited just outside the doors, not wanting to shock the blacksmith if he were inside. "Anyone here?"

"Doesn't appear to be anyone about." Colin stepped back, releasing her arm to survey the stairs leading up the side of the building to a landing above. "That must be their rooms up there."

He started to climb the steps, and Ophelia leapt into action behind him, keeping close pace as they climbed. She held her skirt high to avoid tripping and tumbling back down the steep steps. They appeared clean of dirt and well swept.

A pounding in her chest had her placing a hand over the area as she fought to catch her breath as she climbed. It was not her heart beating erratically, but the pendant swinging and thumping her bosom. Ophelia wrapped the precious stone in her hand and was immediately filled with a sense of comfort. Was it Porter "Fair Wind" Parnell reaching out to her from somewhere beyond her meager existence? The question needed more pondering…but now wasn't the time, nor the place. Or maybe it was the exact place for such consideration.

Making the landing, Colin paused and waited for her to reach his side before he grasped the latch and pushed the door open.

Ophelia sucked in a breath. She'd imagined the door would be locked to avoid trespassers, but they stepped over the threshold without anyone coming to stop them. The room was empty except for two cloth-covered pieces of furniture; one being a table, and the other a large shelf. The hearth was also bare and swept clean of debris.

Colin walked farther into the room, his footsteps kicking up dust from the floor and causing Ophelia to sneeze.

No one followed them, and no footfalls sounded on the stairs outside.

Lady Edith and the others must have remained below.

The windows were shrouded in heavy, brown fabric, reducing the light in the room to a hazy, patchy glow, casting shadows into the far corners not reached by the light streaming in from the open door.

"There doesn't appear to be anyone living here," she mumbled, needing to say something to break the silence. "There is an inch of dust on every surface."

Colin's stare scanned the room once more and settled on the mantel above the open hearth.

A tiny wooden box rested there, devoid of the years of dirt and grime covering the rest of the room. The pieces of a broken lock had been placed atop it, and the latch was sprung.

"Someone has been here"—he paused, scanning the room once more—"and very recently."

"But who?"

He didn't answer, and she hadn't expected him to. As everything else surrounding Fair Wind and his past, it would likely remain a mystery.

Colin approached the hearth—and the tiny box—with caution.

Ophelia could not blame him for his hesitation. Whatever the box held, it was certain to change his life—for good or bad. If it was empty, they'd accomplished nothing in Sheerness. If it held the missing pages, Colin would be forced to return to them Molly and cause more friction between his father and grandmama. Ophelia suspected it would not be so simple to cast aside all his father had believed for his entire life.

Setting the broken lock aside, Colin picked up the tiny wooden box and returned to her side.

"My great-grandpapa, Fair Wind's father, was a master carver." Colin smiled, and Ophelia knew he was in another time, another place. "He lived here, in Sheerness, crafting trunks, boxes, and even furniture for the many sailing vessels."

Colin turned the box over in his hands and held it out for her to see.

In perfect script on the underside of the box was *Parnell*.

"The box could have been crafted yesterday." Ophelia reached out and traced the word with her fingertip. "It is beautiful. Your family has much to be proud of."

"And many secrets to keep hidden, it appears."

She set her hand on his shoulder in comfort but he winced, stepping away from her.

"Shall I wait outside?" she asked. This should be a private moment for him. If it were Ophelia on such a cusp of discovery, she'd need space and time to process everything. "I will join the others downstairs."

She made to turn, but Colin reached out, grasped her gloved hand, and tugged her back to face him. He said not a word, only raised her hand to his lips and placed a light kiss on her open palm. It was an invitation—no, a demand—that she stay.

Here. With him.

No matter what they discovered about his family's past, they would return to London together. She wanted to tell him that she'd be at his side through it all. Whether they returned with good news or no news, she'd be there.

For him.

"Go on, open it," she coaxed in a whisper. "Let us

see what adventure lies in such a tiny box."

He released her hand and focused on the box once more.

For the first time since leaving London, Ophelia was overwhelmed. Her head spun, her vision blurring. Closing her eyes, she took a deep, calming breath, and begged her mind to remain in control of her body. She would not faint…not here, not now. She gulped down another deep inhale and allowed her eyes to flutter open.

"You are beautiful," Colin breathed, taking a step closer to her, the box between them. "Have I told you that today?"

"You've…you've…you've never told me that," she stammered, unable to collect her thoughts with him so close.

"Ah, rest assured, I've been thinking it since the moment I rescued you from Molly's wrath in the Atholl drive."

"Perhaps it is my sorceress spell," she teased. "Beelzebub come to drag you to the Underworld."

"Or, perhaps"—he leaned in so close their lips nearly met—"it is only you and your inner light that has captured me so completely."

"My lord, I must say that sounds far more likely than Molly's accusations of the devil's mark."

This time, it was Colin who moved the final inch and captured her mouth.

Unlike their previous kiss, this time, their mouths met and danced in a light, undemanding cadence. Neither deepening the kiss nor parting their lips. It was a promise of intimate times to come, the assurance that no matter what they found in the box, they'd still have one another. Their time together would not cease once they returned to London. Ophelia wholeheartedly believed that.

She would never be able to walk away from him and not look back.

He'd been burned into her mind. His composed confidence and determination etched there.

Colin was not the arrogant and domineering gentleman Torrington and Montrose appeared to be. He was not the shrewd businessman Luci's father was. He was not the cunning, manipulative lord Abercorn certainly was.

He was something altogether different…and that fact made him all the more special to Ophelia. He'd allowed her this journey, this adventure, never questioning her motives yet believing in her ability to assist him.

"Are you ready?" he said on a soft exhale. She could only nod, not trusting herself to speak.

Clutching the box in one hand, Colin lifted the lid with the other, and they both peeked inside.

Nestled in the emerald green fabric lining the box was an envelope with one simple word written on it.

Molly.

The sure, solid print was unmistakable to Ophelia. She'd read nearly all of Fair Wind's travel log and his bits about Molly and his home. Porter Parnell had addressed the envelope to his wife, the woman he'd loved above all else.

Whoever had broken the lock hadn't taken the letter. She wondered if something else had been housed in the box at some time.

The envelope was too thin to hold all the torn pages from Fair Wind's book.

Ophelia glanced up at Colin to see a single tear slide down his cheek. He'd been so strong and unaffected since their arrival in Sheerness, despite their many setbacks, but it appeared the letter was too much.

She reached in and grasped the envelope. The paper had yellowed with age, and the ink had faded with time.

"It is addressed to your grandmother. Should we take it back to London?"

Colin shook his head firmly, his lips pressed into a frown. "No, we open it here. There is perhaps information we need inside."

Handing the note to him, Ophelia collected the box and returned it to the mantel while Colin studied the letter, pacing from one end of the room to the other. He stared at the note with all seriousness, and Ophelia noticed for the first time how exhausted he appeared. His strong posture had receded, and his eyes were glazed over with fatigue. He'd never given up; however, it was as if he needed a month's worth of rest now that he held something concrete in his hands.

If Ophelia could make this all easier for him, she would. She'd do anything to lessen the burden on Colin's shoulders.

This was where her adventure ended, and Colin's real-life struggles took over.

CHAPTER 20

COLIN HAD IN his hand the one thing he'd been searching for, and he wanted nothing more than to return it to its box on the mantel and run—return to London, tell Molly they'd found nothing, and continue as he had since childhood. Forever in the middle of his family's strife. Would that be preferable to knowing the truth of his family's past? At present, Colin was seriously pondering that exact question.

Until he glanced up at Ophelia.

Going back and forgetting all that had transpired in Sheerness would also mean erasing Ophelia from his life. Forgetting the feel of her soft lips. Putting from his mind the long, silky, auburn locks that even now hung with wild abandon about her shoulders. Most of all, erasing her tenacity and determination to help him in such a selfless manner. She'd risked everything to accompany him—at first, he'd believed she was bored and in need of distraction, but it was so much more than that. Over the last day, he'd discovered a deep-seated, undaunted determination within the woman that he'd come to admire greatly.

Bloody hell, but he more than *admired* her.

He couldn't imagine returning to London, and his life, without her.

Molly had been correct. Ophelia had cast a spell over him, and he never wanted it lifted.

But he needed—*they* needed—to finish here in Sheerness before talks of the future were possible.

Colin smiled, knowing it did not reach his eyes and slipped his finger under the seal holding the letter closed.

When the flap opened, he removed the single sheet of paper and was instantly reminded of the note Molly had sent with her list. Had she known Colin would find himself so enamored with Ophelia? Had she foreseen that the adventure would bring Colin close to Ophelia, closer than he'd ever been to another person?

He shook his head to banish the thought.

Unfolding the note, he read:

My dearest Molly ~

Me love for ye has no bounds—it is not restrained by land, sea, time, or distance. Yet, I find meself here, in Sheerness, and ye in London with Ramsey. Neither of us could'a imagined what the king had planned for me; not the journeys ta Prussia nor the title and land. It was not what we planned, and never what I wanted. But ye believed in a better future for us. London is not me home. I am ever pulled to the sea, but ye draw on me is far stronger than the sea. Me home is where ye are. If'n I destroy all the records of me service ta the king, we can return to Sheerness, live the life we always dreamed'a. Ye with yer family close and me close ta the two things I love: ye and the sea. I am a coward, my dearest Molly. Here I be, where I believe I—we—belong—and I cannot do it. The sea is a dangerous place. Ye be worthy of a good husband, not a man too long at sea, or worse, lost ta the murky depths of the unforgiving waters. Ramsey deserves better—a title without scandal and gossip of times long past attached. Not a scoundrel of a pa. And so, I be leave'n the pages here along with me past and me need for the water—and return ta London the gent me king made me...but I promise ye, we shall return. One day...

With all me heart, Porter, Lord Coventry

Colin reached out and took Ophelia's hand in his as he read the letter several more times before handing it to her. He assumed it had been written not long after his father finished his studies and was taking his place in society as the son of the Earl of Coventry. The letter said so much, yet so little all at the same time.

Porter "Fair Wind" Parnell had been an ally and trusted courier for King George II. That much was certain, but the box did not contain the missing pages. The proof.

His grandpapa had sacrificed his own happiness for that of his son, Ramsey.

He'd remained in London, played the lord, all to secure a better future for Ramsey, and in turn, Colin when he inherited the Earldom. To expose his position as the king's loyal servant, Fair Wind would have been forced to also uncover his jaded past as a smuggler.

Had Molly known all this?

Fair Wind must have spoken of it during the years after his final trip to Sheerness before his passing.

Both Colin's father and Molly had been correct. However, the truth lay far deeper than the surface. Yes, Fair Wind had worked for the king, but he'd been a smuggler, a seaman at heart. He'd given up his life's blood for the two people he loved above all else—including the sea.

The letter was significant proof of Porter's past, yet it had been written during the critical time when Ramsey and his father were feuding. Their family's past hadn't been important until Ramsey discovered other men of the *ton* had long lines of lineage, spanning hundreds of years and a dozen titled ancestors before them.

Ramsey was the grandson of a wood carver and an ale house proprietor from a small fishing town—no more than a village during those times. Even his mother, Molly, had served as a wench in her family's tavern while Porter earned his coin by unsavory dealings at sea.

Society was not particularly forgiving of such dubious past indiscretions.

His grandpapa knew that, and was still willing to all but erase any word to the contrary.

"This is beautiful," Ophelia sighed. "So different from his earlier writings but still very much his words."

Leave it to Ophelia to notice the eloquent nature of the letter, beyond the poignant message given. His grandpapa hadn't wanted anyone to find proof of his past. Without solid evidence, no one could refute Ramsey's right to the Earldom, despite it being awarded by the king. For all intents and purposes, the Parnell family were country folk blessed by a king who needed no explanation for his royal decrees. It had been an intelligent move on his grandpapa's part, and one not appreciated by Colin's father.

"I think we are done here in Sheerness." He turned a weak smile on Ophelia.

"But we have not found the pages." She folded the letter and returned it to its envelope. "They must be here somewhere."

He glanced at the box and back to Ophelia, his excitement over finding the box diminishing. "The lock was broken, and the latch opened. Someone found the pages before us, but I believe the letter will confirm everything for Molly—and my father will have little choice but to end their feud."

She shrugged and toyed with the pendant he'd placed around her neck.

"We will collect our carriage from the inn and return to London by nightfall." His words left him with more force than intended, but he offered no apologies. They'd done as Molly asked and would return home. They should both be satisfied with their discoveries and take a measure of pride in the knowledge they'd be responsible for bringing Molly peace. "I will meet you downstairs."

He glanced at her in time to see her chin lift before

she turned and rushed from the room. Her walking boots barely made a sound as she descended the stairs, leaving him alone in the place Molly and Fair Wind had once called home.

In no way did Colin feel satisfied with the information they'd found, nor pride in the discovery they'd return to Molly.

CHAPTER 21

"I AM COMING with you," Ophelia said with a stomp of her foot, ignoring the audience watching them. "I have had the last several hours to ponder everything, and I have made the decision to be at your side when you speak with Molly."

The evening breeze whipped her hood from her head as she stared Colin straight in the eyes, his carriage horses stamping their hooves with impatience. She'd ridden in Colin's carriage, with Luci and Edith, all the way back to London. The men taking up residence in Montrose's conveyance. Propriety had been maintained, and Ophelia had been able to share the entire story with her friends.

Ophelia suspected her determined demand had much to do with the way Colin had cast aside her words in the room above the blacksmith's shop. She'd thought there was more to find in Sheerness, and he'd dismissed her out of turn, treated her as if she had no say in anything pertaining to their journey.

"My father clearly has a guest," he said, gesturing to the carriage parked farther down the drive. "It is not the best time to discuss this."

Bloody bollocks, she thought, commandeering Edith's most prized expletive.

She narrowed her stare on him, and his nostrils flared ever so slightly with his irritation at her continued insistence. Why had she thought Colin lacked the arrogance and domineering nature so present in Torrington and Montrose? He could be bloody stubborn when the need presented itself. However, Ophelia found herself in possession of a doggedly persistent character, as well.

The Coventry butler held Colin's townhouse door wide, awaiting his entrance, and her friends—with Montrose and Torrington in tow—had all gathered in Montrose's carriage, waiting to deliver Ophelia home.

However, *she* was not leaving.

Not until she and Colin had spoken with Molly and passed on the letter from Fair Wind.

Besides, Ophelia needed to return the older woman's pendant.

It was the least she was owed for agreeing to throw caution—and her reputation—to the wind to embark on the adventure with Colin.

"I said I would call on you in the morning and inform you of how Molly took the news, as well as my father's reaction." His Hessian-clad feet were placed wide apart, his stance unyielding. His voice firm and filled with conviction.

But the man did not know Ophelia well at all if he thought her daunted by his seemingly unwavering determination to see her removed from the final portion of their duty. She would see everything through to completion.

"While that is very kind of you, my lord," she seethed, her hands settling on her hips as she leaned in close, lowering her voice. "I insist on being with you when you speak with Molly."

He sighed, and the tension drained from his shoulders.

With a satisfied smile, Ophelia turned to her waiting friends and shouted, "I will be out shortly."

Luci and Edith waved from the carriage before sitting back in their seats to wait.

"Shall we, my lord?" Ophelia's brow rose in question as she attempted to mask her grin with a serene smile. There was little need to anger him further. She'd gotten her way, and there was no need to rub the victory in his face. Nor do anything that would have him changing his mind before they were securely in the house. "I do look forward to seeing Molly's reaction when she sees the letter."

He reluctantly held out his arm, and she placed her gloved hand into the crook of his elbow. Holding her chin high, they entered the Coventry townhouse.

"I have warned you, Lady Ophelia," he leaned close and whispered in her ear. "My father can be a particularly ill-tempered man if he's interrupted while entertaining."

"As cross as you are now, Lord Hawke?" she asked with a smirk.

"Cross? Heavens, no," he said with a chuckle. "I believe *furious* better describes his nature."

Ophelia swallowed past the lump that had settled in her throat, blocking her airway. She refused to back down or cower. They'd been so close during their time in Sheerness, but it had all changed swiftly after finding Fair Wind's letter—no, correction, after Colin had read the letter, and she'd insisted on searching the town for more information.

If she could take it back, she would. Anything to banish the shadow that had settled on Colin. It was a cloud of unidentifiable darkness. Sorrow? Anguish? Confusion? Disappointment?

Perhaps a mix of all four.

Ophelia's own confusion had taken over during the long ride back to London. She'd meant to support him, be by his side the entire way, but unwittingly, she'd pushed him away. When he'd requested to ride with Montrose and Torrington, Ophelia had been hurt and conflicted. Certainly, she'd wanted some time with her dear friends—to explain everything—but more than anything, she'd longed for a few private moments to speak with Colin. Discuss what they'd found and make some attempt to sort through everything before they arrived back in London.

But she'd been denied that.

"Lord Hawke," the Coventry butler greeted him with a nod. "Lady Ophelia."

He'd remembered her name from her single visit to the Coventry townhouse. Ophelia ignored the servant's startled expression as he caught sight of Molly's pendant around her neck.

"Can you tell me where I might find Molly?" Colin asked.

"The physician departed an hour ago," the servant said, pointing down the hall. "She requested her meal be served in the salon."

"Does she have guests?"

"No, my lord." The butler cleared his throat and glanced down the hall to his father's personal study.

"Matheson?" Colin asked. "Is there something you are not telling me?"

"Well, my lord…it seems… Your grandmother does not have a guest; however, your father has two guests, and I've been instructed to keep the dowager away from his study," he said in a rush. "My lord, your father says I am to use force—if necessary. Force is always necessary with Lady Coventry."

The man worried his hands before him as if he were a debutante attending his first musicale and was fretting over hitting a wrong note. A bit of Ophelia's ire dissipated at the man's unease. She'd been in his position herself but had been on the receiving end of Molly's cane at the time—though, in all honesty, the woman's words wounded far deeper than her walking stick.

"And who, exactly, is my father meeting with?"

Matheson cast a quick look down another corridor before whispering, "Lord Abercorn and his sister, Lady Sissy."

Ophelia and Colin gasped at the same time.

Ophelia rounded on Colin, pushing him slightly when she withdrew her hand from his elbow. "You know Abercorn? Why did you not say?"

"Because I do *not* know Lord Abercorn," he retorted, his eyes narrowing on her.

"How convenient that a man you do not know is even now meeting with your father." Ophelia crossed her arms, her anger returning swiftly. How many things had he failed to tell her?

"How do you know Lady Sissy?" He took a step toward her, lowering his voice.

"I do not *know* Lady Sissy beyond her kinship—and resemblance—to Lord Abercorn."

"Why are you perturbed by Abercorn's presence here?"

"I am far more than perturbed, Lord Hawke," she seethed. "I am—" Ophelia's voice broke, and an uncontrollable shiver ran down her spine. "I am shocked such a heinous man would be allowed within your father's home."

"Then we are much in agreement, although I cannot fathom why Lord Abercorn would put his sister at such risk after what happened." Colin pinched the bridge of his nose before taking a calming breath. "Why do you despise Abercorn?"

"Why would Lady Sissy be at risk?" she demanded.

Ophelia pushed her shoulders back and watched him closely. He could keep his secrets about why he'd rushed back to London from Sheerness and why his demeanor and treatment of her had altered so drastically in a span of only a couple of minutes, but Abercorn was responsible for Tilda's death. If the man were now involved in yet another aspect of Ophelia, Luci, and Edith's lives, then she would bloody well find out how.

"I will ask one more time, my lord." Her pulse thrummed through her, resulting in a deafening echo in her head. "Why would Lady Sissy be at risk?" When he only stared at her, she continued, "Perhaps I should join them in the study and find out for myself."

"My lord, my lady," Matheson squeaked. "Can we not continue this conversation in another, more private room, or better still, on the morrow?"

"You are correct, sir," Ophelia said with a smile, but from the servant's sudden recoil, she could only assume she'd given him a sneer. "I find I wish to join Lord Coventry and his guests. I am acquainted with Abercorn, though we have had a rather tumultuous relationship. Shall I announce myself?"

She only managed two steps toward the study when Colin grabbed her arm, halting her.

"Lady Ophelia, you cannot—"

"I most certainly can." She had little clue what had come over her. The last time she'd knowingly been in Abercorn's company, she'd nearly succumbed to a case of the vapors, but at present, she only felt outrage and venom. She couldn't count spying on the man at Oliver's Book Shoppe because Abercorn hadn't suspected she watched him; therefore, she'd been in no danger. "Step aside, Colin."

He released her, and she started for the study once more, her footsteps sure as she worked through the coming confrontation in her mind.

"Stop, Ophelia," Colin pleaded at her treating back. "Molly and Lady Sissy were involved in a skirmish at a ball many, many, many years ago. It resulted in Molly's final banishment to Tintinhull Court, and Lady Sissy's— along with her brother, the duke's—lifelong dislike for my father."

Her steps faltered and she stumbled, but Matheson caught her arm and righted her quickly. In her fury, she hadn't noticed the servant hurrying to announce her.

"Then why is Lady Sissy here now?" Ophelia asked

without turning.

"That lie'n, slimy, dicked in the nob woman be in this house?"

"My lady!" Matheson yelped as all three turned to face Molly. "May I bring you tea in the salon?"

"Lady Sissy hadn't an ounce of steel in her then, and she sure as the morn'n sun don't have it now." Molly shuffled into the foyer, making a show of looking in every direction for the offending woman before spitting on the floor. "What Banbury stories is that vile bit of muslin spread'n now?" She narrowed her eyes on Ophelia before turning to Colin. "And when did the pair of ye arrive?"

"Only a few moments ago," Ophelia said. She was certain she appeared as frightened at the Coventry butler. "We were coming to find you."

"Did this beetle-browed knave think ta keep me unawares of an enemy in me own home?" Molly lifted her cane and pointed it at Matheson's chest for emphasis. "Ye be dismissed."

With a curt nod for Colin and a low bow for the women, Matheson disappeared toward the kitchens, likely in search of a drink—if he were smart.

"Now—" Molly leaned her cane against the wall and slipped her arm through Colin's before hobbling over and doing the same with Ophelia. "What be the plan ta get this buck fitch and his doxy outta this house?"

Ophelia and Colin shared an uneasy glance over Molly's head.

"I am right pleased ta have the pair of ye home," the older woman said as they reached the door to Colin's father's study. "Not a soul I can trust but ye two."

Ophelia couldn't barge into the room and confront Abercorn without knowing more about the feud between Molly and Lady Sissy. "What happened between you and Lady Sissy?"

"That no-good trollop came at me, right after me Fair Wind went ta the hereafter, accuse'n me family of steal'n her land." Molly glanced up at Ophelia, a crooked, satisfied grin on her face. "So, I shoved her, and she fell over a refreshment table and inta the crowded dance floor. Last time I heard her say anythin' about me family."

"Do you know why she is here now?" Colin asked.

"Ta claim ye Hawke Manor be me guess," Molly shrugged as if Lady Sissy's claim was unfounded and of no consequence. "But I plan ta send her on her way again, ye wait and see."

The door to the study pulled open, slamming upon its hinges into the wall behind it.

Ophelia, Molly, and Colin stood in the path of a very angry, red-faced Lord Abercorn and Lady Sissy.

"Sissy," Molly hissed.

"Molly," Sissy jeered. "So, you have returned to London."

"Lord Abercorn, Lady Sissy," Lord Coventry called from the study. "Please return so we can attempt a compromise."

"We do not compromise with the likes of Satan." Molly released Colin and Ophelia, pushing her way into the room.

Abercorn and Lady Sissy were given no opportunity to flee before Colin entered the study and turned to Ophelia.

"Go back to your friends, have them return you home safely." His stare pleaded with her to understand, but every part of her knew she needed to be in that room, she'd just been given the opportunity to question Abercorn about Tilda. "This is a private family matter. You understand, do you not?"

Ophelia felt her head nodding, but truly, she didn't understand at all.

Lord Coventry's voice rose as he commanded everyone to take a seat.

"Please, go home. I will call on you tomorrow." With one final look, he closed the door, shutting her out for a second time in the same day.

She wanted to slam her fist against the door. Scream that she be allowed entrance. Demand Abercorn answer her questions about the night of Tilda's murder.

She was uncertain how long she stood outside the study door, or when Matheson had appeared at her elbow, but instead of doing what she longed to do, she allowed the butler to escort her to the front door.

What was happening in the Coventry study was a family matter, and Ophelia, despite how close she and Colin had become during their travels, was not his family.

CHAPTER 22

COLIN LEANED HIS forehead against the closed study door, wishing with every breath he took that Ophelia could be by his side in the study. No part of him had wanted to shut her out and close the door in her face. He exhaled sharply, waiting to hear her receding footsteps as she fled his family's home.

But he heard nothing.

Not so much as an inhale—and mercifully, not a sob.

If he had, Colin would have ripped the door from its hinges and taken her into his arms, his family and their dubious past be damned.

He no longer wanted her by his side, safe and protected—he *needed* her there.

This, his family's sordid past now coming back to haunt them, was something she shouldn't have to bear witness to. She deserved a man who was above reproach, a gentleman who'd never cast a shadow over her reputation, and a love that would not tarnish her future.

Colin could guarantee her none of that.

His character was forever blemished by his family's past.

While Ophelia was nothing but goodness,

206 | *Christina McKnight*

compassion, and caring. She'd sacrificed her future to accompany him to Sheerness, and why? Because Molly, his sometimes addlebrained grandmama, had demanded it?

Colin was more to blame than anyone. He'd allowed it all to happen; their journey, their shared private quarters, and their kiss.

Bloody hell, but he would never regret that.

The feeling of Ophelia wrapped in his arms, held tightly against him...his body surged with heat at the thought.

"Colin?" his father barked. "You may go."

He pushed away from the door, and his shoulders stiffened. "This matter has as much to do with me as it does you, Father. I will stay."

"Bollock and toads!" Molly slapped her knee as Colin moved into the room and took the seat next to his grandmama and across the low table from Abercorn and Lady Sissy. "Lad, these filthy scavengers think ta steal your land—twist'n your father's arm the entire time. I not be let'n 'em get the best of me then, and I sure as a rainstorm on a breezy Somerset night won't be consent'n ta them have'n what belongs ta ye now."

"What is all this about?" Colin looked at his father, who paced before the hearth. "And why is my estate involved?"

"That was my dowry, young man," Lady Sissy seethed, leaning across the table toward Molly. Abercorn cast a restraining arm between the women and pushed Sissy back. "Because of your grandfather— that common free trader—it was taken from my family and given to yours."

"You were stripped of your family lands?" Colin felt a measure of sorrow for the woman.

"That is not exactly how everything happened," the earl grumbled. "The owner was heavily in debt, and a note had been placed on the property with three different gaming hells. The king confiscated the land when the men brought legal action against Abercorn's father. It ended the dispute. He gifted the property, with the title, to the first Earl of Coventry for his unborn son—me. The letters from King George II cannot be disputed."

Lady Sissy shot to her feet. "They can be, and I am!"

"Oh, stuff a roast bird in ye mouth and pipe down, ye—"

"Molly!" Lord Coventry warned. "Lord Abercorn came to talk, nothing more."

Colin eyed the man, remembering all that Ophelia had said—and all she hadn't said. The duke was responsible for Miss Tilda Guthton's death. He had wed the young woman, and she'd faced a tragic fall on what should have been the first night of her wedded life. Ophelia hadn't shared Abercorn's name the night she'd told him of her friend's passing, but there was no doubt this was the man whom she'd spoken of.

"I want my land, or"—Lady Sissy held her handbag before her and riffled around before pulling out a handful of paper—"I will take these directly to the *Gazette* or *The Post* and have them published in tomorrow's edition."

Colin didn't need to see the script on the pages to know they were the missing pages from Porter's book. They'd been stored for safekeeping in his and Molly's rooms above the blacksmith's shop in Sheerness.

His father rubbed the back of his neck. "It will not lead to the return of Hawke Manor, I can assure you, Lady Sissy."

The woman sneered, her lips rising to reveal uneven, yellowed teeth. "Perhaps not, but the truth of your family's past will be revealed. The lot of you are nothing but the descendants of a bar wench and a smuggler."

"My father and his vessel were commissioned by the king himself, and Porter Parnell was ultimately

awarded the title of earl and given land and fortune."
Coventry halted and turned his penetrating stare on
Lady Sissy. "I am proud of my heritage and the
sacrifices my father made to assure his family's future."

Colin shook his head softly, making certain he'd
heard his father correctly. Ramsey Parnell, the second
Earl of Coventry, was *proud* of his father? After all these
years of denial, arguments, and ill will toward Molly and
Porter, his father admitted this?

"Now, I think it best if the pair of you depart
before I collect Molly's cane and allow her at you!"

"Whack 'em both over their empty, pea-shaped
heads, I will," Molly said with a triumphant smile.

"Lord Coventry, I do believe this has all been a
misunderstanding—"

"There has been no misunderstanding." Coventry
stepped around the lounge, closer to Abercorn with
each word. "You will leave this house and never, ever
threaten my family again."

Lady Sissy waved the pages in the air before her.
"I'm taking these directly to *The Post*, I assure you."

"You will do what you must, Lady Sissy." The earl
waved his hand in dismissal. "I have faith that my family
will survive—no, better yet, we shall *thrive*."

Lady Sissy shoved the pages back into her handbag
and clutched it to her chest as if she feared Molly would
rip them from her grasp, yet Molly hadn't so much as
moved a muscle since Ramsey's proclamation.

"Matheson!" The butler opened the door a breath
after the earl's summons. "See Lord Abercorn and Lady
Sissy out, please. Do make certain the entire staff knows
they are not welcome on Coventry property—*any*
Coventry property, including Colin's estate."

"Yes, my lord," Matheson said, gesturing with his
arm for the pair to proceed him out of the study. "This
way, please."

Abercorn bustled from the room with Lady Sissy
following a bit more hesitantly, keeping a close eye on

Molly until she'd crossed the threshold into the hall.

Colin watched his father all but collapse onto the lounge next to Molly.

"Father, I—"

"Close the door, Colin," he commanded, though his voice held none of the steel from a few moments before. When he did as instructed, his father continued. "Sit."

He took the seat across from his father and grandmama in the chair Abercorn had vacated.

His father rested his arm around Molly's shoulders, pulling her in tight. It was the first time Colin had ever witnessed any sense of physical love between mother and son. Colin was struck again by how similar the pair looked, in complexion and demeanor.

"Damn it all, but that felt good," the earl whispered.

"Admitting your pride in Fair Wind?" Colin asked.

"No." His father shook his head. "Finally putting that woman in her place. She's been holding our family's past over my head since I inherited the title. Threatening to expose us to the *ton*—all these years. I should have dealt with her ages ago, but I did not want you growing up under a shadow of sordid gossip and scandal."

"You did this for me?" Colin asked, his eyes round in surprise.

"And your mother," Ramsey admitted. "She wed me not knowing our family's past. I couldn't allow her to be ridiculed by society because I was too much of a coward to admit and embrace the Parnell family history."

Colin looked to his side, reaching out, but his hand met with only empty space. Ophelia should be next to him. She'd had a right to witness the culmination of their adventure—or misadventure, as it were—but he'd thrown her from the room.

"Why were you so against us finding the book?"

"Because then I'd be forced to admit everything—

and I was uncertain I could protect you, Molly, and your mother from society's anger."

"Never cared a whit about those insufferable nobs anyhow," Molly grumbled.

"I know, Mother." Ramsey leaned over and placed a kiss to Molly's forehead. "But I spent so many years denying everything, that I was uncertain how to go about fixing things."

"You could have trusted me with the information." Colin had been a fool, gallivanting about England in search of something his father had never needed. Something his father was very aware existed. The one thing his sire had hoped would never be found. "I could have helped you sort through it all."

"Yes, well, when your grandmama came to me and begged me to allow you to search in Sheerness, I could not deny her request."

"Wait. You knew—" Colin looked between the pair. "You knew I went to Sheerness?"

"Of course. Molly said the trip was important and would very likely determine the future of the Coventry line."

Colin returned his focus to Molly, noting the grin she made no attempt to hide…the same smile she'd had just before begging him to travel to Sheerness with Lady Ophelia as she'd entrusted him with her pendant for good luck.

"Molly?"

"Yes, lad." The satisfied smirk only intensified.

"What do you know of this?" He wanted to know, but at the same time, he didn't want to hear her say the words.

"How else was I ta get ye and that fiery-haired siren alone?" She cocked her head to one side.

"Why would you want us alone in the first place?"

She laughed until she doubled over in a coughing fit. "Why? You think'n I didn't see the way ye stepped between us in the drive that day? Ye wanted ta protect her, even if that meant me cane bash'n your skull, lad."

"I would have done the same for anyone," he insisted.

She shook her head vehemently. "Oh no, Colin, you were protect'n her. Any other time, ye woulda stepped in ta protect me."

Colin clamped his mouth shut, stalling his retort as he pondered her accusation. He'd spent his entire life defending and protecting Molly—from anything and everything that would harm her. He'd spent months each year with her at Tintinhull Court so she wouldn't succumb to loneliness and sorrow. Since her arrival in London, he'd barely left her side—except to travel to Sheerness, which he hadn't thought twice about doing.

"See, Ramsey, the lad is in love, sure as the fish swim in the dark." Molly swatted at his father's arm. "Where did she run off ta?"

"I sent Lady Ophelia home," Colin mumbled.

"Oh, ye foolish lad, ye best be goin' after her before she finds—"

Colin didn't wait for Molly to finish as he sprang from the chair and fled the room. His grandmama was correct, as always. Colin had been wrong to send Ophelia away. His boots thundered down the corridor as he shouted for Matheson to have the stable lad bring around his horse. He only hoped that when he found Ophelia, she'd forgive him.

"Lord Hawke?"

Colin slowed his pace, turning toward the voice coming from an alcove nestled below the grand stairs— the Duke of Abercorn sat on the single bench seat. He didn't appear the sturdy, haughty lord from his father's study, but rather a man who'd lived a long life and was…exhausted.

His chin dipped toward his chest, and at some point, he'd untied his cravat as it hung loosely down the front of his jacket.

"May I have a word with you before my sister and I

depart?"

OPHELIA STALKED IN the shadows outside Colin's family townhouse, avoiding the torches lighting the driveway. It would be highly satisfying to hear the stomp of her kid boots; unfortunately, they made barely any sound. She didn't want Luci and Edith to notice her and demand they deliver her home. Colin was in there, and she needed to secure a way to see him—or she'd wait here in the darkness all night long if she had to.

She settled on biding her time until Abercorn and Lady Sissy departed before demanding to speak with Colin. Truly, she had no urge to remain in a room with Abercorn, to sit across from him and act as if her blood did not boil every time she caught sight of the man. Even surrounded by Colin and his family, she'd be vulnerable.

No, Ophelia would bide her time, and then demand answers from Colin.

Why had he all but ignored her after finding Fair Wind's letter?

Why had he insisted on riding with Montrose and Torrington back to London?

And most importantly, why had he pushed her from the study and closed the door in her face as if she meant nothing to him, and him nothing to her?

If their intimate conversation at the inn and their kiss at the docks had meant nothing to him, then he should have said as much, and she would not pester him again. He owed her nothing. Nothing but the truth behind his actions. After that, they could return to their normal lives; she to the London ballrooms, and he to…whatever he did on a usual day.

Her steps faltered, the toe of her boot catching on a slightly elevated cobblestone, and she nearly tumbled to the ground. Pacing in the dark was far too risky. Thankfully, Ophelia caught herself and settled for tapping the toe of her boot, her arms crossed. She kept her narrowed stare on the door, pushing the many colliding thoughts from her mind. They created a din of noise louder than the racket from a hundred carriages. This might very well be her last chance to speak with Colin—she needs must have her wits about her if she meant to gain the many answers she sought.

There wasn't even time to think about Abercorn and his connection to Colin and his family.

Since when was exposing Abercorn not her main priority?

A jolt of guilt coursed through her. Tilda, and bringing down the man responsible for her death, had been Ophelia's main focus since that tragic night. It should *still* be of the utmost import to her—yet, standing here, in the Coventry drive, she longed only to speak with Colin.

Perhaps she should risk it all and knock on the door. Matheson was a kind enough butler, and would certainly not turn her away. If she could only implore him to fetch Colin for her—they would speak, and she could return home, knowing she'd done all in her power to help him, even if her assistance was no longer required or wanted.

Closure. It was about seeing their situation through to the end.

She and her friends had yet to gain closure with regards to Tilda's death, but Ophelia's situation with Colin was not completely out of her control. Yes, she had been curtly dismissed and escorted from his home, but she would not believe it was what he wanted. Not until he looked her in the eyes and told her to go, to leave and never return.

Ophelia yelped when the door opened, and Lady Sissy exited—alone.

The older woman glanced at her carriage parked close to the end of the circular drive. Molly obviously hadn't gotten to the woman with her cane as her hair was still perfectly pinned, and her gown without so much as a wrinkle. The torches positioned on either side of the front door cast enough light to see the woman clearly. She was certainly older than Abercorn by many years, but the resemblance was unmistakable. Her hair had turned from brown to coarse grey, and her skin was sallow. Except for at Oliver's Book Shoppe, Ophelia had never seen the woman in public. She didn't remember noticing Lady Sissy at Tilda's wedding or the following celebrations. If she'd been present, she'd kept to herself and away from the guests.

Yet, she was the daughter of a duke, just as Ophelia was. Why hadn't she wed in her youth, started a family, and created her own home?

As if sensing Ophelia's scrutiny, Lady Sissy turned toward her, spotting her in the shadows.

"Lady Ophelia Fletcher." Her lip turned up in a sneer as she joined Ophelia in the shadows. Unease drained every ounce of anger from her as Ophelia watched the woman move slowly toward her as if she viewed Ophelia as her prey. "I thought you'd hurried home after being dismissed by Lord Hawke." When Ophelia didn't immediately respond, Lady Sissy's brow rose. "Oh, has a cat escaped with your tongue? I had heard you were prone to fainting."

Ophelia suppressed the tightening in her chest. The woman was only baiting her, trying to stir up a reaction because she had pent-up rage.

"Lady Sissy. I can assure you, I am not on the cusp of fain—"

"Pity…" She pressed her finger to her chin and looked Ophelia over from head to toe.

"What are you doing here?"

"I could ask you the same thing," Lady Sissy sneered, taking a step closer to Ophelia. "You and your *friends* seem to pop up and stick your nose in business that doesn't concern you."

Ophelia glanced over Lady Sissy's shoulder as Luci

and Edith exited their carriage that had been waiting on the opposite side of the circular drive from the Abercorn town coach. Satisfaction coursed through Ophelia knowing that Lady Sissy would be irked all the more to see the full trio of women popping up yet again.

"I find it quite peculiar that the more I try to be rid of you all, the more you seem to be underfoot." Lady Sissy pivoted toward the front door and continued pacing. "I thought I'd be rid of the lot of you after that chit was taken care of, but no, then Franny thought himself *in love* with the gangly, raven-haired hellion. Unacceptable."

"Tilda?" Ophelia's voice rose sharply. "What do you know of Tilda?"

Lady Sissy turned back toward Ophelia. The twin pools of light from the torches surrounding her. Her eyes were aglow with—pleasure? Her chin notched up, and her sneer transformed into a genuine smile, yet nothing but apprehension filled Ophelia.

"My brother—may the good Lord forgive me for saying—is a forlorn, senseless, disappointment of a man. He makes promises, only to break them when another light skirt catches his fancy." She shook her head as if what she'd just shared were truly tragic. "Instead of gaining back what belonged to our family— what belonged to *me*—he focused on this chit or that chit."

"Tilda was an innocent, intelligent, kind spirit, not a light skirt."

Lady Sissy waved her hand. "That is of no consequence, now is it? She is gone, and once again, my dear brother—heartbroken and desperate for attention—is devoted to me."

Ophelia blinked rapidly, trying to understand what Lady Sissy meant by all this.

"But then that raven-haired harlot caught his notice," Lady Sissy scoffed. "I thought her safe enough because she was wed, but no, the woman took Franny from me—and again, his promises to me went by the wayside."

Lady Downshire? She must be speaking of Lord Torrington's stepmother who had been Abercorn's mistress.

"Thankfully, the woman disappeared, making it far easier for me." Lady Sissy's demeanor once again shifted, her eyes widening. "But imagine my surprise when yet another dark-haired hoyden cast a wicked spell on my Franny."

A spot of movement caught Ophelia's notice behind Lady Sissy. Luci and Edith crept up the drive, coming ever closer to Lady Sissy, who was so consumed with her own ranting and raving that she didn't notice the women approaching her from behind.

"Do you know what happened to Tilda?" Ophelia needed to keep the woman talking. If there was any hope of finding out the truth—that Abercorn had pushed Tilda to her death—it seemed Lady Sissy might have it. "Please, tell me what happened to my friend."

Lady Sissy cackled, throwing her head back, the disturbing sound echoing in the night. "Did you know Franny was planning an entire year traveling the Continent with his latest bride? It was then I realized the chit had to go. Wedding and bedding Miss Tilda Guthton would not satisfy my brother. No, he wanted a wife and a family. Where would that leave me? What would I have after he produced a horde of heirs and spares with that broodmare?"

Her glare snapped to Ophelia.

"Alone," she seethed. "I would be alone, forever, with no home of my own. All because of the Earl of Coventry."

"But I thought you blamed your brother?"

Ophelia realized her mistake when the woman took a hurried step toward her, her hand rising as if to strike Ophelia, but she halted.

"Francis is a weak, sniveling man." Her hand

lowered back to her side. "If I had been born a man, I would have returned our family's property immediately. However, it is never too late."

"What do you mean?" Ophelia kept her eyes trained on Sissy—and not Edith and Luci, who motioned for her to keep the older woman talking. "Hawke Manor has belonged to the Coventry Earldom for two generations now."

The conversation was moving swiftly between topics, but Ophelia needed to steer it back to Tilda.

"While Franny did not agree with my methods, I have provided the earl with enough reasons to return the property to me—or risk ruination for his family."

That could mean only one thing. "You stole Fair Wind's pages from the box in Sheerness?"

Sissy clutched her handbag close to her side. "Yes, but they will not be with me long, as I am on my way to *The Post*. They will be giddy with pleasure to have such scandalous knowledge of Coventry's past. He—and his family—will never be welcome in polite society again."

"How does that lead to the return of your family's land?"

She shrugged, allowing her bag to fall to her side. "It is of little import. Lord Coventry, the dowager countess—as well as Lord Hawke—will be tarnished. The baron will never find a suitable bride. I suppose our families will be even then."

"Abercorn will find another bride," Ophelia said, hoping to bring their conversation back to Tilda. "It will only be a matter of time before he falls in love once more, and you are cast aside like you feared when he wed my friend."

Lady Sissy shook her head, "Tsk-tsk, Lady Ophelia. When will you learn I am a very resourceful woman? Determined, much like you and your dear friends. I will handle the woman much like I did Miss Tilda."

"You killed Tilda?" Ophelia asked on a shocked exhale.

"I cannot say I killed her, but the fall certainly did. I only helped her along."

"How?" Ophelia noticed Luci clutching Edith's arm several paces behind Sissy as they listened in abject horror. "Luci saw Abercorn flee at the top of the stairs."

"My brother could not harm a fly, I assure you," Lady Sissy spit out. She clamped her mouth shut, as if realizing she'd said too much. But with a nonchalant shrug, Sissy scrutinized Ophelia once more, obviously coming to the conclusion she posed no threat to the woman. "You and your friends were all cozy in my mother's library, talking as senseless chits do. It was not hard to hurry up the stairs, donned in my robe, slip my dear brother a sleeping tonic, and return to have a private conversation with the new Duchess of Abercorn before she joined my brother in his chambers. But the woman would not listen to reason. In fact, she outright refused my request to discourage Franny from leaving England on their trip. The chit thought I had no say in my brother's life. She was wrong...and it was very advantageous on my part that my brother still owned the matching robe I bought him during the previous Christmastide."

"Sissy! What have you done?"

Ophelia turned toward the front door, now thrown open with a gaping Lord Abercorn exiting the threshold and Colin close behind.

CHAPTER 23

"...BUT THE WOMAN would not listen to reason. In fact, she outright refused my request to discourage Franny from leaving England on their trip. The chit thought I had no say in my brother's life. She was wrong...and it was very advantageous on my part that my brother still owned the matching robe I bought him during the previous Christmastide."

Abercorn's entire body tensed where he stood before Colin, and he rushed over the threshold.

The older man stumbled to a halt only a few feet from his sister. "Sissy! What have you done?"

Ophelia and Lady Sissy turned to face them as Abercorn took the final steps and grasped Sissy's arms.

Colin stumbled himself when he took in Ophelia's terrified stare, her hands clutching her throat.

The gravity of the situation sank in, and a void opened in his chest. He'd sent her from his home, only to further put her in jeopardy when Lady Sissy sank her venomous claws into her. Colin should have departed the study with her, delivered her home safely, and returned to his father's townhouse. Instead, he'd been too consumed with his own troubles, his own need to discover what his family had kept from him all these years.

He'd failed Lady Ophelia again.

Colin stood helplessly by as Lady Edith and Lady Lucianna rushed to Ophelia's side, the trio wrapping their arms securely around one another. These were the people who were worthy of a woman like Ophelia. They cared about her, thought of her above all else—they deserved her, and Ophelia deserved them.

What Lady Ophelia didn't deserve was a man like Colin—a man willing to push her aside for things that were nowhere near as important as she was. Trivial details that, in the larger scheme of life, meant nothing to Colin. Yes, they had a jaded past, but that did not determine his future or how he chose to live it.

Ophelia did…or at least, Colin longed to make her such.

"Sissy," Lord Abercorn demanded, putting his finger under his sister's chin and raising her eyes to meet his. "Did you push Tilda, my dearest love, down the stairs?"

"I—well—"

"Do not lie to me!" His hand still held her arm firmly, and he shook her. The woman's teeth clacked together. "Tell me what you did!"

"She was not right for you," Sissy stammered. "I am the only woman you need."

Abercorn released his hold, then pushed her away and turned to Lady Ophelia and her friends, still clinging to one another. "Lady Edith, Lady Lucianna, Lady Ophelia…you must believe I loved Tilda with all my heart. I know there were many years between us, but that did not diminish our capacity to love one another. She was to be my duchess"—his voice broke on the word and his eyes pooled with tears—"was to give me the family I always longed for—"

"I am your family, Franny," Sissy called. "I love you…it has always been you and me."

"I begged you for years to let your anger and resentment go, to find a husband who would make you happy, but you refused my advice at every turn." He turned sharply toward his sister, pinning her with a steely glare. "You are nothing to me," he sighed, his shoulders caving in. "I loved Tilda, and you took her from me, just as you've taken everything from me over the years. I have nothing more to say to you." Next, he addressed Colin. "Send for the magistrate. I will have my wife's murderer sent to the Tower."

"Franny, no!" Sissy fell to her knees, her scream ripping through the cold night air as her handbag tumbled to the ground, forgotten.

Without a second look for his sister, Abercorn nodded to Ophelia and her friends and started for his waiting carriage. He didn't pause or hesitate for even a second before climbing inside and taking off.

Colin envied the man, to be able to rub his hands together and, just like that, walk away from the situation.

"You...you did this!" Sissy pointed her finger in Colin's direction. "If it weren't for you, I would have kept my Franny close and had my land returned."

He glanced over his shoulder to see Molly and his father had arrived to witness Abercorn's departure.

Colin stepped toward Sissy, but Molly sprang from the steps before his father could stop her.

"Me?" Molly strode forth, barely using her cane as she navigated the dim drive toward Sissy. "Ye killed a woman—and for what? A crumble'n estate manor and cropland? You could not convince me then ta return the land, and ye shan't convince me now. My grandson—Colin—he is a fine lad, an honorable lord, and he deserves all that's been given ta him, just as me Fair Wind earned his Earldom and fortune by serve'n the king."

His father set his hand on Colin's shoulder, stopping him from stepping between the women. "Son, allow Mother her say," Coventry sighed. "She's been quieted for too many years."

Instead of interfering with the older women, Colin

moved to Lady Ophelia's side where she and her friends huddled close. He'd thought them terrified a moment before, but when he stepped closer, it was relief he noticed from them all. They weren't huddled close to protect one another, they were supporting each other.

"I should'a thumped ye over the head years ago when I had the chance, mighta given ye an ounce of sense in that addled brain of yours." Molly lifted her cane high. "I suppose it ain't too late."

His father signaled for the two waiting footmen, and they sprang into action, taking Lady Sissy under the arms and guiding her back into the house. He collected his mother and followed, leaving Colin alone with the trio of young women. Holding one another tightly, they murmured softly to each other. In that moment, Colin was the outsider, listening in on a conversation he had no right to hear. But he was helpless to walk away and give them privacy to reconcile the loss of their friend. He was a part of this. As much as he felt otherwise, Colin was inexplicitly linked to Ophelia and her friends. He too had suffered at Lady Sissy's hands. The years of family strife were solely due to that woman, not because Colin's father despised his grandpapa.

In a way, the earl had spent years sacrificing for his family, just as Fair Wind had sacrificed before him.

None of this would have been resolved without Ophelia. There would be no shining light after a lifetime of doubt had it not been for her courageous nature. Even now, Ophelia appeared to be the one consoling her friends. If Colin possessed even a tiny portion of her dauntless daring, he would have set out years before to mend his family's conflict. Instead, it had taken a woman like Ophelia to show him how to accomplish what needed to be done.

Bloody hell, but he could not imagine a day without her by his side.

It was hard to believe it had only been that morning they'd awoken at the inn in Sheerness and went in search of his family's truths. She had utterly taken over his life, and Colin was uncertain he could go on without her. When they'd set out on *her* adventure, she'd been lost and searching for something of her own. Now, she was *his* compass.

OPHELIA BREATHED IN deeply, the scent of Luci's lavender soap and Edith's choice lemon perfume mingling to fill her with a deep sense of rightness. She was exactly where she belonged, with her friends there to support her. She thought she could do everything on her own, break away from Luci and Edith, prove she was more than the sum of her parts, a woman independent of her friends.

But she'd been wrong. They needn't conquer things on their own to prove their worth. They were friends, first and foremost. Their friendship was based on love, understanding, and loyalty. Luci and Edith had come back for her, and when they'd not found her where she should have been, they'd set out to locate her. Not to bring her back or take over his adventure, but to offer their assistance. Ophelia had done everything on her own, she'd been responsible for luring the information from Sissy.

She held Luci and Edith close, each confused and conflicted by Sissy's confession. Ophelia had little doubt they'd each be reeling for days to come. They'd been wrong, so inexplicably wrong in their belief that Abercorn was responsible for Tilda's death. They'd targeted an innocent man.

Lifting her head from Luci's midnight hair, Ophelia noted Colin standing a few feet away, his hands tucked deep into his trouser pockets as he attempted to give them a moment together. Her heart tugged, and she pulled away from her friends. They willingly let her go, and she hurried to Colin, wrapping her arms around his neck and lifting up on her tiptoes to place a gentle kiss to his lips. His hands encircled her waist and held her close.

Ophelia pulled back and stared into his dark green eyes, shrouded in fear. But what had he to be fearful of?

"Thank you," she mumbled.

"For what?" His brow furrowed, and his hold on her loosened. "Lady Sissy could have hurt you, and it would have been all my fault."

In response, Ophelia did the only thing she could think to do, she tightened her arms around his neck and pulled him down toward her, pushing her body close to him. "No." She shook her head, uncertain what she was saying no to. This moment—this was the *moment*—and she needed him to hear her. "You showed me I could do things on my own. I did not need to follow others, remain in the shadows while everyone around me lived. You asked me to accompany you to Sheerness because Molly demanded it, but I think you had other reasons for bringing me."

She released him and scooped up Lady Sissy's forgotten handbag and held it out to him.

"I think this, or at least what's inside, belongs to you." Ophelia gave him a nod, pushing him to take the bag. "Go on, take it."

His eyes searched hers, and Ophelia only hoped he saw what she did. She felt whole, fulfilled, and invincible when she had him by her side. It was those exact things she wanted him to feel, as well, even if it wasn't because of her.

"Lady Ophelia," he said before pausing to clear his throat. "Ophelia, since the moment I saw you stand up to Molly, even with her cane held high above your head, I knew I needed you—by my side and in life."

Tears welled in her eyes. She blinked to hold them back, but one escaped and trailed down her cheek.

Colin leaned forward and kissed along its path, stopping the drop from falling from her chin.

"My lady, I think it best I tell you something. Now, before any further surprises present themselves."

She couldn't help but laugh, a quiet teasing sound that filled her with such contentment and ease. There was little guessing what Colin would say next, but Ophelia knew, deep down, it would alter her life far more than what they'd experienced thus far.

"What is it, my lord?" She kept him close, refusing to give him any opportunity to pull away from her. "Colin…"

"I fear I am in love with you."

"You fear?"

"Yes, I fear. Because my love for you puts me at a severe disadvantage, my lady."

"And why is that?"

He took a deep breath and leaned close, their lips all but touching. "I will do anything, agree to anything, to have you close. You can see how that might—"

"You think I aim to take advantage of your love for me?" she asked. When he only nodded, she continued. "It is a sorry state we find ourselves in then, Colin, for my circumstances may be far more dire."

"How is that?" His breath cascaded along her cheek, and he tensed. "Tell me what I need do to—"

"Because I love you, too," she confessed.

His brow rose in shock, and he pulled from her hold, pushing her to arm's length as he searched her face for any sign she was jesting.

But Ophelia wasn't joking in the slightest. She'd held and hugged her friends, but she longed to have Colin's arms around her. She'd needed his comforting embrace when she learned of Sissy's part in Tilda's death.

It had been only Colin she'd wanted in that moment.

Ophelia did not fight to bring Colin close once more, but took the opportunity to take in all of him— and sure enough, her love was mirrored in his eyes.

She couldn't help but wonder if Luci and Edith had experienced this same life-changing moment with Montrose and Torrington.

Could it be that she'd found her forever love, too?

"Ophelia?" Luci called.

She'd forgotten Luci and Edith still stood in the drive behind them.

With a smile bright enough to light the dark evening, she turned to face her friends, her hand finding Colin's in the space that separated them.

The cold night air blew against her face as she and Colin, hand-in-hand, stood before Luci and Edith.

"I think it best Edith and I return home now," Luci said, her stare remaining on Colin. "What shall I tell your parents? I am certain they will be worried when I arrive home without you."

Ophelia hadn't thought about how worried they'd be—and probably had been since that morning. "I will be home shortly, and I will explain everything, Luci. Will you tell them that?"

"*We* will be there shortly," Colin corrected at her side.

"I can trust you to see her home safely?" Edith asked.

"Of course," Colin issued a curt bow. "It is best you both hurry out of the cold. I am certain Torrington and Montrose would have me strung up in Hyde Park if either of you were to become ill."

Ophelia released Colin's hand and stepped forward, giving both women a quick hug to reassure them that she'd be fine and would be home soon.

"I think it best we visit Tilda's parents on the morrow and let them know what we found." Luci's return to her no-nonsense ways should have been expected. "They deserve to know before all of London finds out."

"I agree." Ophelia nodded, returning to Colin. "But for tonight, we deserve a few hours to allow Sissy's confession and Abercorn's declaration of love to sink in. We've thought for over a year—lived in fear of something similar happening to each of us—that every man we encountered had the opportunity to harm us or another young woman. Abercorn loved Tilda, and if her words on her wedding night were true, she loved him, as well. Tonight, I will sleep soundly knowing this."

Edith stepped forward and wrapped her arms around Ophelia. The woman's blond curls blocked Ophelia's sight, but she was certain she saw Luci brush a tear from her eye.

"Now, hurry home, the both of you," Ophelia said sternly.

The women hurried to their waiting carriage and set off, Ophelia giving them a small wave as they pulled out of sight.

"My lord, my lady?" the butler called behind them. "The dowager and Lord Coventry have requested your presences inside."

"Shall we?" she asked, looking up at Colin. Her heart stumbled as his tongue darted out to moisten his lower lip.

He ran his hand through his hair as his gaze settled on her. "Ophelia, may I—"

"There will be time later to talk privately, Colin." In truth, she was scared to hear what he had to say. Would he take back his confession of love? Would their mutual love not be enough? If there were other factors that would make their relationship impossible, Ophelia didn't want to think about them until tomorrow—or the day after. "Let us not keep your grandmother waiting."

She didn't allow him time for a response as she slipped her hand into the crook of his elbow and started for the front door. It seemed as if hours had passed since he'd pushed her from the study and closed the door in her face, causing her to flee to the driveway. It had probably only been minutes, but more than a lifetime of changes had occurred.

The truth surrounding Tilda's death had been learned. Lord Coventry had exited the townhouse with Molly on his arm. Her friends had whispered their words of praise for her courage. Colin had told her he loved her.

And, possibly the most important occurrence, she'd confessed her love in return.

The stark truth was that she'd felt the blossoms of love since he happened upon her napping in the Atholl gardens with Fair Wind's book open on her lap and dreams of fair-haired, tanned, swashbuckling adventurers clouding her thoughts.

The butler showed them into the study, the same room Colin had denied her entrance to earlier, but now he escorted her by his side across the threshold to face his father and grandmother. Lady Sissy was nowhere to be seen.

The dowager and Lord Coventry made an unnerving pair.

What they probably didn't realize, was that Ophelia had faced far more daunting people—and situations—in her short life.

These past events had thrown her life into chaos and uncertainty.

But this situation, these people, did nothing to deter Ophelia. For once, she was completely confident in her choices, her feelings, and what she wanted for the future.

And he stood at her side.

Ophelia straightened her shoulders when Molly set her hands on her hips and scrutinized her from head to toe. She would not allow the older woman to intimidate her, even though she sensed her cheeks reddening and her heartbeat increasing. Collapsing under the woman's stare was not an option, especially if Ophelia sought a future with Colin.

"I see the lad gave ye me pendant," she said.

Ophelia grabbed the necklace with her free hand,

its warmth infusing her with a feeling she'd never known before. All the while, she knew the time to return the necklace was now. It belonged to Molly, a gift from her true love, encapsulating all that he'd sacrificed for his family.

Colin placed his hand on hers at his elbow, halting her from removing the pendant.

Molly paced toward them, and Lord Coventry stood from his place in a chair before the hearth, uncertain what the woman's course of action was.

In response to Molly's continued perusal, Ophelia's chin lifted.

"I have one question." Her eyes sparked with each word as she moved her intense stare to Colin. Ophelia released a sigh, as it seemed Molly now focused on her grandson, but too soon, her stare swung back to her. "Lady Ophelia Fletcher…"

"Yes, Lady Coventry." It was her proper name as the dowager countess, but it didn't fit the formidable, stoop-shouldered woman before her.

"What, may I ask, are your intentions with me grandson?"

Her intentions…with Colin?

Ophelia fought the smile that threatened to overtake her as the woman's stare softened and she gathered her thoughts.

"Well, my lady," Ophelia started with poise. "My intentions are to make an honest man of your grandson, Lord Hawke. Bare him a horde of fiery-haired hellion daughters, and a perhaps one or two fair-haired, broad-shouldered sons. Love him until my last breath. And make certain he never wants for anything."

Colin tensed beside her. They hadn't spoken of marriage—let alone children.

Lord Coventry chuckled as he moved to the sideboard and poured three tumblers of amber-colored liquid.

But it was Molly who Ophelia kept coming back to.

230 | *Christina McKnight*

She hadn't moved, hadn't uttered a word, and Ophelia feared she'd said the wrong thing. Likely, she'd crossed the line when she mentioned fiery-haired hellions.

Ophelia cared not a whit.

The woman had asked, and Ophelia had spoken the truth.

Her truth.

Her vision for their future.

CHAPTER 24

COLIN HELD OPHELIA close to his side, as Molly stood stock-still, allowing the words to sink in. Hell, he'd need a month of Sundays to truly understand everything Ophelia had proclaimed. She not only loved him, but she wanted to be at his side forevermore. She'd spoken the exact words he'd been thinking and had prepared to say himself—yet she'd proclaimed them first.

"My love for him has naught to do with the devil nor any sorceress enchantment I've cast over him. If anything, Molly, he has ensnared me in *his* spell."

Even if she were proven the sinister being Molly had accused her of during their first meeting, he would thank the devil himself for bringing Ophelia into his life.

If it hadn't been for her, Lady Sissy might have torn his family completely apart as his father tried to keep their family's past hidden, and Molly sought to prove her husband's honor. Without Ophelia, he would have given up hope, and never would have traveled to Sheerness because the book would have never been found.

"Molly," Colin said, his voice gravelly as he fought to keep his own emotions under control. "If it weren't for Ophelia—her wit and many sacrifices—I would have given up hope. So many times, I was prepared to return from Sheerness with nothing, but it was Ophelia who reminded me that all hope was not lost and that we needed to keep searching."

His father returned to the group, handing each a tumbler. Ophelia released his arm and took her glass, eyeing the liquid suspiciously.

Lord Coventry held his glass high, smiling at Colin, Ophelia, and lastly, Molly. "To the woman who put our family demons to rest, brought us all together as we should have been from the start, and put a hex on the most formidable dowager countess."

"She did what?" Molly screeched, her stare darting between Colin and Ophelia. "She cannot—"

"To the woman who taught me how to live—one misadventure at a time," Colin said, raising his own glass. "May our next adventure prove fruitful."

"Next adventure?" Ophelia stared up at him with rounded eyes, her confidence from a moment before slipping slightly. No one else in the room would notice, but Colin did.

"My dear." Colin handed his glass back to his father before plucking Ophelia's tumbler from her trembling fingers. Coventry gladly took the glass from Colin. "It was you who asked for my hand in marriage…and I will not allow you to forget it. You promised to make an honest man of me. There is paperwork to be drawn up, arrangements to be discussed, and my dowry to be settled on."

Ophelia laughed, her eyes lighting with a look of love he was certain she saw in his, as well.

Molly cackled before doubling over in a coughing fit.

Straightening, the older woman held her glass high, clinked his father's tumbler, and they both drank. "Should'a known it would take a siren ta capture Colin's heart." Molly shook her head. "He is far too much like your father, Ramsey."

"How so, Mother?"

"He needs a strong woman ta guide him," Molly said. "Make him the man he was always destined ta be."

Colin pulled Ophelia into his arms, ignoring his father and grandmama as they departed the room. The door closed behind them, and the latch clicked into place.

He didn't know what the future held, where they would go from here, or how they would convince Lord Atholl of their love. However, there was one thing Colin had no doubt of—Ophelia would be his. And he would be hers.

He didn't care where his destiny lay, as long as Ophelia was next to him.

If society found out about the Coventry family's past, Colin knew, without asking, Ophelia would stand by him. She was not the follower she'd always thought herself to be. No, she just hadn't found the situation—or person—worth standing up for.

Ophelia would stand up for him, speak up to protect him, and never allow anyone to speak ill of his family.

And he would dedicate the rest of his life to doing the same for her—starting with convincing her father to allow them to wed.

If there were an emotion deeper than love, adoration, and unwavering commitment; it would be how he felt for Lady Ophelia.

THERE WAS ONLY she and Colin in the room—if anyone else lingered, Ophelia did not notice or care. She looked up into Colin's green eyes and smiling face. Had he ever appeared so happy and…at ease? In all the time she'd known him, he'd always had an invisible weight of sorts on his shoulders. It weighed him down far more than he realized, and Ophelia only understood the

234 | *Christina McKnight*

magnitude of it now that it was gone. He'd lived his life under the burden of his feuding family, always at a loss for where he fit in and searching for ways to stifle the fighting.

Finally, the war between his grandmother and father had come to an end.

It was time for Colin to find out who he was and what he wanted in life.

…and he wanted her.

His finger lifted her chin when she made to look away, bringing her stare back to him. "Ophelia?"

The mere sight of him, his hair disheveled, his shirt wrinkled from their travels, and his satisfied grin had her heart racing. She could end every day looking up at him, just like this.

"Yes," she said with a breathless sigh.

"You are brave." He paused to place a kiss on her forehead. "You are fearless." He placed a kiss on the tip of her nose, and Ophelia stifled a giggle. "You are smart." He kissed her chin. "You are beautiful." He dipped low and pressed a kiss to her chest, just above her beating heart and Molly's pendant nestled against her bosom. "And you are utterly enchanting."

Her chin shook, and her breath caught in her chest. They were words she'd never believed would be spoken to her—about her. Especially by a man she'd come to love and cherish beyond anything. Love and happiness had found Edith and Luci—and Ophelia did not hold their contentment against them, even though she'd never suspected it would one day be hers.

Ophelia longed to tell him it was *because* of him she was all those things. Only a fortnight ago, she would have kept that to herself, never uttered the words, but she could not allow this moment to pass without saying all she had to.

"It is because of your trust and belief in me that I am brave, that I squashed the fear that resided in me and overcame the doubt that plagued me my entire life.

Before you, I did not shine, I was trapped within myself, living a life and following a path that others set for me." She paused, determined to say everything. "But not anymore. My destiny is mine to grasp"—she took hold of his arms above the elbow—"and I choose you, Colin."

There were a million little things she'd wanted to tell him a thousand times during their short acquaintance, like that he made her feel like more than she'd ever longed to be. It was odd that most of their time together had happened away from London and everything that was familiar to her. She'd defined herself as Luci's and Edith's friend, Tilda's champion through her writing for the *Mayfair Confidential*, a duke's perfect, demure daughter, and a confirmed bookworm, but she was far more than those things. She was Ophelia, with or without being all the things she'd thought herself to be, and what others expected of her.

"You've shown me that adventure does not lie solely between the pages of a book. Passion is not reserved for the fanciful tales of old. And love is not meant only for Lucianna and Edith, but for me, as well, if only I am courageous enough to accept it—and remain steadfast in my determination to hold on to it."

Her grip tightened, proving her point that she was never letting him go. Not today, certainly not tomorrow, and most definitely not years from that moment.

"No matter the misadventures to come—and I can assure you, there will be many if I have anything to say on the matter"—he paused, his laugh unforced and relaxed—"you will be at my side. There is no other woman I'd rather be deserted in the Sahara with. No other lady who could lead me safely through the viper pits that are most London soirées. And no other woman I'd trust if faced by a panther in the Amazon rainforest."

Ophelia had to laugh along with him. "I can assure you, there is quite a difference between a ballroom and the wilds of the Amazon. I do not think the two are comparable, my lord."

"Have you ever been to the Amazon?"

"No, but—"

"Well, I have been to my share of London balls, and I can assure you, they are quite daunting indeed."

"Then it is very beneficial that you have selected such an undaunted debutante to have at your side."

"Debutante?" His brow rose in question. "Certainly not, my lady, before long, you will be Lady Hawke."

"We have yet to—"

The door crashed open behind them, slamming against its hinges, causing both Ophelia and Colin to whip around toward the door. For a brief moment, she feared Lady Sissy had escaped the footman and come back, but the thump of her cane against the polished wood floor announced Molly's arrival.

"Enough with the bloody details or the pair of ye will still be yap'n inta next year," she shouted, tapping her cane with each word. "You love me lad, and me lad loves ye. There be nothin' else ta speak of. Kiss the damned woman, Colin!"

"Yes, Grandmama," Colin said, turning back to face Ophelia and gathering her into his arms. "With pleasure."

And kiss her he did.

EPILOGUE

One last word for young women of the ton*: Hold tight to your determination.*
Remain undaunted and steadfast, no matter what life presents you with.
Life is not about becoming what others want you to be, but about trusting your worth, finding your true self, and taking chances—even with a perfect stranger.
Lastly, pay close heed to things you are naturally drawn to; be it person or possession.
Here, you will find your path, passion, and purpose.
Fare thee well, good readers of the Gazette.
-Mayfair Confidential, London Daily Gazette

EVERY EYE IN the dining hall was on Ophelia as she slowly walked down the length of table as she greeted guests and accepted their words of good tidings. It would only last a few short minutes—though it was a time when all attention was on her. She'd never believed she longed for a time when she was the center of everyone's thoughts.

Glancing down the table, he nodded to her, giving her the courage to continue on.

She paused by Lucianna, Ophelia clutched Molly's

pendant close and leaned down to whisper in her ear, "It is lovely to see your mother and family."

Lucianna turned to look up at Ophelia—and she was taken aback by the happiness and warmth in Luci's smile. "Yes, well, my mother and siblings will be staying with Montrose—for the time being."

Or until Lucianna's father relents and approves of her betrothal to Montrose, Ophelia added silently to herself. Not that his disapproval would stop Montrose from taking Luci as wife. They'd agreed on a Christmas wedding, and all hoped Lord Camden would have a change of heart by that time and reunite with his family.

"Ophelia," Edith called from across the table. "I do hope you can spare a few moments after our meal."

"Of course," she conceded with a laugh. "My father's library?"

When Edith nodded and Lucianna laughed, Montrose and Torrington shared a look of question; however, Ophelia and her friends only ignored the men's inquiries. It was a tradition they would continue until each was happily, safely, unequivocally wed—in honor of Tilda, in a way. They would disappear into the library to speak in hushed tones and laugh about the night to come. This will be Ophelia's first wedded night. At Christmas, it would be Luci's.

They'd even invited Lady Prudence and Lady Chastity to join them.

Torrington would certainly not relish his younger sisters being part of such an intimate conversation; however, friends were friends.

And Ophelia was honored to call Chastity and Pru friend.

"I can hardly contain myself and finish our meal." Edith giggled, giving her betrothed a sideways glance. "I most assuredly have things to speak of."

For once, it wasn't Ophelia's face that flushed scarlet, but Edith's.

It would be an utter lie if she didn't admit she was

looking forward to hearing the scandalous tidbits Edith had to share about the marriage bed—though the woman was no more wedded than Lucianna at that moment.

With a wink, Ophelia continued down the table and nestled close to Colin's side, resuming her seat at the banquet table.

Her husband.

Colin Parnell, Lord Hawke, heir to the Coventry Earldom.

The mere thought that they'd met and wed with such haste still had her mind swirling, but Colin was always there to make certain she remained upright with the frenzy surrounding them.

She glanced around the crowded room; row after row of finely dressed men and women ate, drank, and laughed together as course after exquisite course of delicate dishes were set before them.

Ophelia and Colin, flanked by Edith and Lord Torrington on one side, and Lucianna and Montrose on the other, sampled the savory and sweet plates placed before them as all in attendance celebrated the blessed joining of Baron Hawke to Lady Ophelia Fletcher in wedded bliss.

Lady Hawke.

It was quite simply the only decision she'd made in recent months that no one could dare call a misadventure.

No, everything about their whirlwind betrothal and morning wedding in her family's gardens behind the Atholl townhouse was exactly as it was fated to be.

Even Molly had given her blessing—by way of some obscure and intimidating dance ritual that could have as easily been her placing a hex on Ophelia and Colin's entire bloodline. Yet, that did not matter. If Ophelia were cursed, as Colin's grandmother had once thought, then there was no other person she'd rather share a life of misadventure with than the man at her side.

"You are smiling again, dear wife," Colin whispered close to her ear. "If you keep this up, everyone will think you deliriously happy and satisfied in love."

"And if that is exactly what I want everyone in this room—and all of England—to think?" She looked up at him from under lowered lashes with a hint of a smirk caressing her lips. "Is that so awful?"

He placed a kiss to her forehead. "Certainly not; however, we cannot allow all these people to assume we have wedded life figured out. They will demand to know our secrets."

"We will never share our secrets to finding wedded bliss." Ophelia shook her head gravely. "Not unless they hold a burning candle to my toes."

His brow knitted and his tone turned serious. "That is all it would take?"

"Well, that and the promise of plum pudding!"

"Sweets for my sweet?" he said with a chuckle.

Their intimate conversation was interrupted when someone cleared their throat, drawing his and her attention away from one another to the man standing before their table. Ophelia had been so consumed with her new husband that she hadn't noticed Lord Abercorn approach them.

The older man bowed deeply. "May I offer my sincere congratulations on your union, Lord and Lady Hawke. I am ever so pleased to be included in such an intimate gathering."

Ophelia smiled at the man, his cheeks blossoming pink at her attention. Her friends, Edith and Luci, had been as surprised as Abercorn at the invitation extended to the duke, who they'd thought only a few short weeks ago was responsible for Tilda's death. But much had changed with Lady Sissy's confession that night outside Colin's father's townhouse—not only had the woman confessed to pushing Tilda down the stairs, but also to poisoning Lord Abercorn's two other wives.

They were all victims of Lady Sissy's need to control and exert power over all who surrounded her.

"It is an honor to have you among us, my lord." Ophelia spoke each word with a deep-seated conviction and new appreciation for the man. He'd loved Tilda, as they all had, and she'd been taken all too soon. But Ophelia and her friends hadn't been the only ones to grieve her passing. "I do hope your sister is settling in at The Retreat."

Colin placed his hand on the small of Ophelia's back as if to show his support.

Abercorn nodded several times. "She is adjusting to life in York—and the restrictions she must now live within—as well as can be expected. I plan to visit her as soon as the physicians assure me she is stable and that my attendance will not upset her."

"I commend your dedication, Abercorn," Colin chimed in.

"And I very much appreciate your understanding and compassion for my sister's situation." Abercorn gave them both a curt bow and made his way back to his seat.

"Are you certain we did the right thing?" Colin asked as they both scrutinized the man when he regained his seat next to—of all people—Lucianna's mother. "Sometimes, I wonder."

"We must have faith that we did." They'd had the right to see Sissy locked away in the Tower—never to see the light of day again; however, Abercorn was a victim, too and if they'd allowed Sissy to be prosecuted, then Abercorn would have had no chance at a decent marriage or a family. "She will remain in York, unable to harm another person until her last day. Condemning Lord Abercorn to a future outrunning the scandal would only punish him."

"You, my love"—Colin placed a kiss to her forehead—"are a compassionate"—he lightly brushed his lips along her cheek—"understanding"—he lifted her chin when she blushed and tried to hide her embarrassment over his attention—"giving woman. Whom, I might add, I am proud to call my wife."

"I did what I thought was right." Even if Luci hadn't been completely satisfied or in agreement that Lady Sissy had received a punishment worthy of the crimes she committed. Ophelia knew, without a doubt, that Sissy would not have lasted long in the Tower or Bedlam. The harsh conditions prisoners lived under were trying, even on the hardiest of men.

Ophelia looked into Colin's green eyes, the depth of caring for her she saw there never waning, even after they'd been forced to explain to her parents where she'd gone during her absence from London. Even in his wedding day finery with his golden hair trimmed well above his collar, he was still the man who'd protected her from his own grandmother, not that Ophelia thought Molly would have harmed her if Colin hadn't arrived when he did.

"I love you," she sighed.

"And I, you, Ophelia," he declared loud enough for Montrose and Torrington to overhear and give an appreciative celebratory shout.

"Everyone seems to be enjoying themselves," she replied, bringing her sherry goblet to her lips to hide her insanely happy smile. "Do you think every day will be as perfect as this?"

"As long as we are together, not a thing can tarnish the perfection we've created for ourselves."

"Attention, attention!" The Earl of Coventry stood, calling for everyone's notice. When the crowd quieted, and all guests turned their full attention to Colin's father, the man held an envelope high for all to see. "It is with great pleasure that I share with my son—and his exquisite bride—a letter that arrived only yesterday from King George III."

Applause filled the room, nearly as loud as the moment she and Colin had been announced husband

and wife—Lord and Lady Hawke.

Coventry shushed the room before making a grand show of opening the letter. "As you all know, my father, Colin's grandpapa, served our king's father, King George II, as the royal courier between Sheerness, Kent, and Prussia."

Ophelia noticed Colin's chest puff up with pride as his father spoke of Porter Parnell, the first Earl of Coventry. Love swelled within her to see how far Colin's family had come to mending their ties to one another. It had only taken Colin's father admitting that he'd known the truth all along. Once that happened, it was as if the chains holding Colin down vanished.

The earl unfolded a single slip of paper and held it high for everyone to see the royal crest at the top of the page. "He sends his good tidings and blessed wishes for Lord and Lady Hawke's future." Colin's father quieted as he read farther down the paper, his brow rising in surprise as his breath hitched. "This cannot be," he muttered.

"What is it, Father?" Colin sat forward, waiting for the earl to finish reading.

Even Ophelia's own father stood, alarmed at what else a royal letter from the king could hold.

"Well, this is quite interesting."

"Don't be such a tease, Ramsey," Molly huffed, slamming the tip of her cane into the floor of Ophelia's parent's ballroom. Atholl cast a glare in the older woman's direction but had the good sense to hold his tongue. "Is Georgie think'n ta give me Colin a proper wed'n gift?"

"Ummm, no, it is more that the king wishes something *from* Colin and Ophelia," the earl mused.

"What is it, Coventry?" Atholl demanded, drawing back toward his seat. "What can the king want from my daughter?"

Ophelia's heart stopped for a brief moment, her stare moving from her father to Colin's sire.

The Earl of Coventry winked at her, a mischievous grin overtaking his face.

How had she not noticed the elder man's resemblance to Colin?

"As stated here, the king so decrees that Lord and Lady Hawke's first child born with hair the color of pure, red-hot fire is to be named George—after him. If the child is female, she will be called Georgina!"

The silence that had settled on the entire room as they waited in stunned shock to hear what their king demanded of the new couple broke as a shriek echoed through the space.

Molly shot to her feet, lifting her cane and thumping it on the long, wooden table before her. The crystal glasses, now drained of sherry, shook with her forceful strikes, and the other guests at the table—Lady Prudence and Lady Chastity—pushed their chairs back to avoid being caught in the woman's snare.

"That bloody, yellow-tailed, sniveling weasel!" Molly faced reddened deeper than Ophelia's auburn hair. "The contemptible, lick-spittle imp!"

"Mother!" Coventry shouted over Molly's tirade. "I am—"

"The man thinks ta have me great-grandbabe named for him?" she seethed. "Ye bet on everything I possess, no Parnell babe ever be named George—or Georgina!"

Ophelia burst out in laughter, doubling over as the sound filled the room, only to have other sounds of merriment join her own.

"What is so bloody amusing, Ophelia?" Molly demanded.

She sobered enough to notice her new grandmama's injured expression and rushed to soothe the woman's ruffled feelings. "It is only that I am surprised it is a *name* you find unsuitable and not the thought of being the great-grandmama of a red-haired babe."

Molly slumped into her seat with a chuckle of her own, folding her arms. "Don't be think'n the child be escape'n me search for evil marks."

"Evil marks?" Ophelia's father's glare flipped between Coventry, Molly, and Colin before settling on Ophelia, who laughed again—the other guests seeming to enjoy the banter between the newly joined families.

"Do take your seats." Colin stood, resting his hand lightly on Ophelia's shoulder. "Lady Hawke and I thank everyone for bearing witness to our joining on this day. However, I think it long past time my bride and I retire."

Ophelia stood quickly, smoothing the wrinkles from her light blue gown. "Before we go…" She didn't dare glance in Colin's direction. There was much she longed to say, though she'd planned to say nothing. "I have something to share."

All eyes were on her, and Ophelia took several deep breaths to calm her rising nerves. She'd never had the urge to put herself in a place of great attention; however, for the man next to her, she'd live every waking moment in the spotlight of the *ton* if that continued to make him happy and content.

"While many of you were not acquainted with my husband prior to our betrothal, I can attest to his kind heart and giving nature. He loves his family and friends—both new and old," she said, gesturing to everyone in the room. Edith nodded encouragingly when Ophelia fell silent. "I know he will cherish me and our family as much as he does others in his life." She risked a glance at Colin then, her mouth going dry, and her words sticking in her throat. She coughed, gaining a few precious moments to gain her composure. "I am so very thankful that similar to my two dearest friends, Lady Edith and Lady Lucianna, I have found my true path in life. I have been blessed far beyond what I deserve, and though many may consider our meeting a misadventure of sorts, I have come to realize it was far more than a mere adventure—or misadventure—but the first step toward the grandest accomplishment of my life…finding love."

"Hear! Hear!" the guests chanted in unison.

Ophelia made no attempt to hide her tears of joy as they slid unabated down her cheeks.

She was happy—and utterly in love with the man next to her.

She'd feared for so long that love was not something in her future, and even if it were, that there was the chance her life would mirror Tilda's tragic one.

But that was not the only course available to Ophelia and Colin.

No. They were free to love one another without fear or reservation.

Colin leaned down and pulled her body against his, capturing her lips in a searing kiss. One that conveyed the way he felt about her—and her words.

He released her mouth, the same mischievous smile lighting his face as had his father's only moments before. "Lady Hawke, I dare say you have a marvelous way with words. I can only wonder why you have not taken pencil to paper as yet. You would make a fine storyteller—or perhaps, a columnist for the *London Daily Gazette*."

Edith and Lucianna burst into laughter, mingled with the more reserved chuckles from their betrotheds.

Colin waited not a moment longer before bringing his lips to hers—masking her stunned expression.

The cheers that erupted reverberated off the walls and high ceiling, causing a nearly deafening commotion as Colin slipped his arm beneath Ophelia's knees and carried her from the room.

AUTHOR'S NOTES

Thank you for reading *The Misadventures of Lady Ophelia (The Undaunted Debutantes, Book Three)*.

If you enjoyed *The Misadventures of Lady Ophelia*, be sure to write a brief review at any retailer.

I'd love to hear from you!

You can contact me at:
Christina@christinamcknight.com

Or write me at:
P.O. Box 1017
Patterson, CA 95363

www.ChristinaMcKnight.com
Check out my website for giveaways, book reviews, and information on my upcoming projects,
or connect with me through social media at:

Twitter: @CMcKnightWriter
Facebook: www.facebook.com/christinamcknightwriter
Goodreads: www.goodreads.com/ChristinaMcKnight

Sign up for my newsletter here:
http://eepurl.com/VP1rP

**For more information about
The Undaunted Debutantes, turn the page!**

THE UNDAUNTED DEBUTANTES

Three innocent debutantes must work to solve the mysterious death of their childhood friend. With undaunted determination they pledge to not only expose the man responsible for their friend's tragic death on her wedding night, but to also uncover other unscrupulous men of the *ton* who would jeopardize the future of other young women.

The Disappearance of Lady Edith
The Misfortune of Lady Lucianna
The Misadventures of Lady Ophelia

AVAILABLE IN PRINT AND E-BOOK

The Disappearance of Lady Edith
Book 1
Now available

One tragic night changed sensible, proper Lady
Edith Pelton's life: when her best friend fell to her
death, pushed down a flight of stairs by a nefarious lord.
Now, Edith dedicates her time to watching the man she
thinks is responsible, while gathering information to
expose other scoundrels posing as gentlemen of honor
about London. When her spying is noticed by a perfect
stranger, Edith finds herself with two mysteries—what
happened to her friend, and how to win the heart of this
brilliantly handsome lord.

The Misfortune of Lady Lucianna
Book 2
Now available

Lady Lucianna Constantine, a quick-witted hellion,
has no doubt who is responsible for the murder of her
dear friend—and she will stop at nothing from exposing
his transgressions, and those of every despicable man in
London. Though her two dearest friends are unwilling
to point a finger at the dastardly man, Lucianna has
witnessed the cruelty of London's Beau Monde her
entire life…starting with her own father. She is more
than willing to singlehandedly take down every vile man
that crosses her path. However, what happens when a
most honorable man discovers Luci is the abhorrent
woman who ruined both his life and stripped him of his
rightful future?

**Check out Lady Lucianna's journey in
The Undaunted Debutantes in this excerpt from
*The Misfortune of Lady Lucianna!***

An Excerpt From
The Misfortune of Lady Lucianna

It is hereby announced that this writer has born witness to the Marquis of Camden scandalously parading his mistress about in polite society.

As this writer can also attest, Lady Camden and Lady Lucianna were also in attendance at the soirée the marquis saw fit to escort his mistress to.

Shame on a man who does not value family over his own pleasure.
-Mayfair Confidential, London Daily Gazette

Hanover Square, London
March 1815

"PREPOSTEROUS, SENSELESS RUBBISH." Roderick Crofton, the seventh Duke of Montrose, pushed the *London Daily Gazette* away from him on the breakfast table and scowled at his now cold morning repast. "Nothing but a scandal sheet, I tell you. Get this out of my sight."

"Certainly, Your Grace." A footman hurried forward to remove the paper. "May I bring you anything else? Tea, perhaps?"

Tea? No. Roderick did not desire tea. He craved a newspaper that took an interest in reporting true and accurate facts regarding current events, not another gossip rag that took great pleasure in ruining upstanding gentlemen.

Not that Roderick personally knew the Marquis of Camden; however, the *Mayfair Confidential* had set its sharpened teeth upon *him* only two months prior.

"Your Grace?" the footman asked once more.

"No, no, Joshua." Roderick waved his hand in dismissal. "Unfortunately, you cannot provide what I need." When the servant's shoulders slumped, he continued. "However, that is no fault of yours, I assure you."

When Joshua took his place against the wall, Roderick took hold of his utensil and pushed the cold eggs about his plate. If he did not consume at least half the food, Cook would likely chase him down and demand he eat—or else. He'd never discovered what she meant by "or else," and he damn well didn't plan to. He speared a sliver of pheasant and placed it into his mouth and then chewed slowly. Perhaps it would appear he'd eaten more if he remained at the table longer. Blast it all, but he was no longer a boy in knee breeches.

He did not need a woman, no matter that she'd known him since birth, following him like a clucking chicken. If Roderick found he was not hungry, then he would not eat.

Period.

End of story.

Until Cook gained word and saw his untouched plate.

With a sigh, he scooped a mouthful of tepid porridge from his bowl and crammed it into his mouth before he could change his mind.

He supposed someone looking after his well-being was appreciated.

For all the headaches the woman caused him, he was grateful to have her.

Joshua yelped in surprise when the sound of the front door slamming, followed by pounding footsteps, approached the Montrose townhouse dining room.

He raised his brow in question as the dining room door slammed against its hinges, revealing his stable hand, Lucian, his clothes disheveled and his cap clutched to his heaving chest. For all his bluster, he stood silently, staring at the floor, waiting for Roderick to address him. This was the same lad Roderick had gotten into trouble with in their youths for leaving tops on the upper-floor landing—causing not one, not two, but *three* maids injury. And now, he cowered before Roderick as if he would rip the stable hand limb from limb if Lucian spoke out of turn.

"Speak, Lucian," he finally commanded.

"I have news, Your Grace," he mumbled, keeping his eyes trained on the floor.

"And are you worried this news will displease me?" Roderick pushed his onyx hair from his eyes, tucking it behind his ear. He needs must make a note to have his valet trim it or procure a stronger pomatum to keep the blasted strands from falling into his face. "Out with it."

"Your Grace, I…" Lucian started again after taking a deep breath.

"Enough with formalities," Roderick said, pushing his chair back to stand.

"I think I have finally determined the source of the *Mayfair Confidential* column." He dared a glance at Roderick and seeing his pleased expression Lucian continued. "There is a woman. She's come and gone from the *Gazette* on five occasions over the last fortnight. She was there in the late-night hours, and while I have not confirmed, I suspect a new column was printed in the *London Daily Gazette* today."

"You are correct." Roderick nodded to Joshua to remove his plate of hardly touched food. "Have you ascertained the woman's identity?"

A moment of excitement hung in the air.

"No, Your Grace." Lucian shook his head. "I wanted to make certain you approved of me looking further into the matter. I do know she does not find full-time employment at the paper, nor does she have relatives within the *Gazette*. I asked about the business, but no one was familiar with her—or they refused to comment."

"Of course, I want you to investigate further."

Roderick's command thundered, and once again, standing against the wall, Joshua flinched. "This woman, whoever she may be, is responsible for destroying my life. I will see she pays for her actions." He needs must calm his anger, especially if he wanted to keep his footman from expiring from fright. "What can you tell me of this woman? Is it possible I am acquainted with her?"

Lucian pulled at his coat as if noting for the first time his ramshackle appearance. "She arrives in a fancy carriage each time, leaving it down the street. She enters the business without so much as a glance over her shoulder. This was why it took me so long to figure her out. If I were the one exposing men of the *ton*, I would be paranoid and watching my back at every turn. But this woman, her chin is always high, raven hair always perfectly groomed, and her gowns are impeccable, likely made by the finest modiste in London."

"You suspect she is of noble birth?" Why hadn't the notion crossed his mind before? Roderick had suspected the culprit to be a jealous lord, not a woman—especially not a lady of class.

"I have little doubt of it, Your Grace."

"Then you have my permission to look into the woman further; however…" This was not an entirely new venture, sleuthing. He'd been investigating random men and businesses for several years now; though it was imperative that he not draw attention to his activities. "Do not let the woman know we are on to her, or she is likely to vanish."

"Certainly, Your Grace. I will bring you information as soon as I know anything more." Lucian bowed and turned to leave.

"And, Lucian."

"Yes, Your Grace?"

"Do bathe and get some rest before going back out."

The servant smiled, wearily. "Thank you, Your

Grace."

Roderick glanced back toward the footman pressed against the far wall; he seemed unimpressed and no less anxious by the kindness Roderick had shown Lucian.

No matter, he had many important things to accomplish, far more dire than convincing a new servant he was not the beast he appeared to be despite his jet-black hair, severe jawline, and penetrating ice-blue eyes. He only knew these terms for a gentleman's appearance because Lady Daphne was always going on and on about his dashingly handsome face.

His gut twisted at the thought of the young woman, so innocent and shy. It would have been a pleasure to take her as wife and make her the Duchess of Montrose. Yet, that had been another thing stripped from him by the *Mayfair Confidential*. What his father's dastardly friends hadn't stolen from him, the person who'd published the damning column in the *London Daily Gazette* had.

He could remember every scandalous word:

It is hereby stated that this writer has born firsthand witness to the 7th Duke of Montrose, scandalously alone with a golden-haired nymph in his private opera box, all whilst betrothed to Lady Daphne.

As this writer can also attest, Lady Daphne's hair is pure night, compared to the observed doxy's crown of light. Let this article stand as proof that Lady Daphne would do well to find herself another eligible lord to take as husband.

-Mayfair Confidential, London Daily Gazette

Lady Daphne's father had decided to do just that: secure another eligible lord for her to take as husband.

Roderick had been so hell-bent on finding out the truth of his family's missing fortune, he hadn't even thought about the repercussions of being seen in public with another woman. At first, he'd pondered the idea that the *Mayfair Confidential* writer had actually done him a glorious favor. He hadn't loved Daphne. She was sweet, innocent, and beautifully angelic even with her dark locks. And with time, he had no doubt an affection would have grown between them, despite the girl's lack of passion for anything of substance.

Bloody hell. His fury over the situation returned whenever he thought of it; his pulse beating erratically, and his blood hammering through him.

There was no more Lady Daphne in his future. And with her gone, so was the dowry he'd counted on to restore at least a portion of his family's coffers. Admittedly, it was much less than he needed to secure the Montrose line and keep it from ruin, but it would have bought him enough time to find the men responsible for swindling his father out of every coin not nailed down.

He should be donning riding garb and Hessians for an afternoon at Hyde or Regent's Park to socialize and search for a new bride. If he had half the sense he claimed to have, Roderick would be doing just that. Unfortunately, he'd inherited more than just his midnight looks from his father. Apparently, he'd also gained his lack of wisdom.

The time would come to begin his search anew for a wife, but that wasn't now. Perhaps he'd look through the few invitations that had arrived over the last few days and select a few social gatherings to attend. Maybe a ball or a recital.

At the moment, Roderick needed something to ease his fury and cool his heated blood. That was something a ride in Hyde Park could not do.

However, he knew the exact place it was acceptable to thrash another—and it was called sport.

Available in print and e-book now!

ABOUT THE AUTHOR

USA TODAY Bestselling Author Christina McKnight writes emotional and intricate Regency Romance with strong women and maverick heroes.

Her books combine romance and mystery, exploring themes of redemption and forgiveness. When she's not writing, Christina enjoys trying new coffeehouses, visiting wine bars, traveling the world, and watching television.

Email: Christina@ChristinaMcKnight.com
Follow her on Twitter: @CMcKnightWriter
Keep up to date on her releases:
www.christinamcknight.com
Like Christina's FB Author page:
ChristinaMcKnightWriter

PRAISE FOR CHRISTINA MCKNIGHT'S NOVELS

THE THIEF STEALS HER EARL

"When I started reading this book I could not put it down...it caused another book-hangover for me. I wanted to see how things would go when the truth of Judith came out and how Simon was going to handle it...loved it."-*Sissy's Book Review*

"Jude and Cart's story is such a delight! So refreshing to see the hero shy, socially awkward and not super wealthy. I love it...This was definitely one of the best books I've read this summer." -*Reviews from a Thrifty Mom*

FORGOTTEN NO MORE

"This author has made me love historical romance again."
-*TwinsieTalk Book Reviews*

HIDDEN NO MORE

"The storyline was really good, the writing was great. So smooth and engaging, I was able to zip right through the story, it flowed so well. I love finding new to me authors and with this wonderfully written story by Ms. McKnight I've found a new historical romance author." *Bound by Books*

CHRISTMAS EVER MORE

"*Christmas Ever More* was a wonderfully written festive novella full of hope, renewal, love, and new beginnings. If you're a fan of Christina's Lady Forsaken series, this is a must. Even if you aren't caught up, this stands well enough on its own to be a lovely addition to your holiday reading list."-*Literal Addiction*

BOOKS BY CHRISTINA MCKNIGHT